HUNTLEY

LOVING A YOUNG SERIES, BOOK 3

STACY EATON

CHAPTER ONE

DANIELLA

I flexed my hands to ease the tension on my fingers while I sat on my couch in the living room. I'd been typing like a woman possessed as I attempted to get this book finished. I was so damn close—so close—and I was determined to get it done tonight. I had every intention of stepping away from writing for a few weeks and enjoy the beginning of summer. I had one more chapter to blast out, and then I could type my two favorite words: *The End.*

I rolled my shoulders, adjusted the pillow against my lower back, and prepared to get that final chapter underway. Unfortunately, my stomach grumbled madly, and I winced as I glanced at the digital clock on my computer. Holy crap! It was after eight!

When was the last time that I ate? One? Two? I couldn't remember, but that was normal when I was in my writing groove. I could go all day without moving from my spot unless my bladder revolted or something else grabbed my attention.

Like my German shepherd, Tigger, who was now barking at the back door. "Tig, give me a minute."

He growled and began to bark more aggressively, and I

1

sighed as I put my laptop to the side. Maybe he needed to do some business, or more likely, a critter had invaded his back-yard territory.

"Alright, I'm coming," I groaned as I tried to get my stiff body off the couch. I paused to stretch my entire body like a cat, shifting slowly in little increments to get the kinks worked out. I'd been writing since ten that morning; the obsession to complete this story had overtaken all my other needs. The whole time I contorted my body, Tigger barked ferociously at the back door.

"What is your problem?" I asked as I finally headed toward him. I barely had the sliding door cracked when Tig stuck his nose between the door and frame and shoved it a few inches to the side, bolting out the door. "Geez, Tig!" I grabbed hold of the doorframe to keep from falling over after he'd knocked me sideways. "What the heck is out there?"

I closed the door as a trickle of smoke tickled my nose. It was a pleasant night out, but I wasn't going to leave the door cracked like I usually did for him if someone was burning some-thing. When I left the door slightly ajar, Tig would let himself back in once he had finished his business.

He barked wildly near the back fence, and I knew I needed to call him in so he wouldn't disturb the neighbors. Except, I suddenly realized I was in desperate need of using the bath-room. As I rushed down the hall, I considered the time; it was only eight o'clock, not that late. Hopefully, he didn't bother the people around me too much while I took care of my business.

As I finished, my nose twitched again with the scent of smoke. Had I left a window open in my office? I washed my hands and glanced in the mirror.

Holy crap, I looked like hell! The ponytail that I had tossed my long hair up in earlier now poked sideways off my head, and the t-shirt I wore, sans bra, had droplets of coffee down the front from an earlier accident—or two. I hadn't even taken a shower today. I sniffed at my underarm, wincing and then making a gagging face in the mirror.

"Food, chapter, shower, and then bed," I stated to myself as I left the bathroom with a nod. Tigger was at the back door, pawing almost as wildly as he had been barking before he went out.

"I'm coming, boy," I called to him as I slipped into the kitchen and paused at the fridge. I pulled the freezer drawer open and tapped my lip. What would be fast to make and easy to eat while I finished this chapter? I settled on a Hot Pocket, which I knew was not healthy, but it would at least put something into my stomach.

Tigger began to howl at the back door, no longer pawing but outright howling in a low tone. I tossed the Hot Pocket into the microwave and went to let him in. "What is your problem?" I asked as I pulled open the back door. "Get in here and hush. You're going to wake the dead."

In response to my words, Tigger backed up, barking at me, his long fluffy shepherd tail low, his head down, and his fur fluffed around his neck. "What's wrong, Tig? Come here, come inside. I know you want to eat; let's get your food."

He barked more, growling low as he turned to look off in the distance. I frowned at him. "Tig, come here now!" I commanded as I slapped my hand against my thigh. He looked at me, barked once, and then turned and looked away again.

"I'm serious, Tigger, let's go! I have work to do. Stop screwing around and get in here. I'll take you for a long walk tomorrow, I promise."

Tigger turned toward me and started to come in the door, except when he stepped in, he went around me and pushed me toward the opening. "What are you doing? Tig! Stop! I'm not going outside."

While Tig might look aggressive, even downright dangerous to some, he wasn't, especially not with me. That's why when he

3

opened his jaws wide and clamped down on my wrist, yanking me out the door, I finally took notice of his behavior.

"Tig, what's going on?" Apprehension began to shift down my spine as I stepped out of the door. The odor of smoke was much more pungent now, and Tig let go of my wrist and began to run off in the direction he had been watching. I followed his path with my gaze, and my jaw dropped.

"My house!" I screamed. "Oh, my god! My house is on fire!"

The side of my house was indeed on fire, and the flames licked up the structure from ground to roof. I froze for a moment, and then I did what any smart person would do that wasn't thinking: I turned and ran back into my house. As I entered the back, I noticed that there were tendrils of smoke easing down the hallway from the other side of the house.

My heart began to gallop in my chest as I glanced around wildly as Tigger started to bark again. Where the hell was my phone? I ran down the hallway, bouncing off the doorframe as I took the turn into my bedroom sharply. Ouch! I'd have a bruise from that one.

The back bedroom was cloudy with smoke, and I coughed. My phone was right where I'd left it, on the charger beside the bed. I had put it there this morning so it wouldn't distract me while I worked. I grabbed the phone, my fingers shaking so badly I almost dropped it as I began to cough more. The smoke burned my lungs, and I dropped to my knees, remembering the lesson I had learned many years ago in elementary school. Get low, avoid the smoke, and crawl to safety.

I crawled like a woman possessed out of the bedroom, noticing the flames outside the window. Back in the hallway, I coughed again and stood. I raced down the hall, trying to unlock my phone, but I was shaking so much that I couldn't manage to hit the unlock correctly.

It dawned on me as I hit my kitchen that there was an emergency button on my phone. One I had never pushed before on purpose, and I punched the button. Call 911 showed up on my phone, and I hit it as I reached into a closet and grabbed Tigger's leash.

Before I could turn away from the closet, Tigger clamped his teeth on the leg of my pants and yanked; I heard the material rip, and then his teeth were on my ankle. "Tig! Ouch! Stop!"

Tig was still pulling me as a man's voice came over the phone. "Emergency Services. What's your emergency?"

"My house is on fire!" I shouted at him.

"Ma'am, is there smoke?"

As if on cue, I began to cough again. "Yes!"

"Are you still in the house?"

"Yes!"

"Can you get out?"

"Yes, I can. I'm going now."

"Okay, what's your address?"

I gave him the information as I raced through the kitchen to the back door, giving my microwave a cursory glance as I thought about my food in there.

Tigger used his hundred-pound body to push me out the door, and as I rushed off the back porch, another bout of coughing took my breath away. The guy on the phone asked more questions, and I answered them the best I could before he said help was on the way.

No sooner had I hung up than I heard sirens in the far-off distance. I stood staring at the back of my house and heard someone shout behind me.

"Are you alright?" As I turned, I saw movement off to the side near the bushes, but my eyes drifted right past it to his back deck, and I saw my neighbor standing there.

"Yeah, I'm fine, thank you," I told him. I had no idea what his name was, even though I had lived in this house for six months. I didn't know any of my neighbors. I was a hermit.

More sirens rang through the evening air, and I rushed

5

around the side of the house, stepping in something soft and squishy in my bare feet. "Oh, my god! Was that dog poop?"

The scent of dog feces wafted to my nose almost immediately, and I dragged my foot along the grass, trying to rid myself of it the best that I could. I gagged as I felt it between my toes. Another task that I had put off while I was trying to get my book finished. I hadn't cleaned up the dog crap!

A police car zipped into the cul-de-sac where I lived, and I waved two arms over my head—just in case he couldn't see the flames on the roof behind me. Tigger leaned against my side protectively, and I quickly snapped the leash onto his collar so he wouldn't run away—or attack someone. The officer parked as far away as possible as a pickup truck pulled around him, his headlights striking me and making me glance away. Both men looked in my direction momentarily, but neither made any effort to head toward me immediately.

"What are they waiting for?" I asked irritatedly as I glanced over my shoulder. Flames licked sideways over my roof now, and my heart sank. A flash caught my eye, and I noticed red lights bouncing off the houses a street over. The siren of the fire truck echoed eerily in the quiet of the evening. Oh, please hurry! I prayed to myself.

I watched the man from the truck begin to pull things out of the back and start to get dressed in his firefighter stuff as the first fire truck came barreling up the hill and toward my house. A moment later, another one followed. The men in the fire trucks began to scurry around. My gaze went back to the house as they pulled things off their vehicle and stayed there until Tig growled softly. I turned to find a handsome police officer approaching me.

"Friend, Tig," I said to him as I tugged his leash slightly. Tig stopped the immediate growl, although he grumbled in his chest.

"Ma'am, do you live here?"

"Yes, this is my house," I responded.

"What happened?"

"I don't know!" I threw my hand up in the air and watched two firefighters approach my front door, each carrying a heavy-duty tool in their hands. "My dog went nuts, and then I realized my house was on fire."

One of the firefighters held the storm door open and lifted a sledgehammer over his shoulder, while the other one shoved something into the doorframe. "Strike!" the man said, and the guy hit the back of the tool. A loud cracking sound filled the quiet air, and I winced. Oh, my god! My house was going to be destroyed.

As my gaze drifted from the door, it landed on the front window. I saw my laptop through the window, the screen still glowing, the word document barely visible from my distance. My heart seized in my chest! No! Oh, god, no! I forgot my computer! Not my laptop!

Before I could think twice, I shoved Tigger's leash toward the officer and took off running toward my house. There was no way I could allow my laptop to get ruined! I didn't back my manuscript up on my other drive yet. I couldn't lose this story.

Tigger barked frantically behind me, and the cop yelled for me to stop, but I was on a mission. I had to get into the house and get my laptop. Just ten feet into the house, grab it, and then I could get right back out.

Only as I began to near the door, a firefighter barreled out, bent low enough to put his shoulder into my stomach, and effectively halted me from my forward movement. He knocked the air from my chest, and I gasped as he lifted me to his shoulder.

"No! Put me down!" I sputtered on my next breath. "I have to get my laptop!"

"Sorry, darling, you are not going back inside that house."

"Put me down! I have to get it." I slapped his back, kicking my legs as I lifted my head to see the front door getting farther away.

Suddenly, he jerked. "Ow! Call him off! Call off your damn dog!"

I glanced to the side to see Tigger had a hold of his arm. "Tig, stop! Put me down. He won't let you go until you put me down."

The firefighter began to lean forward and all but dropped me right on my ass in the middle of my front yard. "Tig!" I yelled as I winced from the abrupt landing. God, that jarred the hell out of my back. "Tig! Out!"

Tigger immediately let go of the firefighter and came to stand between him and me, growling and pulling back his gums to display his bright-white canines. It was only then that I lifted my eyes to the man's face and sucked in a sharp breath. He could be the hero in the story I was about to finish. My gaze slipped past him to the front window, and I sobbed as I watched smoke filling the room, circling above my laptop—or the one I was going to have to write all over again.

CHAPTER TWO

HUNTLEY

I had just left the firehouse after a long, quiet day. Ironically, we had been joking about the fact that it had been beyond slow in the area for the last few days. Our calls were almost nonexistent other than a small kitchen fire, a lawn tractor that burned down to the frame, and two separate car accidents.

I was almost home when the tones rang out through the radio sitting beside me. I hadn't turned it off yet, and when I heard the location of the fire, I knew I'd likely be the first to arrive. I pulled around one of our local police officers, grinning to myself when I saw Ethan Winston climb out of his cruiser.

Ethan and I were good friends from high school. Our families had been close, sharing many barbeques, carpools, and even a few holidays. It probably had something to do with the fact that like our family, they also had six kids, although Ethan was one of two boys in the family, where I had three brothers and two sisters.

"Hey, Chief," I said over the radio on our private channel. "We have a working fire, single home, enough space between houses to avoid a rollover."

"Okay, thanks, Hunt," he replied as I got out of my truck.

"Hey, man!" Ethan called when he saw me exit. "Looks like you guys finally have some work to do. About time you all get paid for doing something."

I laughed as I glanced at the house, seeing the flames crawling over the roof. The smoke was pluming into the dark sky.

"Is that the homeowner?" I asked Ethan after I'd noticed a woman and dog standing in the front yard.

"Must be," he commented as I pulled on my bunker gear. "Damn, it looks like that lady I was telling you about the other day. You know the hot one I saw at the coffee shop?"

"Oh, yeah?" I squinted toward her, but she was too far away to see details, and it was getting darker by the second.

"Yeah." He grinned. "Guess I'll go introduce myself." He began to saunter off as I chuckled and watched the first of three fire trucks roll past me.

Two of the trucks were there as I joined the group gathering equipment. "Young, Brown, breach the door."

I nodded to my chief, who stood back, reading the fire as it gathered momentum. I grabbed the breach tool and headed toward the front door, glancing at the woman and her dog near Ethan. She was a beauty, even with her messy blond hair and torn pants.

Brown and I took the front door, and I stepped inside to look at the interior. I still needed to get my air pack and mask, so I didn't venture too far in, but I saw enough to tell us that the fire was in the attic and burning through the ceiling. When I turned around to leave, I saw the woman racing toward the front door like she was on a mission, and I stepped off the threshold, squatting down at the last second to catch her. No way she was going inside.

"No! Put me down! I have to get my laptop!"

"Sorry, darling, you are not going back inside that house."

She hit my back, and I chuckled. "Put me down! I have to get it!" I laughed more as she squirmed, and I got a whiff of dog shit right before I saw the dog charging me.

Ethan was rushing after the dog, but it was too late. He latched on to my arm, hard enough to hurt, but I didn't think he had broken the skin through my bunker jacket. "Ow! Call him off! Call off your damn dog!"

She shifted on my shoulder, and I almost dropped her as I tried to keep myself on my feet and dislodge the dog from my arm while I held her balanced over my shoulder.

"Tig, stop! Put me down. He won't let you go until you put me down."

There was no way to do it gracefully, and she flopped off my shoulder and to the ground with a grunt. "Tig! Tig! Out!"

The dog immediately let me go and put himself between her and me. I stared at the dog, afraid to move. For a moment, none of us did, and then she scrambled to grab his leash and get to her feet.

"You have to get my laptop! It's right on my couch! Please!" She begged me. "Please, just grab it! I can't lose what's on that! I'll give you anything that you want; just get it for me, please!"

I glanced back at the house, then at her dog. She'd give me anything for it? Well, that could be an exciting proposition—if it wasn't for her dog. I slowly stepped away from her, and her killer dog watched me warily as I moved.

She jerked the dog's leash. "Friend, Tig. Friend."

Friend, my ass! That dog wanted to eat me for dinner. When was the last time she fed that creature? The dog gave me one last long look before he turned to her, his tongue lolling out the side of his mouth as he leaned against her leg.

Feeling like I could finally turn my back on the man-eating dog, I returned to the front door as a few of the guys entered with a line. I brushed around them and into the living room that was densely filled with smoke and found her laptop sitting on the couch. I yanked the power cord from the side and closed the computer, carrying it outside.

I stopped ten feet away from her, eyeing the dog carefully. There was no way I would approach her with the dog staring at me like he wanted a second chance at my arm bone. Ethan chuckled from off to the side and held his hand out. I happily handed over the computer to him.

"Thank you!" the woman called, and I nodded once as I saw the gratefulness in her gaze and went back to work.

We busted out the house's windows, ripped down the ceiling and walls, and put the fire out. It was a destructive fire, and I felt for the woman who lived here. Hopefully, she had family and friends around who could help her out.

I was standing on the side of the house when I felt eyes on my back and turned to find a man standing in the shadows. He wore a dark t-shirt and a baseball cap, and his complexion was ruddy, his eyes intense as he stared back at me. I turned away; people always came to gawk at fires. Some out of horror at the situation, some because of a sick fascination with destruction.

I glanced the other way; there were several people gathered about on the sides of the scene. I scanned the area but didn't see the woman or her dog. Did she go into someone's house?

Not my business and not my problem. I put out the fires. I didn't get involved with the homeowners or the aftermath.

It took three hours before the fire was ultimately out, and we were packing the truck again. Four fire trucks had responded to the scene, and many of the guys stood around shooting the shit as they finished their tasks and cleaned up.

It was strange—maybe to some—but the atmosphere was more upbeat than it had been in a while. Like me, these guys craved the adrenaline, and after being able to feed that craving, they were on a high that lasted for a few days. It was kind of sick in a way, but that's how firefighters were—police officers too.

I was putting something next to one of the last truck's compartments when I noticed the ambulance parked off to the side. Sitting on the back ledge was the woman and my brother, Henley. Lying on the ground at her feet was her killer dog. He looked like he was resting, but his eyes were watchful, always shifting as they tracked the movement around him. If anyone stepped toward him, he lifted his head and watched until they moved away.

My gaze went to the woman who was hugging her computer to her chest. She swiped at her cheeks as if she were crying, and I glanced back at the house. Her house was a wreck. She'd be lucky to salvage anything from seventy-five percent of it. Maybe a few odds and ends, but not much after the flames, smoke, and water damage.

I felt for her; I did. It was hard to watch someone lose everything in a matter of minutes. My feet carried me toward the ambulance, and Henley saw me. "Hey, there you are. I lost you a few times." He stood as I stopped in front of him and began to remove my bunker jacket.

"I didn't realize you were working tonight," I replied, glancing at the woman who was observing us unabashedly.

"Yeah, took a shift. Roxy is working tonight. Figured I'd make a little extra money; we need to put a new roof on the house. The stupid thing passed inspection, and then a week after we bought the house, we found a damn leak."

"That sucks." I cracked a grin at him. I'd never pictured Hen settling down or owning a home, although I wasn't sure why.

"Yes, it does."

I pulled my jacket back and winced as the material ran over my left forearm. I glanced down at it and saw the start of a bruise on my forearm from the earlier dog bite.

"Whoa," Henley said as he took my arm. "What the hell happened?"

I lifted my chin toward the dog, who sat on his haunches

staring at me, his mouth open, his tongue hanging out. "That happened."

Henley glanced at the dog. "Tigger did that?"

My gaze popped to the woman, and she winced and curled her shoulders forward. "I'm sorry. He's never bitten anyone before."

Henley turned my arm around. "He broke the skin here," he commented and looked at the woman. "Daniella, is he up to date on shots?"

She nodded quickly. "Yes, in fact, he was just there a few weeks ago to get his boosters. I can show you the paperw—" She stopped as her eyes slammed back to her house. "Well, I could have shown you the paperwork, but I don't think it survived."

Daniella, hmm—a beautiful name. It matched her well. "It's okay. I believe you." It would be hard to believe that she didn't take care of him properly, especially as attached as they seemed to be.

She winced again. "I truly am sorry about that. Tigger was so excited by what was going on, and he was only trying to protect me."

"As was I," I told her gruffly.

"Yeah, but he didn't know that," Daniella stated and then pursed her lips. I saw a spark of something in her gaze as if she was preparing to fight.

"Why are you upset with me? I was trying to keep you from getting hurt."

"I only wanted to go into the front room and get my laptop," she said hotly.

"Yeah, well, the house was filling with smoke. I wasn't going to let you get hurt."

She sighed, and the fire that had been in her eyes quickly extinguished as she visually deflated before my eyes. "I know, and I appreciate you retrieving it for me. You have no idea how much I would have lost if it were destroyed." She squeezed the computer tighter to herself.

It was a computer; I'm sure she could have lived without it, but at least I had saved one thing for her. I wondered if she had meant what she had said about giving me anything for retrieving it. My thoughts on the possibilities distracted me briefly until my brother snapped me back to reality.

"Let me get this cleaned for you," Henley said.

"No, it's okay. I'm fine. I'll do it later."

"You should let me clean it, Hunt."

"I told you it's fine." I was going to have a nice bruise, but I'd live.

"Hey, I have a favor to ask," Henley said as I started to step away and return to work.

"Yeah, what?"

"Can you take Daniella over to Mom and Dad's when you get done?"

I blinked, my brow furrowing. "Mom and Dad's? Why?"

"Because Daniella doesn't have anywhere else to go. She doesn't know anyone around here. She sure can't stay here, and I already talked to Mom. She was fine with it."

Daniella glanced between us a few times. "This is your brother?" she asked toward Henley.

He nodded. "Yeah, this is Huntley, the baby of the family."

I smacked him in the gut. "Hey, I might be younger, but I could take your ass in any competition."

Henley laughed good-naturedly. "Yeah, you think so."

I grinned at him as I turned away. "Yeah, I can take her over. Let me get my stuff done first."

"Hey," Henley called, and I turned back. "The service is already on its way. I called them for Daniella."

I nodded. "Okay, we can wait for them to arrive and secure the premises before I take her to Mom's."

I glanced at her, taking in the haunted look on her features as she stared at the smoldering shell of her house. She shivered, and something deep in my chest wanted to reach out to her. I sure couldn't do that, but I could do something else.

"Hen, there is a sweatshirt in my truck; get it for her."

He nodded, and I turned away, wanting to do the opposite, and went back to work before I made a fool of myself or got bit by the K-9 killer again.

CHAPTER THREE

DANIELLA

I couldn't believe this was happening. More times than I wanted to count, I almost broke down into hysterics, but somehow, I held it back. Maybe it was because I was surrounded by testosterone-filled men who would have shaken their heads at me and thought I was a weak female.

Well, I was a weak female, but they didn't need to know that. Henley had been kind enough to bring me over to the ambulance and keep me company. Explaining what they were doing as the firemen around my house worked.

My heart was heavy—my house destroyed. Practically everything I owned was gone. I closed my eyes and tried to memorize the feeling. Not that I wanted to remember, but because one day, I could use this in a book. I could put my thoughts and feelings about losing everything into a story to bring it to life.

"It can be replaced," Henley said sympathetically as if he knew what I was thinking.

I snorted. "Can you read minds, Henley? I was just thinking about how it was all gone."

He chuckled. "No, I can't read minds, but it is written all over your face."

I sighed as a single tear rolled down my cheek, and I swiped it away. "I have no idea what I am going to do now."

"Well, after the fire marshal determines what caused the fire, your insurance company will assess the damage. Then you can work with them to get it rebuilt."

"Rebuilt," I murmured. "Rebuilt. My whole life has been one constant rebuild after another."

He didn't say anything for a while as I dwelled over the mess of my life.

"Do you have friends in the area? Family?"

I shook my head slowly. "No. I've only been here for a few months. I don't know anyone in the area."

"No one?"

I cocked my head. "I think the barista at the coffee shop is Coleen." I frowned. "Or Cathy, or something like that. But I honestly don't know a single person in this town."

He chuckled. "Coral, her name is Coral. She owns the place." He paused. "How long have you lived here?"

"Oh!" I felt my cheeks begin to heat. "Makes sense, Coral's Coffee Cafe, and I've lived here for six months," I murmured, wondering how much of a loser he thought I was now.

"You've lived here for six months, and you don't know anyone?"

I shook my head.

"Why did you move here if you didn't know anyone?"

I glanced at him. "For exactly that reason, I didn't know anyone."

He grew quiet for a few long moments, and then I saw him pull his phone out from the corner of my eye. "Hey, Dad."

I glanced at him, wondering if his phone had rung and I hadn't heard it.

"Yeah, we're at the fire now—pretty bad, which is why I'm calling. The house is totaled, and the owner, Daniella, doesn't have any friends or family in the area. I was wondering if she could stay at your place at least tonight, her and her dog."

I blinked at him. He was asking his parents if I could stay at their house? He didn't even know me, and I sure as hell didn't know them. Why would he do that?

"Okay, yeah, thanks. I appreciate that. I'll talk to you guys a little later."

He hung up the phone and found me staring at him when he turned my way. "You did not just ask your parents to take me in for the night, did you?"

He shrugged. "Yeah, of course, I did. You need a place to stay, and they have the room."

"I can't do that, Henley. As nice as you seem to be, I can't stay with strangers."

"Well, it's either my parents' house or you sleep on the street." He sighed. "I guess someone could give you a ride to Summersville, but that's an hour away, and I'm not sure the hotel there allows pets."

I closed my eyes, feeling the overwhelming urge to curl in a ball and cry until I couldn't shed another tear. Instead, I stared at Tig. He looked at me, his eyes bright, his tail thumping on the ground.

"They don't mind Tigger being there?"

"No, they like dogs. They live on a small farm, so animals are welcome. As long as your dog doesn't bite anyone."

I winced. "He bit one of the firemen."

"Your dog did?"

"Yeah, I was trying to run into the house to get my laptop, and one of the firemen stopped me by picking me up over their shoulder. I was fighting with him to put me down, and Tigger latched on to his arm."

"I'm sure he's alright, or I would have seen him over here."

"I hope so," I said. "I'm not sure I can handle anything else right now."

"So, you willing to stay at my parents'?"

"Tell me about them. I'm not real trusting with strangers."

He grinned. "Dad's mostly retired, although he still owns a construction company, which my older brother, Bradley, runs now. I'm one of six kids. My brother, Huntley, is over in that fray someplace; he's a firefighter. One of my other brothers, Wesley, just got married in March; he's a doctor in Summersville. Riley is my younger sister; she's a teacher, and Kayley lives in New York. She's a real estate agent. Oh, and my oldest brother, Brad, has two kids, and Wes just adopted his stepdaughter."

"Too bad the sister that is in real estate doesn't live around here. I might need to buy a new house."

He laughed. "Nah, they will fix this up. It will be good as new when they finish."

"I don't want new. I want what I had."

"I'm sorry, Daniella."

"Thanks," I muttered, and we grew quiet for a while. Every once in a while, another tear would ease down my cheek, and I would wipe it away. A few minutes later, one of the firefighters approached us, talking to Henley. I quickly realized it was the one that had stopped me from going into my house.

He was also the one that could have easily been my hero, Jake, in my current novel. His green eyes, robust facial features, short dirty blond hair were identical to what Jake had in my story. I eyed him out of the corner of my eye as he spoke to Henley, enjoying the view more than I should have.

Maybe that's why I snapped at him about stopping me from going inside my house. I didn't want to find him appealing. I didn't want anyone to be appealing other than my fictional heroes. Or was I nervous about what he might want after I'd told him I'd give him anything to retrieve my computer? Did he remember that? Would he ask me for something?

I was a little unnerved that he would be taking me to his

parents' house and not Henley. I didn't know this guy, even though he had tried to protect me. I didn't know Henley either, but I had immediately liked and trusted him. What was it about his brother that made me jittery?

Not that it mattered. I didn't have any choice. I had nothing. I sighed as I thought about my car parked in the garage. It was under the worst of the fire—under the hundreds of gallons of water from the hoses. There was no doubt that it was ruined, too.

The only clothing that I now owned was the stained t-shirt and torn lounge pants on my body, and I didn't even have shoes. Speaking of which, my toes were cold—everything about me was frosty—and it wasn't even a chilly night.

Henley walked away shortly after his brother did, and a few minutes later, he returned and held a sweatshirt out to me. I set my laptop to the side, pulling the large item over my head. A spicy scent filled my nose as my head slipped under the material, and I inhaled deeply. Wow, I could stay like this—just like this. I could hide inside here like a turtle, fantasize about my next sexual encounter between characters, and just enjoy this lovely, spicy scent. I inhaled again slowly, feeling better than I had in hours.

"You okay?" Henley asked with a chuckle, and I popped my head through the opening.

"Yeah, sorry." I felt a blush creeping over my cheeks. Hopefully, those thoughts weren't written on my face now.

A few more people arrived in large SUVs and eventually, the fire trucks started to leave. Huntley returned to the ambulance, and Henley stood again.

"You guys done?" Henley asked him.

"Yeah, you can clear," He told his brother before turning to me. "You ready to leave?"

I glanced at him, then my house. "But what about my house?"

Huntley peered back at it. "The fire marshals just arrived. It's going to take them a little while to figure out what caused this. Some people will be here soon to board up what they can to keep people out until the insurance company arrives."

"Can't I go in? I want to see how much damage there is."

He shook his head. "No, it's not safe for you to go in. The house is unstable, and there are still some hot spots."

The tears began to bang on the back of my eyelids, and I blinked rapidly to stop them. A few snuck out and trickled down my face. I batted them away angrily. "I can't just walk away from here."

Henley stepped in front of me, and Tigger got to his feet to get out of the way. "Daniella, there is nothing that you can do tonight. Go to my parents' house, get something to eat, take a shower, and try to get some rest. You can come back tomorrow and see it in the light of the day. There is nothing you can do tonight."

A man approached our group. "Hey, Hunt." He shook hands with him.

"Hey, Broadbent, good to see you."

"Yeah, you too." The man turned to me. "Are you the homeowner?"

"Yes. I'm Daniella Knight." I stood, my legs stiff from sitting so long in one spot.

He put his hand out, "Marc Broadbent." I shook it quickly as Tigger leaned against my leg. Everyone watched the dog for a moment. "Tig, friends."

The men shared nervous looks, but then Marc Broadbent began to ask me questions about myself, the house, and the fire. What was I doing when it started? What happened after the fire started? What insurance company did I have? Had I had any work done on my house recently? The questions went on for quite a few minutes.

"Okay, well, it looks like we are going to be busy here for a while. How can we reach you?"

"She's going to be at my parents' house," Henley supplied.

He nodded. "Okay, do you have a cellphone?"

I pulled it out of the waistband of my lounge pants. "Yeah, luckily, that didn't get left behind." I gave him the number.

"We'll give you a call once we finish, but it's probably not going to be until tomorrow morning. There are still hot spots around the house, and it will be easier to figure things out in the daylight."

"Thank you," I told him, and for a moment, the three men bantered about some sports event before he nodded to me and then walked away.

"Well, Daniella, I'm going to leave you in my brother's competent hands. I'm sure I will see you again. Get some rest tonight."

"Thank you, Henley," I replied and turned to his brother. I suddenly noticed that he no longer wore his fire gear but instead had on snug-fitting jeans and a long-sleeved t-shirt.

"Thanks, Hunt. I'll talk to you later."

"See you later, Hen."

Henley closed the doors to the ambulance, smiled at me, and then disappeared around the side as a box truck pulled up the street.

"Ah, that's the emergency service. Those guys will secure your house and make sure it's good after the fire marshals are finished."

I bobbed my head absently as I watched them park.

"Are you ready to go?"

I turned to him, then sighed. "Come on, Tig."

We walked toward his truck, and I stepped on a rock. "Ouch!" I yanked my foot up, almost dropping my laptop. A moment later, Huntley reached for me, and Tig growled low.

"Woah, boy. I'm just going to pick her up and carry her."

"You don't have to do that," I said, gingerly putting my foot back to the ground.

"We don't need you cutting your feet to pieces. Tell your dog I'm not going to hurt you."

"It's okay, Tig," I said softly, and then Huntley came a little closer, his eyes on Tigger as he put his arms around me and lifted me.

Tigger walked at our side, and I tried not to memorize the feel of Huntley's arms around me. Although on second thought, maybe I should remember this to fit it into my next book or go back and add it to a scene with Jake. Before I had decided what to do, we were at his truck, and he put me down, opening the back door. "Get in, Killer."

I chuckled. "He's not a killer."

"Could have fooled me." He spoke gruffly as he opened the front passenger door and let me get in. Tig jumped in the back, putting his head over the seat excitedly.

The doors closed, and Huntley went around the vehicle. I inhaled deeply, finding the interior filled with the same spicy scent from the sweatshirt, mixed with the odor of smoke. The combination was almost sexual. I needed to figure out what cologne he wore so I could keep a bottle around for inspiration.

Huntley got behind the wheel, glancing at Tigger and me. "He's quite protective. How long have you had him?"

"About a year," I replied.

"Any reason you keep an attack dog around?"

I glanced at Tigger and then him. "No." I wasn't going to share that I had purchased Tigger for just that reason, to protect me and attack the next man who tried to hurt me. Nope, as lovely as it was that he was helping me right now, it wasn't any of his business.

CHAPTER FOUR

HUNTLEY

She looked way too good for my liking in my sweatshirt, but I didn't say anything. I was irritated with myself for even noticing. Since I'd caught my fiancée in a compromising position earlier this year with her boss, I'd sworn off women for a while. I didn't want to notice them, and I sure as hell didn't want to get involved with them.

Unfortunately, I had noticed Daniella, though. Her sad eyes tore at my heart, and knowing that she had lost everything bothered me more than it should have. Picking her up and carrying her had been an idiotic idea because now I knew what she felt like in my arms, and damn, if I didn't suddenly miss that.

On the ride to my parents' house, I kept my attention on the road, although I was keenly aware of the woman, and her dog, beside me. Her dog leaned toward me and sniffed the side of my head, and I didn't move a muscle. The last thing I needed for him to do was to take off my ear.

We were halfway there when I couldn't stand the silence anymore. "So what is so important on the computer?"

"My job."

"Yeah?" I glanced toward her, getting a better view of killer's profile and his vicious-looking canine teeth than I did her. "What do you do?"

She seemed hesitant to talk, but after a moment, she replied, "I'm an author. I'm almost finished with my latest book. I only have one more chapter to go. I couldn't lose it."

Huh, an author. I sure didn't picture that. "You don't have your stuff backed up on a cloud server?"

"No, not until it's finished. I like to keep it on my hard drive until it's done, then I save it there to share with my editors."

I glanced toward her; the dog was staring at me. I shifted in my seat as I put my eyes back on the road and made a turn. "You might want to change that in the future so that you don't lose your work."

"Yeah." She sighed. "I know. My editor tells me that all the time."

"What kind of books do you write?"

"Nothing you would have read," she replied softly.

I laughed. "You don't know that. I happen to enjoy reading."

She peered around her dog as I came to a stop at a four-way intersection. One of her brows was raised in what I took as a sexy challenge. "Oh, do you read romance regularly?"

I chuckled. "Okay, I guess I wouldn't have read any of your work." Why did it seem fitting that she wrote romance? Was it because she was a beautiful woman? Or because she had soulful eyes that could probably dig right through every barrier and see your every desire?

I frowned to myself, more of a reason not to get to know her any better. The problem was that most parts of my body were not paying attention to my reasoning.

"I didn't think so," she said and sat back in her seat.

"I'm sure my sister Riley does, though, Riley, she loves to read, too." She didn't say anything, and I pondered what to say next. Probably better to just remain quiet. We were almost there anyway, so I focused on driving instead of conversation.

When we pulled down the long driveway, she lifted her laptop, hugging it close to her again as if she were putting a barrier between herself and something. I frowned as I parked, wondering why I even thought that.

I went around the truck, and she was climbing out. "Wait, let me carry you again. There is gravel here; it will kill your feet. Trust me, I know from experience."

She bit her bottom lip as I lifted her, and I got stuck on it for a moment. When I lifted my gaze from her mouth to her eyes, I froze. How had I not noticed how pretty her blue eyes were?

We stood staring at one another so long that her dog jumped over the seat and inserted his head between our faces. Daniella laughed. "Tig, stop!" She pushed his furry head away. "Sorry about that."

I chuckled and stepped back. "Come on, Tigger," I called him, and he looked at her. She nodded, and then he jumped down.

"He listens to you well," I commented as I carried her toward the back door of the house.

"He's supposed to do that," she said, keeping her face turned away from me.

"Yeah, I guess he is," I commented, and when we reached the back porch, I set her down. She stepped away immediately, glancing around.

"I bet it's pretty here in the daylight. Do your parents have horses?"

"Yeah, two of them. Buttercup and Fellow."

"Oh, very nice." I glanced back and saw the dog running around the yard and lifting his leg on a bush.

"Come, Tigger," she called and slapped her leg once. He immediately responded to her and trotted up the stairs to her side. I pulled open the back door. "You're sure it will be alright for Tigger and me to stay here?"

"Yeah, it's good," I told her as I waited for her to go in.

"Come on, Tig," she said softly and stepped cautiously into the mudroom.

When she paused, I stepped around her and her dog into the kitchen. "Mom? I didn't expect you to be up."

"Oh, Hunt, when Henley called and told us what happened, I just couldn't sleep. Where is she?"

I stepped to the side. "Mom, this is Daniella and her dog, Tigger. Although you might—" I was going to warn her to be careful of the dog, but she bent down, smiling at him, and he rushed to her, his tail wagging. "Or not."

Daniella snickered. "He likes women."

"Lucky women," I commented dryly.

My mother stood, letting her eyes slip over Daniella quickly. "Oh, dear, come in here. What a night you have had." She went to Daniella's side and put her arm around her. "Let me get you something to eat, and then you can take a shower and get some rest. Things will look better tomorrow."

Daniella's eyes were wide with surprise as she glanced my way as if asking for help. I hid a smile behind my hand for a moment as I rubbed the scruff on my chin.

My mother took her to a chair and all but pushed her into it. "Now, I already have water on, so I'm going to pour you a cup of tea and make you something to eat. Do you have any food allergies? We can never be too careful about those."

"No, I don't, and thank you."

"Don't you thank me, you poor girl, losing everything." She tsked as she turned to me. "Hunt, go shower, you smell horrible. I'll make you something to eat too."

I chuckled. "Thanks, Mom, but I was going to head home."

My mother's head cranked toward me, and then she glanced at Daniella. "And leave her here alone? She doesn't know us. I'm sure she would be much more comfortable with someone she knew here."

"Mom, I just met her tonight."

We turned to Daniella, and I saw the concern in her eyes as she spoke softly. "It's okay; you can go home if you want. I'll be fine."

I stared at her, getting stuck in her beautiful blue eyes again, and inhaled sharply. "I'll go take a shower. I'll stay the night; that way, I can take you back to your house in the morning."

She looked thankful the moment I spoke, and I knew I'd made the right decision. At least for her, it was the right decision. Me? Well, I wasn't so sure about that as I began to walk out of the room.

I glanced back over my shoulder. Tigger had lain down at her feet, and she was staring at me. "I'll be back in a few minutes."

She nodded as my mother responded. "She will be fine, Hunt. Go, you're smelling up my house, and make sure to bring your clothes back down. Don't leave them upstairs wadded in the corner."

Daniella chuckled as we shared a smile, and I dramatically rolled my eyes and left the room as I shook my head. Did moms just assume that their sons never grew up? I had my own apartment, and it was rather neat and orderly. Even though I lived not too far from here, I kept some clothes in my old bedroom for when I helped around the property. I gathered a change of clothes and then paused, staring down at my t-shirts. I dug around until I found one that I thought was soft enough for Daniella to sleep in and collected a pair of socks for her, too— just in case.

I hustled through a shower, worrying that my mom was giving Daniella the third degree. The urge to protect her again striking me in the gut like a fist. I didn't understand that, and I knew she would be okay with my mom. Probably safer with her than me, but that didn't stop the sudden drive to make sure she was.

When I rounded the corner into the kitchen, I stopped.

Daniella was holding up her fork, chattering about something that made absolutely no sense. My mother was hanging on her every word—eyes wide, lips slightly parted.

"Oh, Hunt! Do you know who this is?" my mother said excitedly when she noticed I'd come back in.

"Um, yeah, Daniella, the same person I left down here fifteen minutes ago—I think," I replied.

"Oh, Hunt, you're such a man sometimes." She waved a hand at me. "This is Veronica Raven! She's one of my absolute favorite authors! Oh, my, I'm having a fangirl moment." She waved a hand in front of her face. "You really have no idea how exciting it is to meet you. My book club read your *Turbulent Troubles* a couple of months ago, and everyone just loved it."

Daniella's cheeks pinkened as she peeked my way. "I'm glad you all enjoyed it. I enjoyed writing that story."

"You've read one of her books?" I asked as I approached the table.

"One of her books? No! I have read them all, Hunt! At least, I think I have read them all. How many books do you have out now? I think the last I counted, I owned fifty of them."

Daniella laughed slightly. "I have published fifty-six."

"Oh, then I am missing some. You will have to look at my shelf and see which ones I'm missing." My mother reached over the table, patting Daniella's hand. "I hope you will be willing to sign one of them for me."

"Do you have one in paperback?" Daniella asked.

"I have them *all* in paperback," she quickly replied. "I don't like reading on those machines. I much prefer a book in my hands. Honestly, you do not know how exciting this is to me."

My mother quickly stood and took the clothing from me as I spoke to Daniella. "You didn't tell me you had written that many books."

"You didn't ask," she replied with a quirk in her brow that made her pretty features rather sultry-looking.

"Oh, wait until I tell the girls that Veronica Raven was at my house!"

If I hadn't been looking at her, I wouldn't have seen the almost scared expression that flashed briefly over her features.

"Um, can you not?" Daniella asked in a rush, looking like she was about to make a break for the back door.

My mother considered her for a moment. "Well, of course, if you'd rather me not, but may I ask why?"

Daniella pulled her bottom lip under her teeth and glanced at her plate. She clenched her eyes before she lifted her face to my mom.

"To be honest, I prefer my privacy. That's why I use a pen name. I don't particularly like others to know that I'm Veronica Raven."

"Oh," my mother stated and then smiled kindly. "Of course, that makes total sense."

It did? It didn't make much sense to me, but okay.

"Thank you; I appreciate that." She grew quiet for a moment. "Although when this is over, I'd be happy to sign and donate copies of my newest book to your club if you'd like that."

My mother gasped, her hand going to her chest. "You would do that?"

"Of course," Daniella smiled brightly. "You're letting me stay here tonight; it's the least I can do."

My mother tossed the clothes into the mudroom and came back, retaking her seat. "You are welcome to stay here as long as you need to. Please don't think it's just for tonight. We have plenty of room with all the kids out of the house."

Daniella glanced my way. "That's very kind of you, but I don't want to be a burden."

"No burden at all. I'd be honored to have you stay here." My mother picked up her cellphone and began to type something.

"Mom, what are you doing?"

31

"I'm sending a message to Riley to see if she can bring clothes over for Daniella. They are about the same size."

"That's not necessary," Daniella quickly said, and my mom's brow rose as she chuckled slightly.

"Dear, you can't walk around in that tomorrow. You aren't even wearing a bra or shoes!"

Daniella's shoulder rounded, and her cheeks pinkened as if someone had just poured paint over them. I couldn't help myself as I glanced at her chest; how did my mom know she wasn't wearing a bra? She still wore my sweatshirt, and it covered her well.

I swallowed and looked away quickly—damn.

I peered at my mother, who raised a brow like she knew exactly what I had just been doing. I cleared my throat and pulled the plate she'd left on the table toward me.

"I left a t-shirt on Riley's bed for you to sleep in, Daniella. I figured Mom was going to put you in her room. It was the only one with a light on upstairs."

"Yes, I thought she'd be more comfortable in that one since it's right across from the bathroom."

Daniella turned to me, her bottom lip caught under her teeth. "Thank you."

I stared at her mouth for a moment then forced myself to meet her gaze, noting the dark circles under her eyes as I shifted in my seat. "No problem."

Daniella turned toward my mother as I shoved my fork into my mouth. "Why are you doing this, Mrs. Young? I mean, I sincerely appreciate it, but why would you go so far out of your way for a stranger?"

My mother's features softened. "Oh, Daniella, there is no such thing as a stranger; there are only people we have not had the opportunity to meet yet. Besides, that's what us Youngs do. We help people."

CHAPTER FIVE

DANIELLA

*M*rs. Young was a charming woman who immediately made me feel at ease— especially as she squatted down and rubbed on Tigger again. "Has he eaten?"

"No, I was so busy working before all this happened that I hadn't done so. Poor guy."

"Not to worry, I'm sure one meal off his normal diet won't kill him. We'll make sure to get some of his regular food, but do you think he'd be happy with some chicken and rice for tonight?"

"Oh, yes. Tig would be thrilled with that, thank you."

"How about you? Does that sound alright for you? I have plenty of leftovers in here if you'd like something else."

"I'll take anything. I'm not picky, and I am rather starved, thank you."

I watched her as she began to make two plates, and then I checked out the rest of the room. There were shelves along the wall with a few knickknacks, but most of the stuff that filled them looked handmade. Probably from her children over the years. There were mugs of all shapes and colors, plates with handprints, and a couple of houses built out of toothpicks and popsicle sticks, among many other things.

I scanned further and saw pictures on the wall—lots of pictures—that carried from one wall into the hallway where Huntley had disappeared. This house was a home—like a real home—and I felt both joyed to view it and depressed that I'd never had something like this.

"Come here, Tigger; this is for you." Mrs. Young set a large bowl on the floor, and Tigger turned to me.

"Eat, Tig."

He lifted off his haunches and went to the bowl, digging in hungrily.

"Your dog is very well trained."

"Thank you. He's good most of the time, but he has his moments." Although after tonight, I would forgive him the next time he brought me a dead groundhog or rabbit.

"Most dogs are," she said with a smile as she put a plate into the microwave behind her.

"He bit your son tonight. Huntley was trying to stop me from going back into my house, and Tig thought he was trying to hurt me."

She looked concerned for about three seconds before she asked, "Why would you possibly be trying to get back into your house if it were on fire?"

I put my hand over the laptop that I'd set on the table. "My laptop was in there. I couldn't lose what was on it."

She cocked her head as she stared at the laptop, momentarily. "What is so precious on that machine that you couldn't lose?"

"A book. I'm a writer, and I only have one more chapter to finish this one."

"A writer?" Her eyes brightened. "Do you write under your name?"

I shook my head, nibbling my bottom lip as I contemplated

how to respond. Finally, I figured if she was kind enough to open her house to a stranger for the night and feed both Tig and me, I could at least tell her the truth. "No, I write under the nom de plume of Veronica Raven."

She gasped. "You do not!"

I chuckled at her unexpected excitement. "Yes, I do."

She came around the counter quickly, pausing in front of me. "What book were you finishing? Oh, please tell me it was the next book in the Serenity Forest Series."

I startled back. "You know my books?"

"Oh, dear, do I know them?" She laughed loudly. "I love your books. You are one of my go-to authors! I even get your weekly newsletter, and as soon as a new book comes out, I purchase it."

I was somewhat surprised as Mrs. Young was a bit older than my typical reading fan, but I was very thankful for her.

The microwave dinged, and she went to remove the plate, setting it down in front of me before putting a new one in to warm. Tigger finished his meal and came back to my side, staring at me and then my plate.

"No, this is mine. Don't beg, Tig."

He shifted and curled at my feet.

"So, tell me," she said after the other plate was warmed, and she put it on the table a few chairs down from mine. "Is it another book in that series?"

"Yes, actually it is. It's Jake's book, and I just have the last chapter to write. I had every intention of doing that tonight, but then all hell broke loose."

"Give yourself a day, and you'll be back. Maybe you can finish it tomorrow."

"Hopefully," I told her and took a bite from my plate. "Thank you for this."

"Can I ask you a question?" she queried as she took a seat opposite me.

"By all means."

"Is Markus really on the wrong side of the law now, or did you make it seem that way to throw us off?"

I chuckled around a mouthful and wiped my mouth with the napkin before I responded. "I have been asked that quite often. I'd tell you, but that answer will be in this book."

"You know what I'm thinking—Markus did something wrong, and he's being blackmailed for it. That's why he's doing all that stupid crap, right? I have to believe that he is a good man and that he'll come back to Emily."

I grinned at her, pointing my fork for emphasis. "I will tell you this, Emily and Markus will be back together, but I'm afraid I can't tell you anything else, or it will ruin the suspense."

She glanced over my shoulder. "Oh, Hunt! Do you know who this is?"

He approached the table, and I glanced at him sideways. He was wearing sweatpants and a t-shirt that fit tightly over his chest. Totally Jake material, I thought to myself. Oh, man, was he ever Jake material.

"Um, yeah, Daniella, the same person I left down here fifteen minutes ago, I think."

"Oh, Hunt, you're such a man sometimes." Mrs. Young went on, and I began to blush. I loved to meet my readers, and I was always humbled by the praise they gave me.

Huntley was looking at me carefully, and then his mom as we discussed it. I was a bit overwhelmed that she was not only a fan, but what I'd call a superfan. Someone who read everything I published and collected the books. It made me feel much more comfortable about being here, knowing I was around someone who enjoyed my work—although some people might say it was almost stalkerish. Mrs. Young sure didn't fit *that* profile.

Thankfully she understood that I wanted my privacy, and an incident was averted. I hoped that my consolation of giving her book club signed paperbacks would help ease that along, and it seemed to.

As we continued to talk, she reached out to her daughter to bring me clothes. I found myself overwhelmed by everything that this family had already done for me. Why would they go through so much trouble for a stranger? I'd never really known anyone who would do that. Yes, I knew charitable people, but not ones that would open their doors to someone like me.

"Oh, Daniella, there is no such thing as a stranger; there are only people we have not had the opportunity to meet yet. Besides, that's what us Youngs do. We help people."

I stared at her, in awe of her words, and I glanced at her son to see him smiling tenderly at his mother. The look in his eyes similar to how I imagined Jake would look at Arrabella in my story—as if she were the world to him. There was no doubt that he treasured his mother. God, to have someone look at me with even half that amount of love and tenderness. What must it honestly feel like?

Huntley turned to me, and for just a moment, we studied one another, and I got a brief taste of the love he had for his mother before he cleared his throat and went back to eating with gusto.

"Well, you are too kind, and I can't imagine how I can repay you for your generosity."

"Think nothing more of it, Daniella. I'm glad that we can help you in any way that we can."

I returned to my meal and ate as much as I could with my anxious stomach. Visions of my house burning and the thoughts of what I had lost made it hard to swallow at times, along with the mental exhaustion of writing all day.

I was staring at my plate, pushing food around on it, when Huntley touched my arm, tentatively. "You alright?"

"Um, yeah. I guess I'm totally worn out and just so upset that I can't seem to think straight."

"Well, why don't I show you to the bathroom, and you can take a shower and try to get some rest."

"I think that's a good idea," his mother stated, and I started to yawn.

"I am getting very sleepy."

"It's the tea, dear," Mrs. Young said. "It's a calming blend that is supposed to help you relax and sleep."

"It's working," I told her and then thanked her for the food.

"Does Tigger need to go out again?" she asked, and his head popped off the floor.

"Oh, yeah, I guess he should since he just ate."

"Huntley, take the dog out, and I'll show her up to the bathroom."

Hunt stared at Tigger. "Um, I'm not sure the dog will listen to me."

I chuckled. "Yeah, probably not. I'll just take Tig out quickly." I stood, and Huntley came to my side, his gaze sliding to my chest momentarily before returning to my face. I felt the blush on my cheeks. I guess he hadn't noticed earlier that I wasn't wearing a bra, but now that my laptop was on the table, he could probably tell.

"I'll go out with you," Hunt said, and I nodded.

"Come, Tig. Let's go out." He followed me toward the door, and Hunt grabbed a coat off the hook by the door.

"Here, it's cooler out now."

"Thank you." I slipped it on and passed him as he held the door for Tigger and me. Tigger ran down the stairs and out to the lawn, and I paused at the steps, letting my eyes grow accustomed to the darkness. There was a light over by the barn, and it helped illuminate the paddock area. I'd always wanted to ride a horse, but I'd never had a chance. I had researched horses for a book in my series. So much research that I almost felt like I could climb on a horse and ride like the wind. My luck, I'd be knocked off within a few seconds.

Tigger was sniffing around as he searched for the perfect

spot to do his business. I stared out into the darkness. "I can't believe I lost my house and everything I owned."

Hunt propped himself against the railing a few feet away. "I'm sorry about that, Daniella. I know how difficult that is."

I stared at him. "Do you? I don't think you do." I glanced at the house behind me as if proving a point.

"Hey, just because I have never lost my house in a fire doesn't mean that I don't understand how much that hurts. I've seen it more times than I care to think about."

"I'm sorry. I don't mean to be judgmental. I really don't. I'm just overwhelmed and so damn tired right now." I wiped my hands over my face, trying to gather enough strength not to break down.

I heard his feet on the wooden floorboards, and then he put his hand on my arm to squeeze gently. "I'm sure you are, but you aren't alone here, Daniella. There are people that will help you."

"I know, and I appreciate your hospitality and everything your family is doing for me." His hand trailed down my arm and dropped as Tigger jumped back on the porch, staring at him.

"I don't think he likes me."

I laughed. "Give him time. Once he knows you aren't going to throw me over your shoulder again, he'll come to like you."

Huntley grinned. "Might be worth getting bit again to do that."

My mouth dropped; oh, that was totally something that Jake would say. My mind began to spin as I wondered if I could fit that someplace into my book.

He stepped further back, putting his hands up. "Sorry, that was inappropriate."

"It's okay," I told him and caressed Tigger's ears. "You done, boy?" He stared up at me with loving eyes and his tongue hanging out. "Let's go get some sleep."

I handed the jacket back to Hunt when we returned inside and then said good night to his mother, who was putting the last of the dishes into the dishwasher. Hunt led me through a large living room with almost every inch of the upper portion of the walls covered in photographs. Oh, the stories those photos could probably tell. I was itching to walk along and study them all, come up with my own perceptions of what each picture was trying to say, but then I yawned again. Maybe tomorrow.

I followed behind Huntley and tried not to notice how attractive his backside was in his sweatpants, but my writing brain was blasting words like mouthwatering, luscious, sexy as all get out.

I tore my gaze away as he turned on the landing, speaking in a low voice. "That's my parents' room." He thumbed over his shoulder. He pointed to a room down the hall. "This is the bathroom, and you can stay in here."

"Where is your room?" I asked as I looked further down the hall.

A small crooked smile slipped over his lips. "Why? You plan on coming to visit later?"

Holy smokes! It was like Jake had come to life before my eyes.

CHAPTER SIX

HUNTLEY

*O*pen mouth. Insert foot.

What in the world possessed me to say that to her? I had no clue, but I quickly tried to recover after her eyes widened.

"I'm sorry, I was joking. I guess I'm a little more slap-happy than I thought. It's been a long day."

She looked away, crossing her arms a little tighter over her chest. "It's okay. It has been a long day."

"Well, there is a shirt on the bed and socks. I wasn't sure if you liked to wear those at night or not, but I put some there in case you did. I know Riley likes to sleep in socks. She hates her feet being cold. I'm sure you'll find everything that you need in the bathroom; help yourself to anything." I was babbling, but I wasn't sure what else to do.

"Thank you, Huntley."

"Well, good night, Daniella. If you need anything else, just knock on my door. I'm a light sleeper."

"I will, thank you."

I took a step back, unable to tear my eyes from her beautiful face and the dark-blue eyes that observed me cautiously. She looked away after a moment and went into Riley's bedroom. "Tigger, lay down."

I was closing the door to my room when she stepped out, holding the t-shirt and socks to her chest; she went into the bathroom after peeking my way and giving me a nervous smile.

Tigger came out of the door, stared down the hall toward me, and then curled up in front of the bathroom door. His eyes locked on me as if to say, try it, buddy, I dare you.

I closed the door and sat on my bed. What was it about Daniella that gave me pause? What made me look a little harder, get lost in her eyes? I wasn't generally attracted to blonds, but there was something very appealing about her. Was it the apprehensive look in her eye? The wariness of her trust? The hurt?

I frowned as I pulled the covers back and got in bed. As I did, I heard the water in the shower turn on, and I tried hard not to imagine Daniella removing my sweatshirt along with the rest of her clothes and climbing under the spray.

I rolled to my side and closed my eyes. I didn't need to be thinking of Daniella that way, and I was quite sure that was the last thing that she wanted me to be thinking. I quickly drifted off to sleep and woke with a start.

"No!" I heard shouted from down the hall, and I was on my feet. I opened the door and realized her dog was whining as she called out again, "Stop!" I glanced at my parents' door, hoping that she hadn't woken them. I rushed to her door as I heard her cry out in a strangled voice, and I didn't hesitate to throw it open.

Tigger turned on me, growling slightly, but then returned his attention to Daniella as she thrashed in the bed. "It's okay, Tigger; I just want to help her," I said as I approached the bed, and he looked between her and me.

His ears were back as I reached her side, but he hadn't tried to bite me, not yet anyway. I sat gingerly on the edge, glancing at the dog and then Daniella as she sobbed in her sleep. "No!

Get away! Please, stop!" she called in a slurred voice, her hands batting the air.

I grabbed one wrist so that she wouldn't strike me and put my other hand on her arm. "Daniella, wake up. You're having a bad dream."

She jerked her arm away from me and sprang upright. Her wide eyes locked with mine, and then she did the last thing I thought she would ever do, she threw herself into my arms.

I held her and glanced at the dog. His head tilted to the side as if he were just as confused as I was. "It's okay, darling. It was just a bad dream."

"Jake," she whispered against my neck, and I frowned. Who the hell was Jake? Was that her boyfriend? A man she knew from her past?

I continued to hold her, and she eventually stopped shaking and fell back to sleep in my arms. Well, okay. While I had enjoyed holding her, I was more curious as to who the hell Jake was.

Her body relaxed, and I laid her gently back onto the mattress. Her arms slipped from my sides and fell to the mattress, and Tigger put his face on the bed, whining slightly.

I stared down at her sleeping face; she was incredibly beautiful, and I couldn't help myself when I leaned forward and kissed her brow. I sat back, glancing at her dog. "She's okay; she's asleep, Tig." I reached out a tentative hand toward him, and while his ears twitched, he didn't move otherwise and, more importantly, didn't growl.

I ran my hand over the soft fur of his head. "You watch her, okay?" I said to him before I walked back to the door. I stood there for a moment and looked over her, then the dog. He studied me a moment and then jumped onto the bed, curling his lithe body against her leg. Lucky dog.

I closed the door and returned to my room, wondering who

Jake was and if he was the one that she had asked not to hurt her. He better not be.

It took me a while to fall back asleep, and when I woke next, I heard the dog's nails on the hardwood floor outside my room. I rubbed my eyes, and there was a soft knock. "Come in."

I was rising on my elbow when she opened the door slightly and peered in. "I'm sorry to wake you, but Tig needs to go out, and I wasn't sure if there was an alarm on the door downstairs."

I tossed back the cover. "No, no alarm." As I stood, I realized that was probably a mistake as I'd taken my sweats off and now stood in my boxers, half-hard with my usual morning wood.

I glanced toward her and reached for my pants. She averted her eyes and stepped back. Beside her, Tigger sat, his eyes taking in my every move. She glanced nervously back at me, her gaze hitting my chest and running south, which wasn't helping my condition any.

"I can take him out if you'll give me a minute."

"Yeah, sure."

I noticed as she began to close the door that her cheeks were pink. I'd never seen a grown woman blush as much as she did. It was cute as hell.

I pulled a shirt over my head and then padded out to the hall. She stood near the door to her room, her ripped pants from the night before back on her body, but she still wore my sweatshirt, and damn—did it look smoking hot on her.

Jessica had worn a shirt or two of mine, but she'd never looked that good in them. I frowned to myself. The last thing I wanted to do was compare that cheating bitch with Daniella. "Let me use the bathroom, and I think there might be an extra toothbrush in the closet you can use."

"Thank you," she responded softly, and I let myself into the bathroom to do my business. After I'd washed my hands, I dug around in the cabinet and found a new toothbrush still in a wrapper.

I pulled the door open. "Here you go." I stepped back into the room, leaving the door open as I grabbed the one that I kept there for me. She stepped in awkwardly, and after I loaded my brush with toothpaste, I passed the tube to her.

She peeled back the wrapper and added her paste after wetting the brush slightly. When she stuck it in her mouth, our eyes locked in the mirror, and we both paused. Why had I thought that this would be a good idea?

I glanced away and began to brush again, trying hard not to let my gaze stray back to her, but as she moved, her breasts swayed under the shirt, and I almost choked on the froth in my mouth. I shifted slightly further away, hoping she didn't notice what was going on below my sweatpants.

She focused on the sink as she brushed, but I saw her peek up, her eyes trailing up my body, and back down again, pausing at my hips. I bent over and spat out the toothpaste. I wasn't done brushing, but I didn't need her staring at my aching groin any longer, or I'd be the one blushing.

I rinsed my toothbrush and then the sink before putting the brush in the cup that we kept beside the sink. "I'll let you finish and see you downstairs."

I went to step around her, but Tigger stood abruptly, and I ended up losing my balance. My hand landed on her ribcage, my fingers brushing the underside of her breast as I shifted my feet to keep myself from crushing her over the sink.

The toothbrush jutted out of her mouth, and white foam collected at the corner of her lips. We stared at one another in the mirror. I was almost flush against her back, and there was no way she couldn't feel what was going on behind her.

She swallowed—I swallowed, and something like an electrical surge went straight down my spine, where my dick twitched against her ass. Her eyes closed, and her breath hitched.

I jumped back, dropping my hand immediately and sidestepping her. "I'm sorry, it was hit you or fall over the dog."

She nodded, her eyes now open and following my every move out of the bathroom.

"I'll see you downstairs." I took off without waiting for any type of response, kicking myself the whole way. Holy shit, her body had felt incredible against mine, way too good. "Damn dog," I muttered to myself as I hit the first floor and adjusted myself.

I was putting coffee on when Daniella and Tigger entered the room, and the back door opened. She stopped on a dime in the middle of the room, and Tigger moved instantly to stand in front of her, his ears forward, eyes wide.

"Hey!" my sister's voice called.

"Hey, Riley." I winked at Daniella, and her shoulders relaxed noticeably. My sister hustled into the room, her arms full of clothes.

She stopped when she saw Daniella and Tigger. "Well, hello, and who is that handsome creature?"

"Your brother, of course." I joked, and she rolled her eyes and leaned over to kiss me on the cheek as I approached her.

"I was talking about the four-legged dog, not you, you idiot. God, your head is so big. How do you fit through the doorway?"

I grinned at her. "You love me, little sis. Riley, this is Daniella Knight."

Riley set the clothing on the table and put her hand out to Daniella, eyeing her carefully. "Hi, Daniella. I'm sorry to hear about what happened. I brought over quite a few things. Mom said you were about my size, and I have a feeling these will fit you perfectly. I wasn't sure what size shoe you wore, but—" She glanced at Daniella's feet, and I noticed that her toenails were painted a pale pink. "You will probably fit into at least one pair that I brought over."

"Thank you, Riley. I promise I'll get these back to you as soon as I get a chance to go shopping."

"No hurry. I have a ton of clothes."

Daniella was cautiously checking out my sister, and I wondered what she thought of her. Riley was always so put together—and today was no different. It didn't matter if it was six in the morning or seven at night; she was always picture perfect for the occasion.

"I stopped at the store on the way over and grabbed you a pack of underwear and a couple of sports bras. They probably aren't your type, but at least you'll have something clean to put on."

Daniella looked in awe. "Thank you. Please tell me how much I owe you, and I'll make sure to pay you back."

She shrugged. "Don't worry about it. It wasn't much." She looked down at the dog. "And who is this pretty boy?"

Daniella put her hand to the dog's head. "This is Tigger. Tigger, friend."

Tig immediately stepped forward to say hello to Riley as if he'd been waiting for the introduction, and she squatted and ruffled his fur. "Well, hello there, buddy. Have you been outside yet?"

"No, he hasn't. Let me do that," I answered.

"You don't have to do that, Huntley. I can take him out."

"Neither of you are dressed. I got it." Riley stood. "Besides, I need to let the horses out. He can help. Come on, buddy, let's go outside."

Tig turned to Daniella as if asking permission, and she nodded to him. "I'm not sure how he will do with horses. He's never been around them before."

"He'll be fine. Trust me, Buttercup and Fellow will not let him intimidate them."

I laughed, and Daniella replied with a smile, "Okay, go out,

Tig." He happily trotted after my sister, throwing me a glance as if to warn me that he wasn't going far. Yeah, well, I wasn't either, I wanted to tell him.

CHAPTER SEVEN

DANIELLA

*H*untley left the bathroom, and it took a moment before I could resume brushing my teeth. Had I imagined that he'd been aroused when he'd fallen against me? Was that a reaction to the morning, or me personally?

There was no way it could have been me. I finished brushing and rinsed the brush and sink, staring at the cup where all the other brushes of different colors were standing like lopsided statues. It wasn't very hygienic to stick toothbrushes together. I pursed my lips and then set the toothbrush on the side of the sink near the cup. I was turning away when I suddenly spun back around, snatched the toothbrush, and dropped it into the container with the others. My light-purple brush was now leaning against Huntley's dark-blue one.

I'd never had my toothbrush in a cup. Was it weird that for some odd reason I liked that? I pondered the whys of that as Tig followed me out of the bathroom and down the stairs.

I'd never been part of a large family. I grew up without siblings and went to a local community college while working a full-time job to put myself through school and pay for my small apartment. I'd never had a roommate and hadn't shared any living space since I was seventeen and moved out of my stepfather's house after graduation.

I paused in the living room and glanced around, wanting to look over the pictures—to see what a real family looked like—but I didn't want to appear nosy.

I loved seeing how others lived and loved seeing images of the past where I could develop a story or a scene around it. I got most of my story ideas by doing that. God knew that I didn't have the life experience to write these stories from my memories. Nope, my life had been drastically different than the words I wrote.

Well, once in a while, a hero or heroine brought out a piece of my past, but not often. I didn't want to recall my earlier years, so why would I want one of my characters to have lived through it?

I found Huntley in the kitchen and came up short when the back door opened and a stunning woman with long blond hair came bounding in full of energy, her arms filled with clothing.

The playful banter between siblings enthralled me, and I was amazed that Riley had brought me all that she had. A couple of times, I had to blink back tears as I became overwhelmed, once again, with the generosity of this family.

I watched her lead Tigger out and suddenly became nervous about him being away from me. Not only was he for protection, but he helped to relieve my anxiety. As if he knew, Hunt came to my side and took my hand, pulling me toward a window.

"You can watch from here," he told me after he pushed back the peach curtain. I got lost in his green eyes for a moment, astounded that he had been able to read me so well.

"Thank you." He winked as he stepped away, and I clasped my hand to my belly after he let it go. He returned to the fridge and frowned as if he were thinking about something that bothered him. Was he like Jake, or did I imagine it? Perhaps I only compared them because Jake was a strong, protective man and currently my secret crush? I tended to fall in love with my characters, and Jake was one that I had loved for a while.

Two years and six books ago, I'd introduced Jake as a side character in another book, and he had quickly become a very integral part of my series. His book was the last of this series, and I was secretly sad that it would be over and I could no longer live in the world of Jake and his incredible persona.

Tigger barked and drew my gaze back to the window. He was bouncing around at the barn door as if excited to be going in. "Oh, god, I hope he doesn't hurt the horses."

Huntley returned and stood beside me. "He'll be fine." Tig disappeared inside the barn, rushing around Riley's legs once the door was open. I wrung my hands, and Huntley put his hand to my lower back.

The moment his thumb brushed over my spine, I felt something other than anxiety seeping into my nerve endings. His touch was gentle, nonsexual, and yet parts of my body suddenly took notice.

Huntley chuckled, the throaty sound slithering from my ears right through my veins, and I felt myself shift slightly closer to him. His hand moved, curling around my hip almost possessively.

Tigger was in the paddock with the horses, barking as he ran in circles, and the horses danced around him, tossing their heads up and down and making noises. "Are they upset?"

"Oh, no, they are playing. I told you he'd be fine." He glanced down at me, and I lifted my face to his. We were only a few inches apart, and in my mind, I was instantly writing the scene.

His eyes were so full of life as they stared down, willing me to come closer—almost begging for me to make that next move and show him that I was ready.

51

I blinked and jerked my face away, suddenly mortified that I thought for one second that Huntley would want to kiss me.

"Hey," Huntley took my chin and directed my face back to his, a question in his eyes.

A question that pleaded with me to answer. My heart began to thud harder, and I knew that I could no longer deny the pull that screamed for me to taste his lips. His face grew closer, his incredible vibrant green eyes staring at my mouth as he converged on it. The first touch, so tender that I could have imagined it as my eyes fluttered closed. The second was almost painful in its gentleness as I craved to feel the full force of his passion.

"Daniella?"

My eyes snapped open, and Huntley stood in front of me, a perplexed look upon his face. I jumped back as I realized that I had turned Huntley back into Jake, and I'd been visualizing us kissing. If only the ground would open up and swallow me.

"I'm sorry, what were you saying?"

He laughed slightly. "Are you okay? You looked like you went someplace else for a moment."

"Oh, yeah, I'm fine." I cleared my throat, shifting further away from him. "Is that coffee ready yet?"

"Yeah, it should be. What do you like in yours?"

"A little cream, please." I glanced at the window again as he stepped away. Tigger was playing with the horses as Riley tossed hay around in small piles. Who would have known that Tigger could have so much fun?

I forced myself to keep my gaze on Tigger and not let it stray to Huntley as he moved around the kitchen. Tigger turned to the fence and began to bark, the pitch changing from fun to alert. I glanced the other way out of the window and saw a truck pulling down the long driveway.

"Um, you have someone here in a truck."

"What color is it?"

"White."

"That's Henley." He laughed. "He's probably coming to check on you and make sure you're alright."

The truck stopped, and the door opened with Henley stepping out. Behind him, I saw another two vehicles. "Um, the police are here, along with another vehicle, too."

Huntley returned to my side, his hand once again sliding over my lower back, and I shivered. "That's Ethan and Marc Broadbent. Maybe they have news about your house."

Tigger was barking aggressively, and suddenly, I saw him eye the fence as Riley started calling him to the gate. "Oh, crap." I turned and bolted for the back door as Tigger began to run in a circle. I was bursting out the door as he crested the fence and rushed toward the people who had just arrived.

"Tigger, no!" Tigger slid to a stop, dust clouding up around him as he glanced back at me. All of the men had frozen in place. "Come! Now!" I slapped my leg, and he gave the men one last look before he trotted over to me.

"Good boy, friends," I told him, although I wasn't sure if that was true of all of them. I had to believe that at least Henley was a friend since he was part of the family.

Riley climbed the steps to the porch. "Why don't we take your clothes upstairs and find you something to wear before you give more than my brother something to fantasize about."

I frowned at her and glanced toward the driveway where three men were approaching, all watching me. "Oh, good idea. Come, Tigger."

Riley and I collected the items she'd brought, and Tigger followed along a few steps behind, his tongue hanging from the side of his mouth as he breathed roughly. He needed water; I'd have to remember that when we came back down.

In her room, Riley glanced around. "Did my brother sleep in here too?"

"What? No!"

She laughed. "I don't care if he did. I just wondered if I needed to clean the sheets."

My cheeks turned bright red, and she laughed as I spoke softly, "I just met your brother last night."

"Really? With the way he looks at you, I'd have thought you two were an item."

How did he look at me? "No, you must have misinterpreted it. Your brother is being kind to me, that's all."

Riley laughed as she laid out the clothes into piles. "Hunt is a good guy, but he's probably the least *kind* out of all of us, well, except Brad. He's kind of grumpy."

"Your brother is not grumpy," a deep voice spoke from behind me, and I spun to find a tall, handsome older man. "Bradley is dealing with a lot, and you need to remember that." His voice was stern but gentle with her. When he turned to me, his eyes brightened, and he held his hand out to me. I glanced at Tigger, but he was sitting back on his haunches just watching us. "Hi, you must be the famous author that my wife has been talking my ear off about. I'm David."

I took his hand. "Mr. Young, thank you so much for your kindness."

"You're an author? Wait! No way! Are you Veronica Raven?" Riley rushed to my side, pulling my arm so she could look into my face.

"David!" Mrs. Young appeared behind her husband. "I told you not to say anything. I'm so sorry, Daniella."

"I thought you meant to anyone outside of the house. I didn't know it was a secret here, too. I'm very sorry, Daniella. I won't say another word. I'll let you get dressed and see you downstairs. It sounds like we have quite a bit of company."

Mrs. Young smiled apologetically as she pulled the door closed from the hallway, and I glanced at Riley.

"You are, aren't you?"

"Um," I hesitated.

"Look, there are very few authors that my mother talks nonstop about, and Veronica Raven is one of them. The others all have their pictures on the back of the book jackets, and I know you aren't them."

"Yeah, but it's important to me that I keep my identity quiet."

She shrugged. "So I won't tell anyone." She returned to the bed and bounced for a moment on the side. "I do have to tell you that those sex scenes in *Lost in the Night* were so damn intense, I had to call a friend to relieve the tension after I read them."

Oh, my god, I was going to melt into the floor. I was mortified that she not only knew who I was but had read my books, too. I swallowed, and she barked out a laugh.

"Relax, Dani, I won't tell anyone who you are. I promise." She pulled out a pair of leggings and a long blouse. "Here, this should fit you nicely, and it's probably what you are used to wearing."

What did that mean? Did she think that I only wore leggings? God, I hated that it was what I always wore, and she'd guessed so easily. She messed around with a bag of stuff and pulled out a package of underwear and a sports bra. "Thank you," I told her as I took them from her.

"No problem." She smiled. "I'll let you get dressed, and sorry for that comment about your sex scenes. They are outstanding, though. My brother doesn't know how lucky he is."

She left before the words even registered in my brain. Her brother was what? Seriously? Did she really think I was going to sleep with her brother? She probably also thought that I had personally done those things Stuart and Madeline had done in *Lost in the Night*.

Damn, I wish I had the guts to do some of the things my women did in the books. Maybe if I did, I wouldn't be hiding alone in the middle of nowhere.

I sighed and got dressed, and then Tigger and I went back

downstairs. The smell of bacon and eggs made my stomach rumble, and I glanced at Tigger. I was going to have to find food for him to eat. He couldn't keep eating people food.

When I stepped into the room, I stopped, and Tigger shifted in front of me. People filled the room—not just adults, there were three children in there too, and everyone turned to look at me.

CHAPTER EIGHT

HUNTLEY

*M*y mind was a little boggled as I stood by the coffeemaker and poured two cups. Did Daniella think that I had wanted to kiss her? Had she wanted me to kiss her? It sure looked like she had expected that, or perhaps she'd been wistfully thinking about it as she'd stared at me with glossed over eyes and freshly licked lips.

I had to be making shit up. There was no way that woman had wanted me to do that. My head snapped up as she darted toward the back door, and I set the coffee pot down in a rush to follow her out.

I shook my head as Tigger trotted over to her side. Damn, that dog was well trained. I had yet to see him not listen to her. Again, I wondered why she needed training to that caliber. I knew they weren't cheap. Ethan had talked about the K-9 they had on the police force, and those dogs were expensive to train and keep certified.

After Riley escorted Daniella upstairs with the clothes, the kitchen began to fill up. With Henley, Ethan, Marc, and then my parents entering, more coffee was brewed, and Henley joined my mom at the counter to prepare the morning feast. There was little doubt that the rest of the group, sans Kayley, would show up eventually. As if on schedule, the back door opened, and in came Brad and the kids.

Tyler ran to Ethan. "Hey, Uncle Ethan, what are you doing here?"

"Just got off work, kiddo. What are you doing here?"

He shrugged. "Breakfast, I guess. I don't know. Dad said that we had to come over here for some reason."

My niece, Tonya, smiled at me from across the room and then went to help her grandma and Hen with breakfast as Brad said his hellos to everyone.

A few minutes later, Charlotte joined the party with Marisol, telling us that Wes was working today, and then Riley came back down.

"Is Daniella okay?" I asked my sister as she poured a cup of coffee from the brewing pot.

She hiked an eyebrow sharply at me. "Why are you asking?"

"Because you were just with her, that's why?"

She grinned at me. "Is that the only reason?"

"Whatever, Riley," I muttered toward my sister.

"Riley, cut your brother some slack, please," my mother commented, and Hen laughed.

"No, don't cut him slack. He never cuts anyone else any," Henley blurted.

"I don't know what you all are talking about," I said, but I was not able to hold the smirk off my face.

Ethan slapped me on the back as he went around me to sit down. "Yeah, right."

Most of us were huddled around the table, shooting the shit when Daniella returned and came up short. She scanned the room, her eyes wide, her dog on alert as he shifted to lean against her. I stood slowly and approached her, putting my hand to her lower back as I turned to make the introductions.

"Daniella, you remember Ethan and Marc from last night,

right?" She nodded. "Well, that old guy over there is my brother, Brad, and those are his kids, Tyler and Tonya. The pipsqueak at the counter is Marisol, and that is her mother, Charlotte."

Marisol pouted. "Hey, I'm not a pipsqueak," she said and then saw the dog. "Aww, it's a puppy." She jumped from the stool and raced toward the dog. I was about to grab for Marisol to keep her back, but Tigger's tail started wagging wildly, and he bounded toward her, prancing as he licked her face and caused giggles to erupt.

Daniella peered at me momentarily, saying softly, "Kids aren't a threat."

I frowned, once again wondering why she needed a dog that would be on the watch for threats. Tyler approached the dog a little more cautiously, and Tigger rubbed his body up against him in greeting before coming back to sit at Daniella's feet.

Daniella said hello to my brother, and Charlotte stepped forward to hug her. I saw the surprise spark in Daniella's eyes, but then it vanished quickly. I led her to an empty chair at the table before I went to get her a fresh cup of coffee. Her eyes darted around the room as I put the mug down. She seemed unsure where to look with all the people talking around her. Something told me she wasn't comfortable in large groups, but hopefully, she would realize that no one here wished her harm.

I winked at her while I squeezed her shoulder with my other hand. Tigger pushed against my leg as if to say I was too close. Seriously? Man, that dog didn't like me. Was it just because I had put her over my shoulder at the fire?

As food was prepared and put on the table, Daniella sat quietly, stroking the top of Tigger's head, and a little piece of me felt jealous at the attention that he got from her. Not that I had any right to be jealous at all.

Once the food was on the table and things passed around, I looked down the table. "So, Marc, what did you find out?"

He swallowed the food he had just shoveled into his mouth

and shifted his eyes toward Daniella briefly. She was wide-eyed and watching him.

"We did find the source of the fire. It was at the backside of the house—outside."

"Outside?" Henley and I both repeated simultaneously and glanced at one another. "Jinx," we both said again, and everyone started laughing. Even Daniella cracked a momentary smile.

Marc nodded. "Yeah."

I frowned; what could have started the fire outside? The answer was not one I wanted to consider, but I had to. "You think someone started the fire?"

Marc watched Daniella for a reaction, and she gasped appropriately. He shifted his attention to me as he nodded. "It was intentionally set."

"What? Why?" Daniella whispered, and Tigger stood, putting his face on her leg as if he felt her growing anxiety.

"Someone started the fire at the back of your house, Daniella. Is there someone who would want to hurt you? Is there someone that is upset with you for something?"

She dropped her chin to her chest, but not before I saw how pale her face had become. She shook her head, her blond hair waving back and forth like a curtain. "No," she finally responded, her voice louder than I had expected it to be. She lifted her eyes back to him, and for a moment, they regarded each other until Ethan spoke.

"Are you sure that there isn't someone who wants to hurt you, Daniella?" Ethan glanced at the dog, as did Henley and me. She had that dog for a reason, and I would bet my pickup truck that it wasn't just for companionship.

"No, I don't know anyone who would want to hurt me." She lifted her chin higher, pulling her shoulders back.

Marc nodded. "Well, it could have been random. It wouldn't be the first time we had an arsonist around that wanted attention and to see the thrill of fire. We did speak with a couple of your neighbors, but no one recalled seeing anything, although two of them noted that your dog was barking a lot around the time that the fire started."

Daniella's eyes bounced back and forth, and her brow furrowed as she tried to recall something. "He was. Tig was very agitated at the sliding glass door. I let him out, and he burst out the door and off the porch before I could even get the door entirely open, but I didn't see anything. Do you think he might have seen the person?"

"Maybe he heard them," Ethan commented.

"I did smell smoke, but I thought someone had a fire burning. I never for a second considered the fire was my house." Daniella looked gutted, and I wished that whatever was dwelling in the back of her mind, she'd share. She peered my way, and there was something behind those eyes, something that she wasn't saying.

Ethan and I shared another look, and I was pretty sure that he was thinking the same thing. Maybe after everyone was gone, I could get her to open up to me.

"How much of my house is salvageable?" she asked after a moment of silence.

"Sadly, not much. Your house was like a tinderbox, and it went up like a matchstick."

"What started the fire?" I asked.

"We found traces of what we believe will be accelerant up the stucco wall where it started. Stucco is cement, so it doesn't burn. Pieces of it fell after the roof caught on fire and burned into the beams behind the wall. And of course, on the woodpile that you had stacked back there. It looks like they splashed the accelerant up your wall to make sure it would take to your house. Using the woodpile was a perfect place to start it, especially if the wood was dry, and since we haven't had much rain lately, I have to assume it was. That would have burned hot and fast. Of course, we took a sample to test, but I have a feeling it's going to come back as lighter fluid. If someone sprayed something up the wall, that would make more sense. Gasoline would be splashed and messy. Lighter fluid could have been applied easier."

Daniella hung her head, and I reached for her, but Tig locked his eyes on mine, probably preparing himself to strike. I pulled my hand back and heard someone chuckle softly.

Daniella lifted her head wearily, and there was so much anguish in her eyes as she opened them that I reached out again. To hell with the dog, he could bite me if he wanted to, but I was going to show her that she wasn't alone. I put my hand on her forearm as it rested beside her plate. Tigger's mouth opened again, his tongue peeking out the side as if he were okay with the action. "I'm sorry, Daniella."

She stared at my hand for a moment, then shifted her arm away. "Thank you." I tried not to let that bother me, but for some damn reason, it did.

"Daniella, you are welcome to stay here as long as you need," my mother told her.

"Thank you, Mrs. Young, but I don't want to be a burden on you."

There was laughter around the table, and Charlotte stood to take her plate to the sink, stopping beside Daniella. "You can't burden this family. They live for this stuff."

Henley agreed, as did Ethan. His family would have done the same thing. In fact, had Henley not been there to help Daniella out, Ethan might have stepped in, and she might have been staying at his parents' house, not here. Good thing that Henley was there.

I froze. Why was it a good thing?

"Well, at least when it comes time to rebuild, we know a great contractor," Henley stated as he turned toward our brother, Brad.

She looked confused for a moment, and Henley reminded her that he owned a construction company.

Brad sighed. "As much as I'd like to help, I'm not sure we'd have the time. We have a pretty busy schedule right now."

"Oh, come on, Bradley," my father said. "You can always find more time. This is important."

"Yeah, but so are the other jobs I have," he stated.

My dad looked sternly at him. "Of course all the jobs are important, but I'm pretty sure Mrs. Lang's sunroom could wait a little while, along with the Connors' bathroom remodel, especially if they knew why their jobs were being rescheduled. I doubt either of them would begrudge Daniella from having a place to live."

Brad shrugged, and I wanted to knock him upside the head. Since when did he not want to help? "I could ask, but Daniella might have someone else she wants to do the work."

All eyes turned to her, and hers went wide at the sudden attention. "Um, I don't know any contractors, but if you're too busy, maybe you could recommend someone."

"We'll make it work, Daniella," my father stated firmly toward Brad, then smiled as he shifted his gaze to her. "Even if I have to come out of retirement and do it myself."

Her lips parted in surprise. "Thank you, Mr. Young."

"David, please." He winked at Daniella, and my mother put her hand on his arm, the love she felt for the man so evident in her features.

The conversation took a change in direction, and the kids began to monopolize the talk about events at school. Daniella remained withdrawn as she toyed with her food. Finally, she carried her almost full plate to the sink and handed it to Charlotte, who was doing the dishes.

Charlotte spoke quietly to her, and Daniella brushed her hand down Charlotte's arm, her eyes smiling for the first time in a while as if she approved or appreciated what Charlotte had said to her. Maybe Charlotte was telling her to go with the flow. If the Youngs got something in their mind, they would always follow through. Charlotte had found that out herself when Brad had helped fix a misunderstanding between Wes and her.

Daniella tapped her thigh gently twice, and Tigger went immediately to her side. Without looking at anyone, she headed toward the back door. Marc, Ethan, and I all watched her leave. I was going to go after her when my mom passed me and put her hand on my shoulder. "Give her a few minutes. I think she needs some time to process everything."

I nodded; she was probably right.

Ethan got to his feet. "Well, if you all will excuse me, my shift is over, and my pillow is calling."

"You sure that isn't the teddy bear that's calling to you?" Riley asked him sassily.

He smirked and opened his mouth to respond but thought twice about it as he glanced around and laughed. "Thanks for breakfast, Pat." He kissed my mother's cheek, winked at Riley, and disappeared out the back door.

He was barely out the door when I shot from my seat and went to the window. Ethan approached Daniella as she stood facing the barn, her arms crossed tightly over her chest. Was that a defensive posture or a frustrated one?

I watched them speak for a moment and was about to head out when Henley stopped me. "Let him work."

"He's not working," I said gruffly.

Henley looked over my shoulder. "He's working, Hunt. I'm sure he has questions that he wanted to ask her in private." He paused. "Although, he might be working on her, and not the case."

My gaze snapped back to the window, and some odd feeling punched me in the gut as she started laughing at something Ethan had said.

Henley leaned forward. "Better watch out; he might get the girl."

"Like I care," I muttered.

He slapped me on the shoulder. "Yep, keep telling yourself that, Huntley. You just keep telling yourself that."

I glared at his back, but as I turned, I realized my hands were fisted at my sides.

CHAPTER NINE

DANIELLA

*T*his could not be happening—not again. It had to be a random act; I couldn't be the target—could I? No! I'd been so careful about keeping my location quiet. No one knew where I lived now, only a select few, like my editors and publisher.

I stood outside, letting Tigger run around sniffing the yard and then the fence near the horses. My mind was in turmoil. It had to be bad luck; that's all it could be. My life was always one string of crap after the other—except for my books. My books were the only saving grace in my life.

The door opened behind me, and I assumed it was Huntley coming to check on me; it wasn't, though. Ethan approached, his gaze locked on Tigger as he explored. Tigger glanced at him briefly when he stopped next to me, but his attention went back to one of the horses who was throwing their head up and bouncing at the fence like it wanted Tigger to play with it again.

"How are you holding up?" he asked.

I shrugged. "As well as can be expected. Do you really think it was arson, Ethan?"

"Yeah, we do, Daniella."

I pursed my lips.

"Your dog is a trip. I thought Tigger was going to take Hunt's hand off earlier when he touched your arm."

I laughed. "Yeah, Tig is great around women and kids, but he considers most men threats."

His voice dropped lower. "What's the reason for that, Daniella? Why do you need a dog to watch for threats?"

I turned to him; part of me wanted to explain, the other wanted to forget the past. "Because I wanted a trained dog. I'm a woman living alone." I shrugged. "It's nice to know someone is watching out for me."

"You mentioned that you have only lived around here for a little while. Where did you live before?"

I stared at him for a full three seconds before I averted my eyes. I saw a hundred questions rolling around through his mind. "Does it matter?"

"It might. If the reason you moved here is that someone was trying to hurt you where you used to live, then yes, it does matter very much."

I kicked at the dirt with the toe of the sneaker that I wore. Riley was right; I had found a pair that fit me well enough.

Ethan stepped closer. "Daniella, it's obvious that something has happened in your past. I don't know what it is, but you can trust me. I only want to help you."

I almost snorted with laughter. Yeah, the last batch of cops wanted to help me too, at least that is what they said. The problem was, they hadn't. They hadn't taken my concerns seriously, not until it was almost too late. "I appreciate that, Ethan, but there is nothing to say."

He sighed heavily, then removed something from a side pocket of his pants and retrieved a pen from his chest pocket before he jotted something on a slip of paper. "Here is my card; you can call me anytime, Daniella. My cellphone is on there, too. Anytime you want to talk, or if you remember something, please call me. I really do want to help you. I'm not just saying that."

I took the card, fisting it as I crossed my arms again. "Thank you."

He glanced at the house, then put his hand on my shoulder. "You're safe here. The Youngs will do anything they can to help you, but if you don't feel comfortable here—or safe—you let me know that. I can find you another place to stay, even if it's with me. I can protect you from whatever it is that you're afraid of. I know there is something you don't want to tell us. I hope that you eventually come to trust us enough to know that we want to help."

Stay with him? Trust them? I didn't know these people. Why were they so willing to help me? What did they want from me? People didn't generally do these kinds of things for no reason—there was always an underlying reason.

I finally nodded in response, and he dropped his hand as the back door opened again, and this time, Hunt did make an appearance. Ethan chuckled. "I'll talk to you later, Daniella. Call me; I'm there for anything that you might need."

Was there an invitation to that comment? I watched him walk backward, and he winked before he turned and went to his car as Huntley reached my side.

"What did he want?" His voice was slightly gruff.

"To make sure I was alright," I answered.

"Did he give you his phone number?"

"Yes. Ethan told me to call him if I needed anything or if I remembered anything."

Hunt glared over his shoulder. "Yeah, well, be careful; he might have meant with more than what's going on."

I shrugged. "Ethan seems like a nice enough guy."

"He is a nice guy," Hunt replied.

I almost told him about Ethan's offer of staying at his house but thought better of it. Maybe Hunt was right, and Ethan was looking for something else in return. I did remember seeing Ethan once before at a coffee shop. He had been observing me, and I'd heard him whispering to the barista, asking who I was. I had kept my attention on my computer until he was leaving. Then he lifted his cup to me and graced me with a very sexy smile.

Ethan was attractive, but not my type. Not that I had a type —at least not one in the nonfiction world.

"I'm sorry about your house, Daniella. I'm sure this is pretty scary."

"Yes, it is. Can I see my house now?"

"Marc said you could. I'll take you over in a little while. You'll have to be careful. There was a lot of damage." He looked at my feet. "My mom might have boots you can wear."

I looked down. "I'm going to have to get a car, go shopping."

"I can help you out until you get one," he said.

I let my gaze slip over his face. He was such a handsome man, and I didn't need that in my life. "Thanks, Hunt, but I know you have other things to do. As soon as I speak to my insurance company, I'll figure out where to go and how to get back on my feet. If there is anything I can do, it's figuring out how to get back on my feet."

He seemed confused. "You aren't going to stay here?"

I shook my head. "No. While I appreciate the hospitality, I don't think it's a good idea to remain longer than I have to."

"Why?" he asked sharply.

I stared at him. "Your family has been very kind, Hunt, but I can't take advantage of their hospitality. It's going to take months to get my house fixed. I can't stay here all that time."

"Yeah, you can."

I laughed uncomfortably. "No, I can't."

He frowned. "Then stay with me. I'll sleep on the couch."

I jerked back. "Um, no. Ironically, Ethan said I could stay with him too, but that's not happening either. As much as I appreciate it, I don't need a knight in shining armor to protect me. I will be just fine on my own."

Hunt had jerked back. "Ethan asked you to stay with him?"

I winced. I hadn't meant to let that slip out, but I was frustrated. "Yes, he did. That wasn't the point of what I was saying. I'm not going to stay with either of you."

"Why? Because of Jake?"

My brows popped. "Jake? Um, no."

"Who is he? Did Jake hurt you?"

My brow lined. "Why are you asking me about Jake?"

"Because you called me him last night."

My jaw dropped. "I most certainly did not."

"Oh, yeah, you did. You had a bad dream. I came in, and you were begging someone not to hurt you. When I woke you up, you called me Jake and threw yourself into my arms, Daniella."

My face heated until I knew it was a deep shade of crimson. How had I not remembered that? Suddenly, I began to recall a slight memory. Holy crap, I had! "I'm sorry that I bothered you, Huntley. Tigger, come!"

I spun away from him, and he pulled me to a stop. "I'm not, Daniella. You were upset by something. Did someone hurt you? Did this Jake guy hurt you? Because if he did, you tell me, and I'll take care of him for you."

I started laughing. "Take care of him?" I barked out a louder laugh because that is precisely what Jake had said to Arrabella earlier in my book about a guy who was bothering her. "Hunt, Jake doesn't exist."

"What?"

"He's a character in my book series."

"You were calling out for a character in a book? Why?" He looked utterly bewildered.

"When I write a story, Huntley, I live and breathe my characters. I've been so immersed in this last one that I was most likely dreaming about him. I do that quite often. It's how I work through scenes."

"Work through scenes? You were scared—like really scared. That can't have been from a book, Daniella. Even Tigger was worried about you."

I sighed as I glanced at Tigger, who was now sitting beside us, watching us as if he were waiting for something to happen. "I'm sure whatever I was dreaming about was a combination of my book and what happened last night. It was horrifying watching my house burn. What if I'd been sleeping?" I paused. "Yeah, that's what I was dreaming about; I'd been in bed, and my house was on fire. When you woke me, I had also been dreaming about my book. I mistook you for him. I'm sorry, Huntley."

So, I lied. That was not what I'd been dreaming about, but Huntley sure didn't need to know that. The dream came back over me, and I suppressed a shiver. There was no way I was going to tell him that I was being chased, and Jake had rescued me. Only Jake's fictional image had morphed into that of Huntley.

"Are you serious?"

Huntley stared at me like he was trying to comprehend a foreigner. "Hunt, it was just a dream. I appreciate you coming to check on me, but it was just a dream. I didn't mean to make you uncomfortable."

He opened his mouth to speak, and a voice off to the side grabbed our attention.

"Dani!" Riley waved at me from the porch as if she needed me for something.

"Excuse me, Huntley, I have to go call my insurance company and tell them what's going on."

Tigger followed me into the house, but I didn't hear Huntley behind us. Riley stood at the door, holding it open with a grin on her face. "You looked like you needed a rescue."

I laughed. "Thanks."

"Yeah, Hunt can get his tail feathers in a ruffle every once in a while," she said as she closed the door. "He might not be the most caring, but when he does, he gets a little intense."

"Well, there is no reason for him to do that," I told her. "If you'll excuse me, Riley, I'm going to go up to your room so that I can call my insurance company."

"I'll keep him busy." She winked at me as we entered the kitchen, and Tigger went over to Mrs. Young, who was setting food and water down for him. Knowing that both of us were safe for now, I went upstairs and left him there.

It took me a little while to find my insurance agent's name and then a number, only to find out that she was unavailable. Thankfully they connected me with claims after I explained why I was calling.

"I need to report a house fire," I told them.

He asked me several questions to confirm my insurance policy. "How much of the house was damaged?"

"The whole thing. It was pretty bad."

"So, you'll be needing housing, correct?"

"Yes, but I need housing that will allow a dog. I have a German shepherd."

I heard him typing. "Yes, I see the additional insurance policy that you have on him."

Yep, I had an individual insurance policy on Tigger. Not in case he got injured, but in case he hurt someone else. Because of his certified level of training, he was considered a dangerous dog. I'd been required to get a one-million-dollar umbrella policy to protect me from being sued should someone come after me again, and my dog attacked them.

I could understand if Tigger bit someone who wasn't dangerous, but I didn't know why I had to have the policy to protect an intruder or someone who would want to cause *me* harm. They had explained that even if someone broke the law, they could still sue me civilly. Some laws were so stupid—very, very stupid.

The man asked me a few more questions and told me that an adjuster would be calling me soon. I hung up as the anxiety built in my gut. What was the adjuster going to tell me? What about my car? A place to live?

As kind as the Young family was, I couldn't stay here. Not if the fire at my house was intentionally set. Were they wrong? Or had it been arson, and I was just a random victim?

I lay back on the bed, staring at the ceiling. He was still in jail, so he couldn't have done this. I frowned. Was he still in jail? It has been almost a year; how long was his sentence? I sat straight up; his sentence had been nine months to two years.

My heart was hammering in my ears. Had he gotten out early? How could he have found me? I dug through my phone, noticing that my battery was getting low, and I didn't have a power cord. I glanced at my laptop and winced; I didn't have one for that either. Damn. I was going to need to buy those at least. Maybe Huntley wouldn't mind taking me to a store today. But where could I possibly find a replacement cord for my laptop?

I pulled up a phone number and hit send. It rang once and then went to voicemail. I waited until the recording ended, and it beeped, "Hi, this is Daniella Knight; I'm not sure if you remember me, but you helped me a while ago. I have a question about my case and was wondering if you could give me a call when you have a chance." I left my phone number and then hung up. With any luck, he'd return the call soon.

There was a knock on the door, and then it cracked open. Tigger pushed the door further with his nose and ran to my side as Hunt leaned against the doorjamb, his arms crossed, his eyes shifting down my body slowly and then back up. Such a Jake move.

Except it wasn't from a scene that I'd created; this was real, and the man who stood ten feet away was flesh and blood, not black and white words on a page or a fantasy in my head. I shivered as his gaze came back to my face.

A wicked smile slipped over his lips. "So, you think I'm like Jake, huh?"

I hiked a brow. "No."

He stepped into the room. "But you called me Jake."

"I was sleeping." I sat up, realizing I was in a dangerous position with the look on his face, and scooted to the edge of the bed.

"My mom said I look a lot like the character," he said huskily.

I laughed and stood. "Yeah, well, I created the character way before I knew you."

He stopped a few inches away. "Maybe you created him so well that he came to life."

My lips parted in surprise, and I couldn't help but stare at his mouth as he gave me a lopsided grin.

The undeniable urge to devour his sexy mouth was all I could think about. His body, mere inches from mine, screamed for my hands to crawl over every inch. I wanted to slip my hands under the hem of his charcoal t-shirt and explore every nook and cranny of his powerful chest. I could practically taste his skin on my tongue, and I craved the taste of him.

"Daniella." Hunt's husky voice brought me back to the here and now. "If you don't stop licking your lips, woman, I'm not going to be responsible for what happens next."

CHAPTER TEN

HUNTLEY

I stood outside for a few moments staring at the back door. Marc stepped out and headed toward me. "What time are you going to take her over?"

"Whenever she wants to go."

"Okay, keep her away from the backside. That part of the house, especially her bedroom, has a lot of damage, and after the water, the floor is going to be rather unstable."

"Gotcha," I told him and said goodbye before heading inside.

I poured more coffee after my mother said Daniella had gone to make a phone call. Tigger was lapping at his water bowl, and I was surprised that he wasn't with her.

I sat down. "So, Mom, tell me about this Jake character."

My mom lifted her eyes to me. "What about him?"

"What Jake character?" Charlotte asked.

Riley turned to me. "Are you talking about Jake from Veronica's books?"

I nodded. "Yep."

"Wait, Veronica Raven? I'm reading the third book in that series," Charlotte said quickly with a bright grin on her face.

"Why do you want to know about a hunky character from a book?" Riley asked wryly.

"Because Daniella was dreaming about him last night. She thought I was him when I went into her room to check on her."

All three of the ladies stared at me—hard. Riley shrugged her shoulders.

"You do resemble him," my mom said.

"Man, I'd totally do Jake," Charlotte said wistfully as she put her hands over Marisol's ears. Then she looked at me. "The character, not you, brother-in-law, but I can see it."

"Oh, god, yeah, don't let his head get any bigger," Riley hissed playfully.

"Jake is a strong man," my mother said. "He's determined and demands his way. He loves the ladies, and they love him back. He is very sexy."

"Yes, very sexy," Riley said. "Which you are not."

"Hey," I snapped at her. "Of course, I am."

"No, you're not," Riley replied. "Besides, you're my brother, and I can't think of you that way."

"Oh boy, alright, kids," My father stood. "Let's go out to the barn and muck the stalls. Ya'll don't need to hear this foolishness."

Tyler, Tonya, and Marisol took off with my father.

Riley's comment was true enough, I guess.

My mother asked, "Was Daniella having a bad dream?"

"Yeah, she was telling someone not to hurt her."

"Well, that wouldn't be Jake," Riley said. "He wouldn't hurt a woman he cared about. I can't wait for him to get together with Arrabella in this book."

Charlotte put her hand up. "Wait! He gets together with Arrabella? I thought he was going to be with Pam?"

"Oh, no, Pam moved away," my mother said. For a few minutes, I watched them discuss the characters like they were living people. Brad and I shared a confused glance.

"Do you guys seriously get that into romance books?" I asked.

Henley started laughing as he spoke. "Dude, Roxy read that series in like a week, and we had the best time after she finished each book."

"What?" I stared at him, completely confused.

Riley barked out a laugh. "He's saying that her books are incredibly steamy. Like holy crap, sexy hot!"

My brows popped, and I glanced toward the hallway. Huh, again, never pictured that about her.

"Wait—why would Daniella say you were like Jake? Has she read the books, too?" Charlotte asked.

"She wrote the books," Riley replied, and my mother glared at her. "What, I thought the secret was only here in the house? Dad did, too."

Charlotte's jaw was hanging open. "Daniella is Veronica Raven?"

"Yes, she is, and she'd like to keep that quiet, so please, let's not mention it again that she is the same person," my mother stated firmly.

"Will she give me her autograph? I have to get her to sign one of her books." Charlotte was going on and on, and Henley laughed.

"I don't get it. Why is it such a big deal that she's an author?" I asked Henley. "They act like she's famous or something."

"Because she is famous," Riley blurted. "She's a New York Times Bestselling Author, and they are getting ready to release one of her earlier books in the theaters."

"Wait, as a movie?"

"Yes, as a movie, you fool," Riley replied with a laugh. "She's a big deal in romance, but it's not just romance. She adds these crazy twists and turns to her books so that they have just that perfect amount of suspense."

"Huh," I said.

Riley walked out of the room and a few minutes later came back, handing me a book. "Check it out. Just make sure you have some time to satisfy yourself afterward."

Henley barked out a laugh, and my mother tsked at my sister, but she had a smile on her face.

"I'm not reading this," I said and put the book on the table as I stared at the couple in a romantic embrace on the cover.

Charlotte chuckled. "You might want to if you want to find out more about Jake."

"Whatever." I grabbed the book and went to leave the room. "I'm going to go check on Daniella and see when she wants to go see her house."

I flipped the pages of the book as I hit the stairs. There was no way I was going to read this. I was about to knock on her door when I heard Tigger coming up the stairs behind me. I went to my room and tossed the book onto my bed before knocking on her door.

The second the doorknob was turned, Tigger burst inside. I stood, checking her out as she lay on the bed, my gaze drifting over the curves of her body, and I wondered if she did write as they said.

"So, you think I'm like Jake, huh?"

A sassy look came over her face for a moment. "No."

"But you called me Jake."

She shifted to the edge of the bed. The sassy look vanished, and instead, she looked slightly unnerved. "I was sleeping."

"My mom said I look a lot like the character."

"Yeah, well, I created the character way before I knew you."

Like a magnet was pulling me into her room, I went to stand in front of her. "Maybe you created him so well that he came to life."

Daniella stared up at me, her dark-blue eyes getting the glazed look about them again as she shifted, and her eyes ran almost hungrily over my face and down to my chest. Holy shit—

"Daniella, if you don't stop licking your lips, woman, I'm not going to be responsible for what happens next." I was pretty sure that if she didn't wipe that look off her face soon, I was going to get bit in the ass by Tigger because I'd have attacked the woman.

She blinked and shuffled back, her legs hitting the edge of the bed, and she began to lose her balance. I instinctively reached for her, pulling her to me—and Tigger growled.

I froze. I didn't want to move a muscle for fear of what the damn dog would do, but I wasn't the only one not moving. Daniella stared up at me, her hands clenched around my biceps.

If I kissed her, would I get attacked by her dog? I had a feeling I might, especially if she didn't want me to. I did not doubt that dog was one hundred percent tuned into her moods.

I took the chance, sliding my hand up her arm to cup the side of her face, lifting her chin with my thumb and her lips parted, her eyes partially closing. "I want to kiss you, Daniella."

She didn't reply, but I knew she heard me; her hands tightened on my arms, and I felt the slightest tug closer. I descended on her, brushing our lips twice before I tilted my head and covered her mouth with mine.

One of her hands drifted to the side of my face tentatively, brushing her fingertips over my rough stubble as our tongues swiped almost teasingly. My arm wrapped tighter around her.

She whimpered softly, and suddenly, I was rock-hard. I deepened the kiss, the energy between the two of us building as she clung to me, her arms wrapped tightly around my neck. I wanted to lift her in my arms so her legs could wrap about my hips. I didn't, though. At that very moment, Tigger pushed his head between our thighs, and his hot doggie breath rushed through the crotch of my pants. I knew without a doubt that if I did anything to cause anxiety to rise in her, he'd probably take a bite at the first thing he could reach, which at present was perilously close to something I'd prefer not get bitten off.

I slowed the kiss, allowing room to come between our bodies again. As I pulled back, I stared down at Daniella. Her face was flush, her eyes glassy with desire. Please let that be a desire for me and not some fictional character.

"Sorry, that's not why I came in here."

She blinked a few times, the desire vaporizing into the air, and she stepped back, looking down at Tigger. "Wow, I'm surprised he didn't try to bite you."

"I was a little worried about that for a few moments."

She averted her eyes. "I'm sorry, Huntley, that shouldn't have happened."

"But it did, Daniella, it sure as hell did."

She opened her mouth to speak, but her cellphone rang. She spun away and bent over the bed to get it. My gaze went to her ass in the tight yoga pants that she wore. I clenched my hands at my side and stepped away from her before I could grab hold of her glorious hips and rub myself against her soft backside.

I glanced at the dog; his bright-brown eyes watched my every move like he knew what I was thinking.

She spoke to the person on the other end, and it sounded like it had to do with her house. I stepped out of her room and closed the door to give her privacy. In my room, my jeans and shirt from the day before were clean and lying on my bed now. I would change clothes and get myself under control.

What was it about her that caused me to lose control of myself? I'd never been like this before. Yeah, Jessica had turned me on, and we'd had a pretty decent sexual relationship, although the fact that she was cheating on me made me wonder.

If anything could have calmed the hormones surging through me, it was the memory of Jessica riding her boss on the couch. Yep, that did it. I yanked my t-shirt over my head as there was a knock on my door. "Come in."

The door opened, and Daniella stood there, her eyes locked on my face. "That was the insurance adjuster. He's actually in the area and wondered if I could meet him at the house in about forty-five minutes."

"Yeah, that works," I said a little gruffer than I had meant to, and something passed over her face.

"Hunt." She began to step forward. I held my hand up to her.

"Don't come in here, Daniella. Not unless you want to take back up where we just paused. One step closer, and I'm going to have you back in my arms."

Her lips parted in surprise; her pretty blue eyes went wide, and she immediately stepped back. "I'll wait downstairs."

Before I could respond, she was gone. Obviously, that was not something that she wanted, and I sighed. I shouldn't want it either. I didn't—liar.

Jessica's face came to mind, and I clenched my jaw. The last thing I needed to do was get involved with anyone when I was still smarting over the end of my relationship with Jess.

I turned to leave my room, and my eyes drifted to Daniella's book on the bed, the head of the woman thrown back as the man kissed his way down her neck. I clenched my eyes closed and left my room.

CHAPTER ELEVEN

DANIELLA

I tried to listen to the guy on the phone; I really did. But I would have failed if there had been a quiz. My head was reeling from the kiss with Huntley. What had possessed me to allow him to do that? Had I subconsciously wanted to know what it would be like to kiss the fictional character I loved so much?

It had been everything that I could have dreamed of and more. The problem was that it wasn't a fantasy kiss; it was with a real man, and although he reminded me of my created hero, Huntley was most definitely not Jake.

I managed to get my mind in the game and told the guy on the phone, whose name I couldn't recall, that I would call him right away if for some reason I could not be there shortly. Luckily, Hunt was willing to take me over.

I had wanted to apologize to him for my behavior, but the look he gave me and his huskily spoken words scared the crap out of me. I wasn't even sure if Jake could have looked at Arrabella with that level of scorching heat. Yep, not going there.

I did what I did best. I turned and ran right down the stairs.

Safely surrounded by people, I announced to everyone that Hunt was taking me over to the house.

Henley put his hands on my shoulders as he stepped around me. "You be careful over there. I'm heading home to get some sleep; it has been a long few days."

"Thanks for all your help, Henley," I told him as he said his goodbyes.

"I have to head out too," Brad said. "It was nice to meet you, Daniella; let me know when you have things settled with your insurance company, and we can sit down and talk."

"Thank you, Bradley, but if you are too busy, I'm sure I can find someone else."

He put his hand up. "Don't think about it again. My father is right; these other projects are nothing compared to rebuilding your home for you."

"Thank you."

He waved again and was gone, leaving me alone with the women. I sat, Tigger laying at my feet, and Mrs. Young studied him.

"You aren't going to take him with you, are you? It won't be safe for him to be there."

I frowned. She was right, it probably wouldn't be safe, and Tigger would want to get in the way.

"Leave him here. Tigger can play with the kids," Riley said. "Brad is working today, so the kids are hanging out here, and Charlotte and I have some plans this morning, so all three kids will be here. I'm sure Tigger will be fine."

Tigger sat up as if he wanted to weigh in on the conversation. "I've never left him with strangers."

"Ah," Mrs. Young bent down. "Tigger wants to stay and play, right, Tigger?"

He rushed to her, his tail whipping back and forth happily. "You won't mind?"

"Not at all. You don't need the dog there."

I gnawed on my bottom lip as Riley spoke. "Besides, Hunt will keep you safe, Dani."

"Why are you calling her Dani?" her mother asked. "Her name is Daniella."

Riley rolled her eyes. "Yes, Mom. I know that, but Daniella is too long and formal. Dani is easier and more fun."

I chuckled. "I don't mind. I have gone by Dani many times over the years."

"See!" Riley spiked a brow sassily. "How about after you check out your house and deal with what you have to over there, you join Charlotte and me this afternoon. We can take you shopping and then have dinner. Roxy is joining us tonight for our bi-weekly girls night."

"Well, I do need to get a charger for my phone and laptop," I said.

"There you go!"

"Wait!" I smacked my forehead. "I can't go shopping. I don't have any money right now. My credit cards and purse were in my house, along with my driver's license. Holy cow, I don't even know if they survived or where they might be."

"Well, you go with Hunt and find out. We'll cover you until we can get you set up again; don't worry about it." She waved a hand at me.

Yeah, famous last words. What Riley didn't know was that I worried about everything. I hated owing people anything, and running up a tab with them wasn't my idea of relaxing. I was already more indebted to this family than they realized.

"Let me see how it goes with the house and insurance," I told her.

She sighed dramatically. "Fine, but I guarantee you that by the end of the day, you'll be dying to get away from my brother and have some fun."

Charlotte laughed. "It would be great to have you join us, Dani. We try to get together at least every two weeks to do this."

When was the last time I'd gone out to dinner with friends? Did having dinner with my editor count? Ugh, speaking of my editor, I needed to call her. I winced, thinking of how my cellphone had next to nothing left on its battery. "Mrs. Young, do you mind if I borrow your house phone? My cell is about to die, and I just remembered that I need to call my editor and tell her that it's going to be a few more days before I can get this story over to her."

"Of course, dear, but only if you stop calling me Mrs. Young. It's Patricia, and David has a phone in his office down the hall. You can use that for some privacy," she told me.

I thanked her and went to find the phone. The office looked like it belonged to a man with its wood finishes and dark colors, but it also included many family touches. More pictures adorned the walls, and there was a bright-yellow clay cup on his desk that held pens and pencils. I sighed as I realized that I truly loved this house, and I tried to absorb every detail of it to use in another story.

I dialed Bea's number from memory and waited for her to answer. "Hello?"

"Bea, it's Daniella."

"You're finished?" she asked excitedly.

"No, not quite," I told her slowly.

"Daniella, we need that manuscript. I thought you were going to finish it yesterday."

"I would have, Bea; in fact, I only have one chapter left to write."

"So, why are you on the phone with me and not zipping those fingers over the magic keyboard?"

"Because I had a fire at my house last night."

"What, holy shit! Are you okay?"

"I'm okay—physically—but my house wasn't so lucky."

"I'm sure it's not as bad as you think it is."

I shook my head. "Oh, no, it's worse. I lost everything; at

least I think I did. I'm getting ready to meet with the insurance adjuster and see it in daylight for the first time. I had four fire trucks at my house last night, and probably over seventy percent of it is destroyed."

"Oh, Daniella, I'm so sorry." She was quiet for a moment. "Wait, Daniella, did you lose your laptop? Please don't tell me that you lost it in the fire. This is why I tell you to back everything up on the cloud!"

"Bea, relax. I got the laptop out of the house. That's the only thing I got out." I sighed. "I have to get a charger for it and my cellphone, though. They are both about to die, hence the reason I am calling you from a different number. It's going to be a couple of days before I can complete the manuscript. I promise I'll get it to you as soon as I can."

"Are you still using the laptop that I bought you for your birthday?"

"Yes."

"I'll overnight chargers to you. I have the receipt for your laptop, and we have the same phone, so I know what kind of charger you need for that. I'll order them right now. What else do you need?"

A sound came out of my throat that sounded like a wounded animal. "Everything. I only have the clothes on my back, and trust me, they are not anything to be proud of." I sighed. "Actually, can you send me a few gift cards so I can at least buy something. I lost everything, and I'm sure my credit cards and wallet were destroyed."

"I can do that. Tell me what hotel you are staying in."

"I'm not in a hotel."

"Then where are you?"

"I'm staying with a local family."

There was a long silence. "Say what? You? Daniella Knight staying with strangers?"

"They are nice," I said softly.

She laughed. "Okay, did you hit your head when you were running out of the house?"

"No, I didn't." I proceeded to explain to her how I'd met the family.

"Wow, nice people around there. No one in New York would do that," she said after I'd finished.

"Yeah, I know, not in Ohio, either." I sighed as I stared out the window behind me and gnawed on my bottom lip. "Bea, the fire was arson."

She paused for a long time. "Are you serious, Dani?"

"Yeah, that's what the fire marshal told me this morning. Someone poured accelerant over the firewood behind my house and up the wall to my roof and then lit it."

She was quiet for a few seconds. "Is he still in jail?"

"As far as I know. I'm waiting for a call back to confirm that."

"Daniella, are you safe where you are? Maybe you should come to New York."

"No, I need to stay here, Bea. I have to deal with this mess. Speaking of which, I need to get going. Hunt and I are meeting with the insurance adjuster."

"Hunt? Now that's a sexy name."

I chuckled. "You don't know the half of it."

"Is he as sexy as he sounds?" I recalled the image of him standing upstairs, his gaze drifting down my body, and I shivered.

"Think Jake times ten," I replied as I heard a sound and turned to find Hunt standing at the door. My cheeks blossomed red, and I turned away from him. "I have to go, Bea. I'll talk to you later."

"Be careful, Daniella."

"I will, Bea. I'll be in touch soon."

"Oh, wait! I need the address to mail this."

"I'll have Huntley text it over to you; that way, you'll at least have one way to locate me if you need me. This number should be good for a couple of days too."

"Perfect. Talk to you soon."

When I hung up, I set the phone down and braced myself to see a knowing look on his face; only, there wasn't. Hunt leaned against the doorframe, filling it with his broad shoulders.

"Who am I texting?"

"My editor. She's going to mail me a few things."

"You ready to go?" He nodded as his crossed arms unlocked and hung to his sides. "You can send her a text from my phone on the way."

"Okay, sounds good." I followed him out of the office, finding my gaze locked on his backside. How I wish I could reach out and touch that, I thought as we entered the kitchen.

We said our goodbyes, and before I left, I turned to Tigger. "You stay, boy. Be good." I squatted down and rubbed his head. "I'll be back."

Tigger stared at me, and then I kissed his head and walked past Hunt, who was holding the door open for me. We didn't speak until we were in his truck.

"Everything okay with your editor?"

"Yeah, I needed to let Bea know what was going on and tell her it was going to be a little longer for the book than anticipated."

"I thought you only had one chapter left to write."

"Yes, I do, but after I finish a book, I go back to the start and begin reworking the first draft. I make notes along the way as I write, of things that need to be changed earlier on in the book and add in details that I might have missed the first time I was writing. It takes me a couple of days to do that, and then I can send the first draft over to her to read over."

"Then are you done with it?"

I laughed. "Oh, far from it. Bea reads it, then sends it back to me with notes on what it might be missing or what could be confusing. I do another edit, and then it gets sent to the editors."

He glanced my way. "Then it's done?"

"Maybe for some people, but I'm very protective of my work. The editors work on it, but then I get it back from them to approve their changes. Sometimes I like what they change, and sometimes I do not. After we go back and forth a few times, then my part is mostly done. They finish the edits, then get it proofed. I'll read it one more time before it goes to publishing."

"Wow, I had no clue that there was so much involved. I thought you just wrote a book and handed it off."

I chuckled. "Far from it. It's a long process. When I first started, I did it all myself, oversaw all the processes, hired the editors and graphics people because I self-published my books. A few years ago, one of my stories took off, and a publishing house came to me. I signed on with them, but I demanded to keep my rights. It's part of my contract."

"How long have you been writing?"

"All my life. Well, not all of it, but I've been writing since I was in middle school. I loved to read and write, and when I was a teen, it helped me escape."

He glanced my way again, his eyes solemn, and I tried not to wince as I saw the unasked question in his gaze.

CHAPTER TWELVE

HUNTLEY

$\mathcal{I}$ stood outside the door to my father's office, listening to Daniella speak to someone on the phone. Her voice was low, but I could hear it well enough. She was talking about the fire and how she came to be staying here. I shouldn't have been eavesdropping, but I couldn't help myself.

I heard her mention my name, and I stepped forward, suddenly feeling guilty for being there. She said something about Jake times ten, and I wondered what that meant. Her face turned red, and I had a feeling that it did have something to do with me, only because she seemed mortified that I had shown up when I had.

Before we left, I waited for her at the back door as she spoke with her dog. While she approached me, the dog and I had a moment of our own. Tig's stare was intense, and I could practically hear him growl, *don't mess with my human.*

I got this, Killer. I'll keep her safe. I tried to convey that to him, and then I shook my head. Did I really think I was having a conversation with a dog? I'd lost my mind.

On the way to her house, I listened to her talk, asking questions about how things worked in the author's world. A lot occurred before a book was published, and I'd always taken it for granted. When a new book came out, I bought it, enjoyed the story, and moved on. I never considered how much work went into it.

I had always enjoyed reading. Back in college, I'd gotten pulled into an espionage series that led me to some other mystery, suspense, and thriller novels. I wouldn't say I was a voracious reader, but I read a book or two a month. That was more than some men I knew.

Daniella mentioned that she had started writing as a teen girl for an escape, and my interest was immediately piqued.

"What did you have to escape from?"

She looked away quickly, clearing her throat. "Nothing really, just—I don't know." She grew quiet, and I contemplated a way to get her talking again, but after a moment, she sighed heavily and spoke in a low voice. "My mom died when I was nine. I started reading a lot after she died to hide from my feelings, and then eventually, I started to write, and it helped me deal with her death."

"I'm sorry, Daniella," I replied as I clenched the steering wheel. I could not even begin to comprehend a world where my mother was no longer a part of my life.

"Thanks. My stepfather took care of me after she passed. He didn't have any clue what to do with a kid. He was older than my mom, never had kids of his own, but he was nice enough—I guess. He drank a lot, so while he was around—sort of—I was kind of left to fend for myself. I was lucky he wasn't a mean drunk. He was a happy one; he'd even laugh in his sleep."

"Are you serious? Where was your real father?"

She shrugged. "I have no idea. I think my mother said that he left when I was like three. I don't have any memories of him, or maybe I do, but they are fuzzy. We never heard from him again, as far as I know. When my mom died, a part of me thought that he might come back for me, but he didn't."

"Daniella, I don't even know how to tell you how sorry I am."

Her laugh sounded slightly bitter. "It's okay, but that's why I started writing. I created worlds to live in where there were mothers and fathers that loved their kids, where they didn't go away, and life was good—happy—complete."

My chest ached—it truly ached. I had been so damn lucky. All of us Young siblings had been. I pulled onto her street, and she grew quiet again. I was still trying to wrap my head around her taking care of herself at the tender age of nine.

"Wow," she breathed as we rounded the corner at the top of the hill, and she got the first glimpse of her house. "It really is destroyed."

I parked, and we sat there in silence for a few minutes. I knew this had to be hard for her, and I would wait as long as she needed me. From the back seat, I pulled out a pair of boots. "Here, Daniella, put these on. They should fit or be close enough. They are my mom's."

She took them from me, changing out of the sneakers that Riley had brought for her. After she was done, she put her hand on the door handle but didn't move further. "Where do I even start, Huntley?"

Her sad voice stabbed at my heart. "Well, how about we just get out and walk around for a little while?"

She nodded and exited the truck as another car pulled into her cul-de-sac. A man exited the sedan with a clipboard in one hand and a camera in the other. "Ms. Knight?"

"Yes," she replied to him. He shifted his clipboard and shook her hand, turning to me.

"Cliff Zeer," he said, and I introduced myself to him before he turned back to Daniella. "Sorry about your place."

He explained what he was going to be doing, and we stood with him as he took photos and wrote notes near the front of the property. "Any idea of how it started?"

"Yes, on the woodpile out back," Daniella answered, and he

glanced at her, frown lines marring his brow, and then looked at me.

"Marc Broadbent, the fire marshal, said that they believe that it was arson," I explained to him.

"Arson?"

Daniella bobbed her head up and down, and his voice grew gruffer. "And where were you when this started?"

"Sitting in my living room working. My dog, Tigger, started barking like crazy. I let him outside, and then he tried to get me to come out of the house."

"Your dog tried to get you out of the house?" His voice was skeptical.

She nodded. "Yes, he's a German shepherd trained for protection."

He cocked his head, skimming his gaze over her. "Is there a reason you need protection?"

Now wasn't that the million-dollar question. Daniella shifted while I replied. "Marc thinks that it might be random. We had an arsonist around here a few years back, and he was going to check into the guy, see if he was still incarcerated or if he had been released."

Cliff frowned and blatantly looked Daniella from head to toe again. She was shifting nervously from foot to foot. Did he think that she had set her house on fire?

"Daniella, are you behind in your mortgage?"

"Excuse me?" she asked, her eyebrows popping high on her forehead as she instantly stopped moving.

"Are you behind on your mortgage? It's not unusual for people to get behind on their bills and start their houses on fire to get some relief with the help of their insurance."

Her jaw dropped, and indignation exploded from her eyes. "I most certainly did not! I just moved into this house six months ago, and I pay my bills just fine—and on time—thank you very much. How dare you accuse me of that! I just lost everything—

everything! Do you honestly think that I would burn down my entire house just to make some damn money?"

"It happens more than you might think," he stated, not seeming the least bit concerned that he had upset her.

I shifted toward Daniella. "Cliff, I was one of the first firemen to respond to the scene. Daniella was adequately scared and confused about what was happening. I can assure you that she didn't have anything to do with this."

"What is your relationship with her?"

"Just a friend. In fact, we just met last night."

He nodded and asked me for my personal information. I had nothing to hide, so I gave it to him. Daniella was still steaming mad, and her arms were wrapped tightly over her chest.

"Well, I need to do my thing." He handed Daniella a few sheets of paper. "I'll need you to make an inventory of your house. You need to include what the item was, a description, value, and how long ago you purchased it."

She stared at the paper, then her house. "For the entire house?"

He nodded.

Her gaze went wide. "You want me to remember everything that I had in my house, and how long I have had it? Are you serious?"

"I know it might be hard," Cliff told her. "But you will need to do that to get the money for replacements."

"Oh, my god! How am I going to remember everything in my house? That's insane!" She turned to me, and I wasn't sure that she wasn't going to break down in hysterical sobbing.

"Any chance you have pictures of the rooms inside your house? If you do, I'd suggest looking at them; they can jog your memory," he stated and walked away.

"But it's going to take more than this piece of paper to list everything," she called out.

He paused and turned back to her. "That's just a template;

you can write the list or type it up. A lot of people make their lists on a spreadsheet on the computer. My email is on that cover sheet, along with your claim number. Just make sure to reference that number anytime you email me."

He walked away, and she stared at his back. "Ass," she muttered when he was a good ten feet away. I had to agree with her. The moment he found out that this was a case of arson, he had treated her like she was a criminal, not the victim here.

"Don't stress over it, Daniella. I can help you with the list."

She turned on me. "Don't stress about it? How are you going to help me, Hunt? Seriously, how can you possibly help me? You have never been to my house before; you have no idea what I had in there."

"You're right, I haven't, not until the night of the fire. Do you have any pictures of your place?"

The frown lines on her forehead grew deeper as she considered my question. "Maybe." She turned and looked at her house again. "I have to wait for the charging cable for my cellphone to arrive. I might have some on there. I did send my editor a few pictures of the place after I moved in."

"Okay, well, that might help. Today, while we are looking over things, I'll take pictures with my cellphone. They might help jog your memory, too."

"Or give me nightmares," she murmured before she released a dramatic sigh.

I put my hands on her shoulders, "I know this is hard, Daniella. It's going to get harder before it gets easier. I'll help you as much as I can."

Some of the tension slipped from her shoulders. "Thank you, Huntley. I know you are trying to help."

She looked so lost and upset that I couldn't resist pulling her into my arms. She rested her head on my chest, one arm around my waist, the other dangling at her side, holding the papers. I almost kissed her forehead as I stepped back but didn't.

"So, why don't we take the boards off the front door and go in?" I asked her before going to the back of my truck to remove some tools. "I have a hard hat for you to wear and flashlights and gloves too."

"Why do I have to wear a hard hat?" she asked as she followed me.

I glanced at her house. "Did you not notice that most of your roof is gone? Something from the attic might fall as we move around in there; you don't want to get hit in the head."

"Ah, true. The last thing I need on top of everything else is a concussion."

I snickered as I pulled things out of the bed of my truck. I kept a hard hat back there for when I helped my brother on construction jobs, and of course, I had my fire helmet with me. I adjusted the inside straps of the hard hat for her and set it on her head. Damn, if that didn't make her even cuter than she was.

After grabbing a crowbar, my helmet, two pairs of work gloves, and a couple of reliable flashlights, we approached her front door. "You ready?"

"No, but what choice do I have?"

It took a moment, but I got the board off the front door and set it aside. The odor of the charred interior, smoke, and water dribbled out, and Daniella backed up, putting a hand to her nose.

"Gross!"

"Yeah, between the fire, smoke, and water, it's not going to smell very good, and it's only going to get worse in the next couple days as the mold starts to grow. If there is a room you want to work in, we can remove the boards to let more air inside."

"We need to get through this as fast as possible," Daniella said, glaring at the dark interior.

"Wait, let me grab a couple of dust masks. At least that will keep us from inhaling ash as we move around."

"Yeah, okay," she said with a sigh, and I returned to my truck. I found a couple of masks in one of the totes I kept back there and brought them back. She was standing on the front stoop, shining her flashlight into the doorway. "It looks spooky in there."

Knowing that someone had started the fire made it a little more eerie to me, but I wasn't going to voice that.

CHAPTER THIRTEEN

DANIELLA

*M*y emotions were on a roller coaster ride—one with a ton of loops and corkscrews. Once upon a time, I had liked riding those—today—not so much. One minute I was ready to curl on my side and bawl like a baby; the next, I wanted to scream and throw anything I could get my hands on.

The insurance adjuster hadn't made me feel any better, either. How the hell was I going to do an inventory of my house? How did someone possibly do that? How could you make a list of everything that had been destroyed? Was that even possible?

I stood on the front step, staring into the creepy darkness that had a blue cast to it—thanks to the large tarp covering the roof. It was like a scene from one of my books.

Jennifer didn't want to know what was in the darkness, but she knew that she had to find out. There were too many things that had happened recently, and she had to put a stop to it. She stepped forward slowly, her hand guiding her through the dark as it slipped over the smooth wall surface.

"Here."

The deep voice startled me so badly that I yelled as I spun around, my hand slapping against my chest to hold my heart inside as the hard hat flew off my head and bounced along the concrete porch.

Hunt started at me—shocked. "Um, you alright, Daniella?"

"Jesus." I bent over at the waist, putting my palms on my knees. "You scared the crap out of me, Hunt."

"Okay—" he said slowly. "Where was your head?"

I grabbed the hard hat and put it back on my head as I stood. "Not here, that's for sure. I didn't hear you come back."

"Daniella, you know if you aren't ready to go in, we can wait. We don't have to do this now."

I glanced over my shoulder; he looked worried. I turned slowly and touched his arm. "Hunt, I'm alright. When I was looking into the house, I was thinking about a story that I wrote, and then you spoke, and it startled me. I'm really alright."

"You were thinking about a story?" He looked puzzled as he asked.

I nodded, and his brow furrowed before he shook the lines away. "Here is your mask. Let me go in first, please, so I can keep an eye on the floor. I'd hate to have you break through a soft spot."

"Like it's any better if you do it?" I asked him.

He chuckled. "No, it's no better if I do it, but I know a little more of what to feel for as I walk around."

"Fine, whatever." I shrugged and removed the hat again before I put the mask over my face.

Huntley was already inside the house after I'd gotten situated, and I followed him in. Five feet into my living room, I paused and glanced around, instantly wanting to run back outside and throw myself to the ground as I wailed.

While there was a section of the ceiling in the living room and dining room still in place, it was drooping and stained from the water. The once white ceiling was now a variety of shades of gray. The living room furniture didn't look damaged, but I was pretty sure that it was. The fire might not have gotten to it, but the smoke sure had.

Less than a day ago, I had been sitting right there on the couch. The only worry in my world had been bringing Arrabella and Jake together in the final scene.

I stepped further into the house, glancing into my kitchen, and saw that while the ceiling was mostly gone, the ceiling fan was still suspended from the rafters. The blades were warped and hanging at weird angles. I glanced in the closest cabinet where I stored mixing bowls and other baking supplies. They were dirty, but they had survived. I opened another cupboard and saw that the plates and bowls were also the same. Well, at least it looked like the majority of my kitchen items would be okay after a thorough scrub and run through the dishwasher.

My eyes dropped to the dishwasher, and I frowned. Had the water damaged that?

"All of your appliances will need to be replaced," Hunt said behind me, providing me with my answer.

I left the kitchen and headed down the hallway that led to the back of the house. "Let me go in front of you, Daniella." I paused, putting my hand against the wall to steady myself as Hunt stepped around me. I removed my hand and stared at the wall. There was now a perfect handprint on the surface, and I stared at the palm of the glove. While the gloves hadn't been new, they hadn't been that dirty—they were now.

My nose twitched. Even with the mask on, the odor of the fire was almost overwhelming. There was stuff littering the hallway as we walked, and I had to step over a box that I knew had previously been in the attic. I glanced above me, the ceiling here gone entirely, and the tarp wavering slightly in the outside air was pretty much all there was to see above me.

Hunt stepped into my bedroom, and I glanced around at

what was left of it. The odor in here was much more pungent, and the carpet felt crunchy and wet under my feet. The entire back wall was gone, and if the plywood hadn't been there, I would have been looking at my neighbor's house. The mattress burned halfway through, and the box spring was almost unrecognizable. The clothes that had once hung in my closet were in an ashen heap on the floor. The door to the closet was hanging at an angle, heavily scorched.

A wave of nausea washed over me, and I closed my eyes. I turned around and walked out without a word, heading toward my office. At the door, I stopped and felt everything around me shift. I knew the floor was solid here, but at the moment, it didn't feel quite so stable—or maybe that was my mental status.

In front of me, my desk was charred; the bookshelves along the walls were heavily damaged. The books that had once been proudly displayed were charred, waterlogged, and scattered around the floor. I glanced down to see a copy of *Summer's Sunrise* lying on the ground, a massive bootprint over the cover.

Tears coursed down my cheeks, and I swallowed the lump in my throat. I picked the book up off the floor and wiped the cover, smearing ash as water dribbled from the spine. I stared at the shelves where my accomplishments had once stood. Side by side, every book that I had published had been there, two copies of each one.

"You alright, Daniella?" Hunt's voice was soft, and I could tell he was only a couple of feet behind me. I shook my head, and a moment later, his hands were on my shoulders in a comforting manner. "What was on the shelf?"

"These shelves—" My throat closed for a moment with emotion, and I had to clear it to continue. "These shelves had all of my first books. Every time I published a book, I would order a few of them. I always took the top two out of the box and put them here. The first one I wouldn't even crack the cover; I would just hold it, enjoy the accomplishment, and then in the second one, I'd open the cover and put the date."

I heard his soft sigh, and then he squeezed my shoulders. "I'm so sorry, Daniella. I know that nothing can replace those first books, but you can build your collection again."

"It won't be the same," I said as I wiped at my cheeks.

"I know it won't." He turned me to face him. "I know that you can never replace those or other things in your house, but eventually, you'll have more first books to put up on a new shelf. It's going to take a while, but you'll get there."

I nodded as I closed my eyes, trying to gain strength to continue. When I opened them, I stared at the corkboard that hung by one nail above my desk. The board was toast, and all my notes and timelines that I had posted there were flakes of ash now scattered over the desk surface. At least most of those notes were saved on my computer, and I could reprint them.

We heard footsteps in the house, and Hunt stepped into the hallway as the adjuster joined us. "You have a lot of damage."

Ya think? I wanted to snap back at him, but I kept my mouth shut.

"I'm going to take pictures of the inside." He looked to Huntley. "Was the basement finished?"

I nodded. "Yes, there is a family room off the garage, laundry room in the back section, and a small exercise room. I guess I need to see how damaged that is."

The adjuster took photos while we waited, then the three of us returned to the kitchen where the stairs to the basement were located. The men went ahead of me, and I stared into the dark abyss below and shivered. Hunt paused at the bottom. "Hey, Daniella, why don't you go around the front of the house to the garage door. There is standing water down here. I'll open the garage door, and you can check out your car that way."

I wasn't opposed to that. The thought of going down into

that darkness and stepping into the dark water did not thrill me in the slightest bit. Hunt disappeared before I could respond, and I quickly went out of the front door, pulling the mask from my face and filling my lungs with fresh air.

I took the concrete steps down to the driveway and heard Hunt in the garage, speaking to the adjuster. The garage latch clicked, and then he was pushing it up. Water trickled out of the doorway, and I watched it as it spread over the macadam.

I stared at my car as Cliff began to speak. "Beamer, huh? Well, if you hadn't left your windows open in your car, it wouldn't have been so bad. Unfortunately, the water from upstairs is now in your car." He turned to me. "Are your car payments up to date?"

"It's a lease, and yes, they are." I practically hissed toward him. "I had nothing to do with this! Some crazy lunatic started the fire, and I have no idea why."

"You sure about that?" he asked.

My eyes popped to Hunt's, who was observing me, too. I put my shoulders back and lifted my chin. "Yes, I am sure about that."

Of course, that could be a lie, but I didn't know that. In the past, when Larry had been stalking me, he had left me notes, flowers, candy. He hadn't done anything dangerous, and he'd never threatened to harm me. Not until the day he showed up on my doorstep.

I turned away so neither of the men could see my face. My past was just that—the past, and it had nothing to do with the present. It didn't.

Cliff spoke with Hunt about a few things and then went up to his car to write more notes. Before he left, he came to say goodbye and told me that he'd be able to have a check cut for me on Monday so I could start replacing some things.

"What about a place to live?"

"I'm pretty sure the office is working on that. I only appraise the damage; I don't deal with the rest of that."

I thanked him and watched as he drove off. I turned back to my house, glancing at Hunt. "Well, where the hell do I even begin?"

CHAPTER FOURTEEN

HUNTLEY

To be honest, I wasn't sure where to start either. I scanned the garage, my hands on my hips as I pondered the answer. When I heard a vehicle pulling into the cul-de-sac, I turned and laughed. "Looks like the cavalry is here."

Daniella looked up her driveway where not one, but four vehicles came to a stop. Bradley and my father were in the first truck. Riley and Charlotte were in her SUV, Henley in his pickup, and Ethan and Evan, his brother, in the fourth vehicle.

"What are they all doing here?" Daniella asked in surprise.

I took her arm, leading her up the slope of her driveway to the street. "Let's go find out."

Riley grinned as she came around the hood of her SUV. "Charlotte and I decided that our afternoon manicures could wait."

Daniella glanced over the group. "You all came to help?"

Henley stepped toward her. "Yes, we came to help."

Her mouth opened and closed like a fish out of water, making her look pretty damn cute. "Why?" she finally stammered out. "Henley, you and Ethan have been working all night. Don't you guys need sleep?"

Ethan and my brother shared a glance and laughed. "Sleep is overrated," Ethan replied.

"I just don't understand why you all are doing this for me. You don't know me. This doesn't make sense."

There were a couple of chuckles around the group, and then Henley, Riley, and I all said at the same time, "Because that's what Youngs do."

My father grinned, the pride filling his gaze.

"We collected plastic totes and boxes so we can start bringing things out of the house and sorting them," Riley said.

"I called a buddy of mine; he will be dropping a large refuse container off here later today so we can start discarding things," my brother Brad added.

I glanced at Daniella and saw a tear slip from her eye, and she swiped at it quickly, leaving a streak of ash in its wake. "I don't know what to say."

My father stepped forward, taking her by the shoulders. "You don't need to say anything, Daniella. Just put us to work."

She nodded, and my dad pulled her in for a quick hug. Henley and I shared a glance, and he grinned widely at me. I wasn't sure what that was for, and I wasn't stupid enough to ask.

"Well, maybe Riley and Charlotte can start in the kitchen and living room area. They can pull things out that can be saved by cleaning," I announced to the group. "Ethan, Evan, and Henley can work in the basement. Dad, Brad, and I can work through the bedrooms and office since that is where the worst of the structural damage is."

"What about me?" Daniella asked. "I can't stand here and do nothing."

I laughed. "Trust me; you'll be busy making sure we are doing our jobs. Besides, you'll need to move between the places when we have questions about stuff."

"Oh."

"I brought the smaller generator with me, so we'd have power if we need to use tools for anything, and light," Brad said. "I'm assuming that the basement is pretty dark."

"Yeah, and someone will need to get her car out of the garage."

Evan, who could have been Ethan's twin but was two years younger, said he'd deal with the car. It was like someone had said, okay, team, hands in, and let's go! Because suddenly everyone turned and got to work.

Daniella still looked shocked, almost somewhat bewildered as her eyes skittered after each one of them. "Why don't you help Riley and Charlotte get the boxes and totes out of the vehicles?"

I started to step away, and she grabbed my arm. "Huntley, I don't know how to thank all of you for this."

"It's okay, Daniella. All you have to do is speak the words."

Her eyes were crystal clear as she stared at me, and then she surprised me by popping up on tiptoe and placing a tender kiss on my lips. "Thank you."

I wanted to spear my hands through her hair and hold her to me, but my hands were dirty, so I didn't. Trying to make light of the situation, I gave her a lopsided grin. "You aren't going to thank everyone that way, now are you?"

She chuckled, and her cheeks began to fill with color as she stepped away, walking backward. She grinned at me and spoke teasingly. "Maybe."

I watched her spin around and move toward my sister. I couldn't help but watch the way her hips shifted from side to side as she went.

A FEW HOURS LATER, my father told us that my mom was bringing us lunch. We were sitting outside in the front yard, all of us wet and covered in soot and ash, when she arrived with the kids and Tigger. Around us were boxes and totes filled with objects rescued from the house. Most of it was from the kitchen and living room, but we'd found a few things that were salvageable from other parts too.

Daniella was laughing about something when the back door to my mom's SUV opened, and Tigger sprung out. He went right to her, practically knocking her down, sniffing and licking at her face as she petted him. After Tig knew she was alright, he began to sniff around at the others with us. He came to me last, not coming close enough that I could touch him, but staring me right in the eye for a moment before his tail swished, and he jetted off to sniff every single item that had come out of the house.

Mom and the kids joined us on the front lawn, and we enjoyed a picnic lunch. Despite the destruction behind us, the mood was light, and even Daniella, or Dani, as everyone had started calling her, seemed to be in a better mood.

Tigger didn't want to leave when my mother began to gather the kids back in her vehicle, but Daniella coaxed him back to the SUV. He looked at me again for a long moment. The intensity of his stare let me know that he was leaving her in my hands again, and he expected me to keep her safe. At least that's what I imagined the dog was saying. I could have been wrong.

After lunch, we went back to work, and by five, we were tossing things into the large commercial trash dumpster that had arrived. I was impressed by the amount that we had gotten done today. Everything collected was stowed in the garage until Daniella could go through it all again and decide what needed to be kept or thrown away. Brad and my father finished up by securing the boards over the windows and doors again.

Daniella stood in her front yard, two totes at her feet of

things she wanted to bring back to the house and clean up. She stared at her home, arms crossed tightly over her chest, brows furrowed in stress. I wanted to go to her, but I also didn't want to crowd her. Ethan came over to say goodbye, and when we turned to Daniella, we found Riley and Charlotte attempting to talk her into going out to dinner with them.

Ethan and I joined the conversation. "You sure you don't want to go out and unwind? Have a drink and relax a little bit? It might be good for you after a stressful day."

She pursed her lips and then sighed after a few seconds. "I'm sure it would be nice for most people, but that's not what I usually do to unwind."

"Yeah, and what do you do?"

"Um…" Her cheeks turned pink as she looked everywhere but at me, but finally, she turned back to me. "To be honest, I'm exhausted, and I think I'd rather take a shower and crawl in bed."

Ethan piped in. "You look like you could use a good night's sleep, and that is exactly where I'm going myself." He laughed, and I found myself frowning at him. Was he inviting her to join him? My gaze passed over Daniella to my sister, who had her lips pursed.

Daniella stepped toward Ethan. "Yes, please go home and get some sleep. I can't believe you and Henley helped all day after working all night." She put her hand on his arm and squeezed. "Thank you. You have no idea how much I appreciate it."

He winked at her and covered her hand with his. "You're welcome, Dani. You have my number. Call me if you need anything."

"I will. Thanks again, Ethan."

Henley joined us and said goodbye, and he ended up hugging Daniella. When she stepped back from him, she looked exhausted.

"Let's get you home. You're dead on your feet." We loaded

the two totes into my truck and said goodbye to everyone else before we left.

When we arrived at my parents' house, she was yawning. "I'm not sure I'll make it up the stairs."

"You want me to carry you again?"

She laughed as Tigger burst off the porch toward us, barking. "No, I think I can manage." She reached for the door handle. "Thank you for everything, Huntley."

"You're welcome, Daniella."

She sighed wearily as she got out of the truck, and Tigger bounced around her, sniffing every part of her that he could to make sure she was alright.

"Hey, buddy," she said to him as she ruffled his fur.

I climbed out and gathered her two totes. "I'm going to put these inside the barn. There is a large utility sink in there that you can use to clean things up when you are ready."

"Thank you. That will work out well." She followed me, opening the barn door for me and then following me inside. Buttercup rushed in from the outside and whinnied at me.

I set the totes down and then rubbed her nose. "Hey, Buttercup." She snorted out a burst of air and raised her head away from me. She never did like the smell of smoke.

I glanced back at Daniella. She was scanning the inside of the barn. "You can use that area over there to clean things."

She nodded, and then I said goodbye to Buttercup as we headed out of the barn again.

Daniella started to walk toward the house, and I began to veer off toward my truck. She paused. "Is there something else in the truck?"

"No, I'm going to head back to my place and take a shower."

Lines marred her dirty forehead. "I forgot that you don't live here."

"Nope, I don't, but I'll see you tomorrow. Hopefully, by tomorrow, we can have most of your house cleaned out."

She followed me to my truck and waited as I got in. "I know I already said this, but thank you, Hunt." She put her hand onto the windowsill of my door. "For everything. I really do appreciate everything you and your family have done for me."

For a moment, we stared at one another, and I almost covered her hand with mine but held myself back. "You're welcome, Dani."

We stared for another few seconds, and then she stepped back. "Have a nice evening. I'll see you tomorrow."

"Get some rest."

She smiled sweetly. "Thank you."

I put the truck in reverse and began to back away as Tigger barked once at me. I put my head out the window. "Bye to you too, Tigger."

His tag wagged briefly, and then he sat down on his haunches beside Daniella and watched me leave. In my rearview mirror, I saw Daniella and Tigger heading toward the house. How I wished I could go back, but I needed to get home.

The entire time I drove—and showered—I thought about Daniella. I was proud of her for holding herself together today. I did not doubt that if she had let herself, she would have fallen to pieces, but she didn't. That counted for something in my book.

I made myself something to eat and kicked back on the sofa, staring at the book in my hand that had somehow ended up in the back seat of my truck. I flipped to the first chapter and, while drinking my beer, began to read the first romance I'd ever read.

The writing was excellent, and even though it was supposed to be a love story, I found myself immediately drawn into it. There were quite a few elements that gave it a suspenseful feel, and in the fourth chapter, I finally got a little glance at the chemistry that Jake had with Arrabella.

She wasn't my usual type; in fact, I'd never been attracted to blonds before; typically, it was redheads that caught my eye. Arrabella was different, though; she always had been. The first time I met her, the fear in her eyes had wrapped around my heart and squeezed, and my feelings for her had kept on strangling it every fucking time she was around me.

I had been fighting it for months, but now as she stood in front of me laughing, I had the undeniable urge to weave my fingers through her hair and bring her luscious mouth to mine. I didn't want to fight it anymore, didn't want to deny that this tiny woman had burrowed her way into my chest and carved out a place in my hard, dark heart.

I drew her to me, her blue eyes sparkling as I leaned in, and her lips parted in anticipation.

This was a bad idea; I knew it was. I was supposed to be protecting Arrabella, and I knew that I couldn't defend her adequately if I stepped over that invisible line. Unfortunately, my need to taste her was more substantial than my will to stop just then, and I curled my hand around the back of her neck. My other around her hip, cupping the gentle curve and then sliding to her back to rest in that sexy as fuck curve above her ass.

Our lips brushed, and every ounce of blood fled my brain and headed south. Arrabella fisted my shirt, whimpering into my mouth as our tongues began to duel.

I jumped when my cellphone began to ring. I found myself laughing slightly as I realized how engrossed I'd been in the story. I glanced at the clock on the wall as I reached for my phone. Damn, I'd been reading longer than I expected.

"What's up, Kayley?" I said as I answered. "How are things up in New York?"

"Hey, you. Busy as usual. How are you? I heard that there has been some excitement there at home."

I chuckled. "Nothing too exciting."

"Oh, you mean the sexy blond famous romance author staying in Riley's room right now isn't exciting news?"

"How did you hear about that?"

"Ry."

"Ah, of course, Riley would call you. What did she say?"

"She told me about the fire and how you brought her home to stay with Mom and Dad."

"That was Henley's idea, not mine."

"Yeah, right." She laughed.

"I didn't even meet her until after he'd already made arrangements. He was on duty, asked me to drop her off."

"Really?"

"Yes, really."

"Um," she murmured. "Well, that's no fun. I was going to bust on you for having a new girl."

I laughed. "Sorry to disappoint you. There is nothing going on between Daniella and me."

"Do you want there to be?" she asked, almost excitedly.

"Well, let's just say that if something did happen, I wouldn't be disappointed." My eyes shifted to the book sitting beside me. I would most definitely not be disappointed.

CHAPTER FIFTEEN

DANIELLA

*I*t felt weird letting myself into the Youngs' house, well, for me. Tigger didn't seem to mind as he burst through the door the minute I opened it.

The smell of beef and gravy filled my nose, and I practically floated toward it. "That smells delicious," I said as I entered the kitchen to find Patricia and David standing behind the counter.

Patricia looked past me. "Where is Huntley?"

"He went home," I replied.

Patricia frowned. "I expected him to at least come in for dinner."

"He told me he had things he had to do down at the firehouse," David replied. That was news to me. He had just told me that he was going home to shower.

"Well, he could have made sure Daniella got inside alright. How did the rest of the afternoon go?" I went to open my mouth, and David put his hand gently on her shoulder.

"Patricia, let the poor girl shower and change, then you can grill her over dinner."

Patricia looked immediately contrite. "I'm so sorry; David's right. Go get yourself cleaned up, and then we will eat."

I glanced around the kitchen; dinner looked like it was ready to be put on the table at any second. "You don't need to wait for me."

She held her hand up. "Don't say another word. We aren't starving. Go take care of yourself, Dani, and take your time. Don't rush on our account."

"Thank you," I said and looked down at my feet, spinning around and going back into the mudroom. "Sorry," I called out as I saw the mess I'd tracked in behind me. I took off the boots that I was wearing and gnawed my bottom lip as I tried to figure out where to put them when David stepped in behind me.

"Here, let me take them. I'll knock the worst off and then rinse them off."

"Okay, thank you," I said quietly as I handed them off to him. I glanced back at the track of dirt I'd brought into the kitchen with me. "Um, do you have a broom?"

"Don't you worry about that, Dani. We will take care of it while you shower. Now go take a few minutes to unwind under the hot water."

"Thank you, David."

"You are very welcome, Dani." He winked and carried the boots out the back door. I slipped back into the kitchen and found it empty. I frowned at the track of dirt that I'd left, but instead of cleaning it, I hustled from the room. In my room, I dug through the clothes that Riley had brought me and suddenly had the urge to cry. This family—this family had done so much for me, and I wasn't sure how I could possibly repay them.

Before I could start blubbering, I hustled into the bathroom and turned on the water. All the emotions of the last two days began to overflow, and I couldn't staunch the flow of tears as I rid myself of my filthy clothing. I was barely under the water when sobs racked my body, and I curled in on myself and let it all out as quietly as I could.

I cried for all I had lost, for all that I had endured. Fear squeezed my heart that this could all be related to what I'd gone through a year ago. Please do not let it be connected with that. Please just let it be bad luck. I continued to cry until I couldn't produce another tear, and then I slowly washed. I didn't have any clue how long I'd been in the shower, but by the time I turned the water off, the only thing I could do was pull on the clothes and drag myself across the hall to the bedroom. I sank on the bed, intent on only resting for a moment, but after only a few seconds, I felt pulled into the darkness, and I didn't have the energy to fight it.

I WOKE to the sound of Tigger's nails on the floor in the hallway and sunlight peaking around the curtain. There was a thick blanket thrown over me, and the door was cracked open. I sat up, rubbing my eyes and wondering what time it was.

I heard a car rumbling over the gravel in the driveway and stood to peek out the curtain. Huntley's truck was coming to a stop, and I heard Tigger barking downstairs for a moment before the sound traveled, and suddenly Tigger was making a beeline for Huntley as he got out of his truck.

The two of them regarded one another, and Tigger wagged his tail at him but didn't approach him. I could see Huntley's mouth move but couldn't hear what he was saying. Tigger's ears perked, and then he turned and ran toward the house as Huntley grinned.

I glanced down at my clothes and then dashed across the hall to use the bathroom. One look in the mirror made me groan as I took in my rat's nest of hair. I hadn't even combed it last night after my shower. I glanced back over my shoulder and quickly discarded my clothes as I turned the shower on again. Yes, I was clean, but I wouldn't be able to do a thing with my hair in the mess that it was.

I washed and conditioned my hair in quick order before I was out and drying myself as quickly as I could. I heard footsteps outside of the bathroom and paused in mid-dry. Tigger's nails clipped past the door, and then the footsteps came back, and Tigger's followed again.

Had Huntley come up to find me? Or go to his room for something? I quickly finished drying, put my clothes back on, and worked a comb through my long hair, taking a moment to snag my toothbrush out of the cup and brush my teeth quickly. Finally, I took a long look in the mirror, noting that I still had dark circles under my eyes, but at least I didn't look like I was a zombie anymore.

I pulled open the door and stepped across the hall to my room, intent on putting on socks when I came up short. Huntley was kicked back on the bed, his long legs crossed at the ankle, one arm tucked behind his head, and holding a book in his hand. He looked as if he'd been lying there reading for a while.

When I saw the book that he held in his hand, heat burst into my cheeks—*Smoldering Nights*. The most intense and sexual book that I had written. My editor had told me to see just how far I could go without crossing that erotic line, and I had gotten right to that edge and almost fallen over. Where did Huntley get that? Please tell me that he was not reading that.

"What are you doing?" I burst forward and ripped the book from his hands, closing it and pulling it to my chest.

He smirked at me, letting his gaze drift to my chest and back up before he slowly sat upright. "Just trying to learn a few things about you."

"From this?" I squeaked. "Where did you get this?"

"From my mother's collection." He grinned as he threw his legs over the side of the bed. "Why don't you want me to read that? It's interesting to see what comes from your mind. I'm learning a lot about you."

"Oh, my god! This is not me!" I held the book up. "This is just a book—just words written for entertainment."

He laughed, a deep husky vibration that slithered down my spine just as I imagined Jake doing to other women so many times. I had to force myself not to sag under the sexual weight of it.

"But you wrote it."

"So?"

He cocked his head to the side. "So I'm learning the way your mind works."

"First of all, why would you want to know how my mind works? Second, just because I wrote that stuff does not mean that is how I am or who I am."

"Who are you?"

I blinked. "What do you mean, who am I?"

He studied me carefully for a moment. "Who are you, Daniella Knight?"

I crossed my arms over my chest. "I'm me."

"Yeah, but who is that?"

I frowned at him. "I don't know what you are talking about."

He stood, and I automatically stepped back. "I think you need to figure that answer out, Daniella. What I see is a woman who is hiding from something—maybe someone. I see a woman who lives life through words on a page, but who secretly wants to walk in those characters' footsteps."

"You don't know what you are talking about, Huntley." I bristled at his words—the audacity of him to say such things to me.

He stepped closer, and I forced myself not to back down. "Then how can you write such incredible stories about love and sacrifice, and then blush when a man looks at you with any type of interest?"

My mouth parted in surprise, and before I could even think of anything to say, Huntley stepped around me and paused at the door.

"When you figure out who you are, let me know, Daniella. I want to get to know that woman"—he peered slightly over his shoulder—"all of that woman."

I stared after him, shocked at what he'd said. Where did I even start with that conversation?

I sat on the edge of the bed, frowning as I ran back over what he had said, and a minute later, I heard an engine start. I looked out the window to see Huntley turning his truck around in the driveway, and then he drove away.

IT HAD BEEN a week since I'd come to stay at the Youngs. Every day I thought of how I was overstepping their hospitality, but Patricia would tell me repeatedly that I was welcome as long as it took.

The insurance company was having a hard time finding a place for me to stay that would allow my dog. They had a few, but they were over two hours away—if they didn't find something soon, I would take what they had offered. I did have a car now, and I'd gotten a replacement credit card, so at least I could make my own purchases—one of them was groceries for the Youngs to thank them for all that they had done for me.

I'd also gotten my book finished. I'd spent Sunday morning getting the last chapter written and then the week doing rewrites on it when I wasn't over at my house cleaning it out. I hadn't seen Huntley since our exchange in the bedroom, but that didn't mean I didn't think about him. I did—like almost every waking minute. It was hard not to as everywhere I turned, there were pictures of him.

I dwelled over what he had said to me. About how he wanted

to know who I was. Did he really think that I wanted to be like my characters? How did he even know about my characters? Had someone told him more about them?

During the week, I had different people helping me. David and Henley helped me the most, although Ethan and his brother had also come two days. I'd heard Henley talking to Ethan about how busy the fire department had been this past week. It sounded like there had been a couple more big fires, which explained why I hadn't seen Huntley—or did it?

It was Sunday, late afternoon, and I was working on an interview that my editor wanted me to complete for a new release. I heard noises in the back of my mind, but I was so focused on what I was typing on my laptop that they didn't register.

"See, she couldn't care less if we were here." Huntley's voice reached me, and my chin popped off my chest so I could see over my laptop screen. In the doorway stood Riley and Huntley.

"She cares," Riley said with a grin. "She's just busy being famous."

I chuckled as I closed my laptop. "I was finishing an interview that my editor wanted me to do."

"Are you done?" Riley asked as she stepped into the room.

"Almost."

"Good, then when you're finished, you need to stop working and come down to relax."

"What's going on?"

"Nothing exciting, just Sunday dinner with the family." Riley shrugged. My eyes slipped to Huntley's, and for a moment, our gazes locked. All the thoughts I had about him this last week crashed over me, almost overwhelming me.

I finally tore my gaze from his. "Okay, I'll be down in a few minutes."

"Alright, we will leave you alone to finish your work, but hurry up." She turned and stepped out, grabbing Huntley's arm.

"I'll be down in a second; I want to talk to Daniella for a moment."

She whispered something, and Huntley rolled his eyes. "Go away, Ry."

She giggled as she disappeared from view, and Huntley stepped over the threshold. I set my laptop to the side, swinging my legs over the side as he approached.

"How are you?"

"I'm fine—busy, but that's nothing new."

He nodded as he paused in front of me, his bright- green eyes drifting over my face as if he were searching for something. "Did you get your book done?"

"I did."

He nodded. "That's good. So Jake got together with Arrabella, right?"

I laughed as I stood up. "What do you know about Jake and Arrabella?"

He smirked. "Would you believe me if I told you that I had read the entire series this week?"

My jaw dropped, and he laughed. "Is it that hard to believe?"

"Um, I never expected you to read any of my books, Huntley. Why did you?"

"Because Riley told me that if I wanted to know who Jake was, that I should read them. So I did."

"You read them to find out who Jake was? Why, because I called you by that name when I was in a dream state?"

"Yeah."

I laughed. "Okay, well, then you read my books. Tell me, Huntley. What did you think of them?"

He shuffled a bit closer, running two fingers down my cheek after he'd stopped. "I think you are a compelling writer, Daniella. I think that you can pull anyone into any type of a story and make them feel things that they didn't know they could feel."

CHAPTER SIXTEEN

HUNTLEY

$\mathcal{A}$ ll week when I wasn't working, my mind had been on Daniella—mostly because I'd been reading her books every available moment. After starting the one last week, I realized that book was in the middle of a series, so I downloaded the books that came before that to my reading device and brought it with me everywhere.

I figured if I were reading on my device, fewer people would ask me what I was reading. I could just imagine the guys at the firehouse seeing the covers of these books. I'd never live that down.

I had wanted to spend time with Daniella in person, but because I worked full time for the fire department, and we'd had a couple of fires this week, I'd been on the clock when she had been over at her house. Henley and my father kept me updated on the progress. Riley and my mom kept me updated on what Daniella was doing at the house—which was mostly keeping to herself.

Mom had told me that now that Daniella had a car, she came and went as needed but kept to her room, except for dinner. At dinner, Daniella would join them and tell them about her progress on the house and the work she was doing on her book.

I know that she had also started sending lists to her insurance company of items she'd remembered in her house. I'd created an album of photos, and everyone who had helped last week had added photographs they'd taken while there. I knew this would help Daniella create her list to submit to the insurance company. My mother said she was very grateful for the shared album, although she hadn't reached out to me directly.

Now it was Sunday, and I planned on spending time with her and getting to know her better. The last time I had seen her, I'd left her with something to think about, and I'd wondered all week if she'd come up with an answer.

"I think you are a compelling writer, Daniella. I think that you can pull anyone into any type of a story and make them feel things that they didn't know they could feel."

She blinked up at me. "You came up with that by reading my books?"

"Yes." I studied her for a moment. "I would never have read any of your work if Riley hadn't pushed me to, but then I started reading, and because your stories were interesting, I went back and read the whole series so I could understand it all. You really do pull people into your stories. The suspense is real. You can literally see it happening to people. The relationships that you build seem like you might be talking about my own family. Damn, I mean, Wesley and Charlotte had a romance story all their own, and Henley and Roxy had to overcome some shit to be together."

She continued to stare at me, not saying anything, so I continued. "It's like your writing nonfiction, real-life stories of people that you could meet anywhere. Like I could walk into the coffee shop, and Jake would be sitting right there, reading emails on his phone, or Arrabella would be playing her music loud in her car as she drove down the street. I almost feel like

I'm walking around now, expecting to see these characters in person. That's how real you have made them."

She began to smile. "I'm glad to hear that because sometimes I feel like they are real."

"You are a fantastic writer, Daniella," I paused. "But do you ever feel like you spend more time living through your characters than you do living?"

Lines marred her brow. "Excuse me?"

"You seem so focused on your writing and your books that I wonder if you ever take the time out to experience life yourself."

She shuffled back slightly. "What are you talking about, Huntley? Of course I live my life."

"Do you? Because I have read a lot of the interviews that you do, and they all talk about how hard you write, even your weekly blog talks about how hard you work, but it never mentions what you do in your personal life."

"Because my personal life is no one's business, Huntley." Her voice had a hard edge to it. "I can't believe you are stalking me now."

"I'm not stalking you, Dani. I'm trying to learn more about who you are."

She laughed. "And that's not stalking? If you wanted to know who I was, why didn't you just come and ask me?"

"I did ask you, and you didn't answer me. Remember? Last week, I asked you who you were, and I told you that when you figure that out, I wanted to get to know you."

She turned away, crossing her arms over her chest. "Well, I appreciate that, Huntley, but I'm sorry. I'm not interested in getting to know anyone right now."

"Why?"

"Because I'm not at a place in my life where I have time to be involved with anyone. My life is hectic, and right now, I'm trying to rebuild it. I don't have time for complications and relationships."

I laughed. "Are you serious?"

"Yes. I appreciate everything that you and your family have done for me, I really do, but I need to stay focused on my career and my own life right now."

I nodded slowly and stepped back. "Well, okay. I guess I don't have a choice."

"I'm sorry, Huntley. I do think you are a very nice man."

A laugh burst from my mouth. "A very nice man, huh? Well, that's not one I have been called recently. Alright, well, I'll leave you alone to finish yet another interview about your writing career and your wishes and hopes for more successful books."

I turned and left her staring after me. I was heading down the stairs, wondering how I was going to be able to remain here and calm after that conversation when I got a text message from one of the guys at the firehouse—the perfect excuse to leave.

"Hey, Mom," I said as I slipped into the kitchen. "I'm gonna have to scoot. I just got a text from Boyer at the house. He needs help with something."

"Huntley, I haven't seen you all week. Are you sure you have to go? I'm sure Daniella will be very disappointed that you aren't going to be here."

"I doubt that, Mom, but if I get the chance, I'll swing back around later." I kissed her cheek, ruffled Marisol's hair, and then high-tailed it out of the house.

Maybe I was acting like a stalker, but that was only to understand more of who she was and where she was coming from. There was so little about her personal life online and even fewer pictures of her. I just didn't get why she hid so much from everything.

I sighed as I climbed in my car and started my truck. I glanced up at Riley's bedroom window and saw the curtain pulled back. I couldn't see into the room, but I knew she was there watching me. What was she thinking? Did she really not want to get to know me? All of our previous interactions seemed like she did. She'd kissed me back, gazed into my eyes like she was interested. Why the change now?

I guess it didn't really matter, now did it? I put the truck in reverse and turned myself around. The last thing I needed in my life was a complicated woman. Nope, no, thank you.

I NEVER DID MAKE it back to my parents' house that night, or any night this last week. In fact, I'd gone to work and then gone home each night and curled up on the couch to read more of her work. Not that I really got into the romance part, but I enjoyed her stories, and oddly, it made me a bit closer to her.

I was kicked back on the couch on Saturday night, a beer in my hand and my ereader in my lap when someone pounded on my door, and it burst open. Henley and Ethan entered, grinning, and I tossed the device aside like a hot potato, embarrassed to be caught reading it.

Henley followed the device as it flew to the other end of the couch, and he cackled loudly. "Are you reading her romance books? Wait, did you get to any of the hot parts yet?"

I could try to deny I was reading it, but why should I? I shrugged. "Yeah, a couple."

Ethan retrieved the device and then gave me an odd look. "Why are you reading a romance, dude? Do I need to worry?"

"No, you do not need to worry!" I grunted at him.

"Daniella wrote it, and Riley and Charlotte told him to read it," Henley told Ethan.

"Hey, you're supposed to keep that quiet," I snapped toward my brother, and he shrugged.

Ethan glanced at us and then back to the book. "Damn, and there are hot parts in here? How do you know that, Henley?"

"Roxy reads her books. Every time she finished one of the sex scenes, she was hot and bothered." He laughed.

Ethan wiggled his brows. "Does Riley read these?"

"Yeah, why?" I asked.

Ethan looked thoughtful for a moment. "No reason, just wondered."

"So, why are you two here?"

"We thought we'd go out for a beer, and we wanted you to come too. Wesley is also meeting us," Henley replied

"Wes is coming out?"

"Yep," Hen said.

"Why is he coming out here?"

Ethan and Henley shared a glance. "Because it seems that all of our women are seriously enjoying themselves, and someone is going to need to get them home safely. Roxy met up with them for dinner and called to let me know that they are three sheets to the wind at Donny's bar."

"Oh, really?" I hadn't missed the part where he said all of *our women*, and I glared at Ethan again. No way was I going to let him get his hands on Daniella. Nope.

"Let me throw jeans on," I said and disappeared into my bedroom. I was back a couple of minutes later, slipping my wallet into my pocket as I grabbed my truck keys.

"We'll see you down there," Henley said as we left my place, and he jumped into Ethan's truck.

I followed behind them and wondered what Daniella was going to be like on the intoxicated side. Was she going to be more open? Or would she blush even more than she usually did? What if she got pissed off that I was even there?

When we arrived, Wes was just parking. We went inside and glanced around. "Holy smokes," Henley said as our eyes followed his to their table.

The women were cackling madly, slapping their hands on the surface and wiping under their eyes. Whatever was so funny had brought them to tears.

"Oh, this is going to be good," Wes said with a grin as he

started toward their table. We followed behind him, and my gaze locked on Daniella. She looked more relaxed now than I had previously seen her, and I grinned as we reached the table.

Wes went to Charlotte; Henley kissed Roxanne's cheek, and Ethan ended up standing near Riley. The two of them stared at each other. Well, that was interesting. Not interesting enough to keep me from turning my attention to Daniella. Her eyes were bright, her cheeks a little flushed, and her gaze drifted brazenly down my body and then back up as she pulled her bottom lip under her teeth. Holy. Shit!

"Looks like you guys are having fun," Ethan said.

"Oh, Dani has been talking about her books," Riley said. "We're dying here with how she comes up with some of her stories."

I eyed Daniella, who was still staring at me unabashedly. "I'd like to hear some of those stories."

Roxy laughed. "Oh, maybe you'll be lucky enough that she'll show you, Hunt."

Daniella's cheeks turned a bit pink as she glanced away, but the smile that remained on her lips made me wonder if maybe I just might be lucky enough to have her change her mind about getting to know me.

CHAPTER SEVENTEEN

DANIELLA

*H*e had ruffled my feathers. If I was honest with myself, he did more than that, but I didn't want to admit it to anyone—especially not myself.

The fact that he had researched—I was trying to avoid the stalking word—my writing had flattered me. Okay, it did more than flatter me. The man had been reading my books because he said my writing was good. I had thousands of reviews, and yet his simple words had meant so much more. Why was that?

Was it because I wanted him to approve of what I did? Did I want him to think of me as someone special and not just some random woman who wrote love stories? Maybe.

Or perhaps I wished for his approval because I just wanted his personal male approval. If Jake were real, would he approve of what I did? Hadn't he scoffed at a character for writing silly tributes to something that did not exist? He had before he had found true love for himself.

Had I based all male opinions on that of my stepfather? He had never called me silly for writing my stories, but he had never praised me either, and he sure as hell had never read any of them, not even the ones that I'd won awards for in middle and high school. After a while, I had stopped showing him my work and kept them all to myself until I finally found a way to publish them. I had published my first book at the age of twenty-four, and now ten years later, I had a lot of books on my shelf.

When I first started publishing, I was all over social media, but after what happened last year, I'd gone through a lot of trouble to erase a lot of myself. I'd shut down accounts, created new ones, and hired people to oversee them for me. They posted information and made it sound like me, but it was never personal—never.

I sat there and thought about what Huntley had said last week. Who was I? I wasn't the woman I once wanted to be; that was for sure. I had always dreamed of having good friends and a relationship to rival my romances, where I did wonderful things and always had fun.

I sighed as I leaned back, shutting my laptop and closing my eyes for a moment. Huntley's face came to me immediately. Every time I closed my eyes, his face showed up in my mind, and instead of pushing it away as I usually did, I took a moment to let the memory associated with it replay. It was the moment he had first kissed me.

I'd been lost in the feel of him, the taste of his tongue on mine. I hadn't even taken the time to memorize it. I'd just lived in the moment that one time, and I still remembered every second of it. From the feel of his soft full lips to the way his hands had run along my back, I could remember it all. But more importantly, I could remember the apparent sexual desire straining behind the zipper of his pants. I could recall every second of it vividly. Those few moments were worthy of any romance scene I'd ever written.

I sighed just as a knock sounded on my door, and I shot up, hoping it wasn't Huntley. "Come in," I called out, and Riley slipped her head inside. Tigger got to his feet and went to say hello to her.

"What's going on?" I asked her as she stood back up.

She glanced at my computer. "Please tell me you are done working for the day."

"Why?"

"Because we want you to come out with us."

"Who is going?"

"Charlotte, Roxy, and me. We are just going out to have dinner and maybe a drink or two." I hesitated, and Riley spiked her brows. "Do not tell me you have something better to do. I know you rock your romances, but girl, you need to come out and let your hair down! You need to have some fun!"

Hadn't I just been thinking about that?

She stepped forward and took a seat on the bed beside me. "Come on, Dani. It will do you good to have some girl time. I promise you will enjoy yourself. Our antics might even give you some ideas for another book scene."

I chuckled. "Okay, fine, but we won't be out late, will we?"

"Nope, I promise, only a couple hours of girl time, and then you can come back here and hide in this room again and write to your heart's content."

"You make me sound like an hermit."

She grinned. "Aren't you?"

"No."

"Dani, you have lived here in town for six months, and you don't know anyone. You said it yourself; you never leave your house. That is hermit behavior. If you don't want to be a hermit, get dressed in something cute, and let's go have some fun!"

"Okay, fine. Give me about twenty minutes."

"Perfect!" Riley squeezed my arm. "I promise you won't regret it."

I wasn't sure about that, but I'd have to trust her. I dug through the clothing that Riley had brought over for me since I hadn't had time to go shopping for clothing and found a pair of jeans that fit like a second skin. I also found a blouse that was a little lower cut than I typically preferred, but it looked fantastic. Especially with the sports bra that I wore as it pushed my boobs right up into the low V-neck. What would Huntley think of this if he saw me in it?

I guess it was a good thing that I wouldn't find out.

Riley and Charlotte were waiting for me downstairs when I came down, and I stared at Tigger again. "Patricia, you don't mind watching him again? I feel like I've just dropped my problems right into your lap."

"I absolutely do not mind, Daniella. Go out and have some fun. You need to let off a little steam."

"As long as you are sure."

"I am sure. You girls have a good time and behave yourselves." She stared at Riley pointedly as she spoke, and Riley pretended to be offended.

"I don't know what you're talking about, Mom."

"Uh-huh," she said with a frown, then immediately morphed into a wide grin as Charlotte put her hand on my arm and pulled me toward the door. I called out a goodbye to Tigger, and we headed to Riley's SUV.

"Roxy is meeting us at dinner," Charlotte said.

"And who is Roxy again?" I asked from the back seat.

Riley frowned. "You haven't met Roxy yet?"

I shook my head. "No."

"Roxanne is Henley's fiancée," Charlotte answered. "She's a wedding planner. Luckily, she had a day wedding that ended early, so now she can join us. Usually, she has to work late on Saturdays, so we usually do these things on Sundays. Which kind of sucks because we all have to work on Mondays."

"I look forward to meeting her," I said, and I meant that. So far, I adored this family. Even though they were a bit pushy, they meant well, and I appreciated it. What I loved most about the family was how well they all got along. The love that they had for one another was impressive, and a little part of me was extremely jealous of that.

"You're going to love Roxy," Riley said. "I'm not sure how she puts up with my brother, but she's been good for him. He's almost tolerable now."

"How long have they been together?"

"Since Valentine's," Riley stated as she glanced at me in the rearview mirror.

"They have been together since Valentine's? How long have they been engaged?"

Charlotte tapped a finger on her lip. "Um, it was shortly after Valentine's Day, I think."

"They met and got engaged that quickly?"

Charlotte laughed loudly. "Yep, seems like the norm in this family. Wesley and I were engaged within a couple of weeks and married a few months later."

"Seriously?" I barked. "How can you marry a man that you barely know?"

Charlotte leaned to the side so she could peek around the seat. "What are you talking about? Your characters do it all the time."

"Yeah, but that's fiction. That doesn't happen in real life."

She barked out a laugh. "Yes, it does. Time has nothing to do with falling in love. If it's meant to be, it just happens."

"Have you ever been married, Dani?" Riley asked.

"No, and I haven't been engaged either," I stated and frowned. "To be honest, I haven't even dated much, and I've never been in love."

Riley stared at me in the mirror. "How do you write those fantastic love stories if you have never been in love?"

I shrugged. "It's all fantasy to me. I write what I dream could happen one day."

"Wait." Charlotte spun in her seat at an awkward angle. "Are you telling me that all that stuff you write is from fantasies? You've never done that stuff?"

I shook my head, feeling slightly uneasy. "Would it be weird for me to say that I don't believe in love?"

Riley was turning into a parking lot. "That's bullshit! You have to believe in love. If you didn't, you wouldn't be able to write the way you do."

I honestly didn't believe in love. The last time I felt like anyone cared about me was when my mother was alive. After she passed, I was alone, and I never got over that. I'd had few friends that weren't fictional, and even less in the way of relationships. Yes, I had been with men—two to be exact—but neither of them had blown my mind or made me feel like fireworks were exploding over my head. It had been sex, and both times it had been because I wanted to know what it was like, not because I was swept up in a passion that I couldn't deny.

The stories I wrote came from my fantasies, and now that I was in my thirties, I was beginning to believe that it would never happen for me.

"We are totally going to talk more about this later," Riley said as she parked. "But we need alcohol and food first."

"Roxy is already inside. She has a table for us," Charlotte said as she looked at her phone while she climbed out of the vehicle. She waited until I was out. "And Riley is right; we need to discuss this more."

I followed them into the restaurant and was introduced to a bubbly blonde that bounced in her seat when she was introduced to me. "Holy cow! Do you have any idea how exciting it is to meet you?"

I stared at her, and then Riley leaned over. "Yeah, I had to tell her who you were. It was only fair since she is part of the family."

I sighed in resignation, put a smile on my face, and told her how much I appreciated Henley's help these past two weeks.

Within minutes, I was laughing with them as if I'd known them for ages. Our waiter was a handsome young man who kept drooling over Riley, and she toyed with him, smiling seductively every time he came to the table.

"You are so bad, Riley," Roxy said as she bumped her shoulder and then picked up her martini glass and held it up. "To girls' night, and our new friend, may we have many more!"

An overwhelming feeling blossomed in my chest as I lifted my glass. I couldn't remember a time that I had ever been as accepted as I was here. I tapped my glass to theirs and sipped the chocolate martini that I'd been talked into getting.

"Holy shit, that's good!" I said before taking another long sip.

"Just be careful," Charlotte said with a laugh. "Those go down easy and then slam into you when you aren't looking."

"Don't tell her that," Riley joked. "She needs to let loose, unwind a little bit and get drunk! Shit, if I'd lost everything I owned, I'd be shitfaced in a minute."

"You're always shitfaced," Roxy said to her with a grin, and Riley shrugged.

"Keeps my life interesting."

"Speaking of interesting, who are you doing now?" Charlotte asked as she leaned on the table.

"No one," Riley replied.

"No one?" Roxy burst out laughing. "You are never doing no one, so who is it?"

"Seriously, I'm not seeing anyone right now."

"That's a first," Charlotte said with a teasing grin.

"Actually, it's not. We need some new blood in town. Maybe Kayley had it right by moving away."

"Oh, don't give me that," Roxy said.

Riley turned to her. "Hey, look who is talking. Both of you found my brothers in other towns. I never leave this place. I know all the men my age, and I've either slept with them or wouldn't touch them with a ten-foot pole."

"What about Ethan or his brother?"

Riley's jaw dropped. "Oh, my god! That would be like sleeping with my own brother."

Roxy leaned closer to her, her eyes wide. "Are you saying that you've never slept with Ethan?"

"No! Yuck!"

"Wow," Roxy murmured. "With the way that he looks at you, I would never have guessed."

"What do you mean the way he looks at me?"

"He looks at you like he wants to eat you alive, Riley," Roxy stated.

Riley glanced at me as she rolled her eyes. "No, he doesn't, but he has checked you out a few times."

"Me?" She nodded.

"He's totally been checking you out." Riley grinned at me.

"Yeah, well, Ethan might have been checking her out, but he knows better than to try anything," Charlotte said.

Not that I was interested in Ethan, but I was interested in what she meant. "Why would you say that?"

Riley and Charlotte both laughed as Riley responded. "Because if he even laid a finger on you, my brother would take his arm off."

"Wait!" Roxy said. "Are you saying Hunt likes her?"

"Likes her?" Charlotte laughed loudly. "The guy is gaga over her. I know he's a Young, but when Dani is around, he's strutting around like a peacock and watching her every move."

"He does not," I said quickly as my cheeks warmed.

They both nodded dramatically. "Oh, yes, he does." Charlotte said. "And he looks like Jake! So it's a win-win situation for you."

I lifted my glass and downed the rest of my drink. The waiter just happened to be passing by, and I held up my glass. "I need another one of these."

"So, now that we have some alcohol in you, you need to

explain that comment in the car about never being in love before."

"I don't think I've had quite enough to drink for that," I muttered.

"What do you mean, you've never been in love before?" Roxy was quick to jump on Riley's comment.

"Yeah, she said in the car that what she writes is fantasy. She's never experienced it before," Charlotte added, and I felt my cheeks burst into flames. Was that the alcohol or the conversation? Probably both.

"No way!" Roxy said. "There is no way you couldn't have used personal experience in those stories. They are so heartfelt and sensual."

I shook my head, the strong alcohol easing through my system and lubricating my lips. "Nope, I've been with exactly two men in my life, and neither of them gave me anything worth writing about."

"Then how do you do it?" Charlotte asked.

"I research."

Riley busted out laughing. "Research? How the hell do you research romance?"

"I read lots of blogs, and—" I hesitated. Would they think me odd if I said the next sentence? Whatever. "I watch porn. Well, soft porn meant for women. It's sexy and romantic."

Charlotte's jaw dropped, and Riley had a brow peaked my way. It was Roxy that reached over the table and put her hand on mine. "I need those websites."

"You know, Riley, if you found a man, you wouldn't need a drawer full of toys," Charlotte told her.

"My toys don't talk back to me, and I don't have to cook them dinner or be nice to them. When I'm done, I can wash them and put them away. They don't keep talking or try to make excuses for leaving."

"That is true," I agreed with her. "No wasted time. No worthless foreplay. You just get down to business and then move on."

"Wait—" Roxy said quickly. "Do you use toys?"

Riley slapped her hand on the table. "The woman researches romance and sex off websites. Of course, she uses toys." She put her hand up for me to high-five, and I did as my next drink arrived at the table.

"You know, I'm amazed," Charlotte said, eyeing me seriously. "If you haven't done the things that you write about, how do you identify with the characters?"

I shrugged. "I don't know. I guess I just make it up."

"If you could be any character from your books, who would you be?" Riley asked as she leaned forward.

"Oh, that's easy. I would want to be Jocelyn. I loved writing her. She has such a fighting spirit, eager sexuality, and she does what she wants when she wants."

"Then you should try to be more like her," Roxy said. "I loved Joceyln, too. Riley is a lot like her."

"You think so?" Riley asked her before she downed the rest of her drink.

"Oh, yes," Charlotte answered.

After dinner, we walked two doors down and found another table near the back of a small country bar. It was dark and crowded and usually wouldn't be my type of scene, but after three chocolate martinis, I wasn't feeling like my usual self.

I laughed more in those couple of hours than I had in my entire life, and at one point, I sat back and listened to Roxy and Charlotte talk about some wedding plans, and I realized that I felt happy. I only hoped that I could continue this friendship with them once I was back at my house.

I was sharing with them how I had come up with one of my recent story premises when we all almost fell off our stools from laughter. I knew that tomorrow, my diaphragm was going to be sore from the hours of constant cackling.

"Oh, boy, don't look now, but the men are here," Charlotte said softly, and we all turned to look at the men approaching us. Wesley, Henley, Ethan, and Huntley sauntered toward us.

Hunt had a cocky smile on his lips as he paused a foot away, and I couldn't help but let my gaze caress its way down his body and back up. I already knew his kisses were incredible, but would having sex with Huntley be anything like the scenes in my stories? Right then, I was seriously tempted to find out.

CHAPTER EIGHTEEN

HUNTLEY

*T*he sound of her laughter was like a drug that made me instantly high. The more boisterous that she got, the higher I became. We ordered a round of beers as the ladies continued to cackle and joke amongst themselves. All of us men remained relatively quiet as the ladies kept us entertained with their antics.

I noticed that while Wes looked tired from his shift, his eyes lit up brightly as he watched Charlotte. His arm was around her shoulders, and her fingers thread through his loosely. Her thumb stroked over his platinum wedding band.

I shifted my focus to Henley as he leaned forward and whispered something into Roxy's ear. She pushed him with her shoulder playfully and then kissed him before turning back to the conversation. The look on his face was one of pride, and you would have to be blind not to see the love in his eyes.

I flipped my gaze back and forth between my brothers. Damn—I wanted that. I wanted to feel what they did. I wanted a woman to love, build a life with, and create a family with. My focus fell on Daniella, but I frowned and looked away.

I glanced to my side and then did a double take as I noted

Ethan's expression. No—fucking—way. Was he in love with my sister?

Riley didn't seem to notice, or maybe she didn't care. Ethan stood beside her stool, not touching her in the least, but that didn't mean he wasn't devouring her with his eyes. I frowned. Was there something going on between them, and Riley didn't want us to know? I was going to have to ask Ethan about that later.

The band up front began to play a song, and Charlotte grabbed Roxy's hand over the table. "We have to dance!"

"Okay!" she shouted back, and then Riley was scrambling off her stool too, and Charlotte tugged at Daniella's arm.

"Come on, Dani! You have to dance."

Daniella's expression should have been comical, but I saw the fear jump to the surface, and then Charlotte leaned forward and spoke softly to her. I got pushed out of the way by my sister as she came around and grabbed Daniella's other arm.

"It's time to be Joceyln," Riley stated loudly, and Roxy and Charlotte laughed. For a moment, Daniella's eyes struck mine, and the fear in her blue irises was gone, replaced by a heated expression that shocked the hell out of me.

The four women hit the small dance floor, and all of them began to sing. Roxy, Riley, and Charlotte immediately began to cut a rug, but Daniella held herself back and glanced around nervously, shuffling her feet. Ethan came to stand beside me.

"Am I the only one who notices how nervous she gets in social settings?"

I shook my head. "No, I see it, too."

"She hasn't told you anything, has she?"

"No, but I haven't been around either. I need to get closer to her and see if I can earn her trust. It's so damn obvious she's hiding something."

Ethan nodded his agreement. "Yeah, well, when she tells you, let me know. It might help us investigate this."

"I will."

As the song progressed, Daniella's tension lessened, and she began to get into the music. So much so that Henley whistled low beside me as she rotated her hips seductively. She closed her eyes, and her head fell back on her shoulders, and one of her hands traced the elegant curves of her body. I was utterly enthralled.

Ethan slugged me in the shoulder. "Lucky bastard." I nearly fell over, but Wes caught me, and his deep chuckle made me glance his way.

"You should probably go out there and claim that before someone else tries to." He nodded toward two guys who were staring at her.

"Aw, hell, no," I growled, took a quick gulp of my beer, and then slammed the bottle on the table.

One of the guys was already off his stool, heading toward Daniella. She had her arms over her head, her eyes half open, and he reached her before I did. He put his hand on her hip as he began to dance with her. She froze, her eyes snapped wide open, and the fear from earlier surged into her features so quickly that anger erupted in my gut. He didn't seem to notice or didn't care as he tried to grind against her.

Riley stepped toward him; her face a mask of fury a moment before I reached the floor. Two more steps and I was behind the guy, but I sidestepped him and put my arm around Daniella's waist and between the two of them. I literally lifted her off her feet and turned her away from him as I growled, "Back the fuck off."

In my arms, Daniella quivered, and the guy glared at me for all of two seconds before he glanced over my shoulder and then put his hands up and stepped back. I shot a look over my shoulder and found Ethan standing there.

Either the guy knew Ethan was a cop, or he didn't want to get into it with two guys. He stepped backward, and I spun

Daniella slowly in my arms just as the music changed to a romantic ballad.

I took one of her hands in mine and curled my arm around her waist. My hand landed in that spot on her lower back that Jake had mentioned in the book. What had he said? Sexy as hell? Something like that, and damn if he wasn't right.

Daniella stared at my chest, and I whispered in her ear, "You're alright, Daniella. You can relax. I got you, darling."

As if I had given her permission, her body began to uncoil, and she stepped closer, shifting her hand to my shoulder. "Thank you, Huntley."

"You're welcome."

For a few moments, we danced, and I let Daniella have control of the moment. She slowly grew closer to me, her chest coming in contact with mine, her hand slipping to the nape of my neck. Her fingernails teased over the sensitive skin, and she rested her forehead against the side of my chin.

I curled our hands in closer to our bodies, my eyes closing as I tried to memorize the moment. She felt so perfect in my arms. Jessica and I had danced a lot, but she had never fit so exact, and she sure as hell never had me as turned on as Daniella did with the subtle shifts of her body against mine.

Daniella turned her head, lifting her chin, and her glassy eyes paused at my lips, then drifted over my face before settling on my eyes. Her fingers tickled over my neck, and I couldn't help myself. I leaned forward, brushing my lips over hers.

Daniella let go of my hand and wrapped both arms tightly around my neck, pushing her chest against mine as if she couldn't get close enough, and she opened for me. I suddenly realized that I could drown in this woman.

As much as I wanted the kiss to continue, this was a public location. I pulled back a moment later, brushing my knuckles down the side of her face and running my thumb over her bottom lip.

"You are so beautiful, Daniella." She frowned and looked away. "Hey, you, don't you look away from me when I say that. Don't you know that you are beautiful?"

She shook her head slightly.

"How can you not know that? Jesus, woman. Do you not ever look in the mirror?"

She scoffed, "Not really."

I cupped her face, waiting for her to look at me again. "Well, you should. You are stunning, Daniella Knight."

"Thank you," she murmured. I winked, and the music changed again to a faster song. She dropped her arms immediately. "I should probably get home."

"Alright, I'll give you a ride," I told her as we began to walk back to the table—my hand on her lower back.

"You don't have to."

I took hold of her arm. "Not sure you noticed, but none of you women are capable of driving tonight. Why do you think we showed up here? It wasn't to bust in on your fun; that's for sure. It was to make sure you all got home safely."

"Oh," she said and drew her bottom lip between her teeth. Why did that turn me on so much?

"Alright, well, I would appreciate a ride home—or I mean— to your parents' house."

I chuckled. "I know what you meant. Let's go say our goodbyes."

The two of us joined the group and realized that they were all ready to leave too. The ladies converged on one another as we headed out, and I was glad that Daniella was getting along with them. She had obviously enjoyed herself tonight, and I had a feeling she didn't do girls night very often.

Daniella hugged all the women goodbye, and as Riley and Charlotte began to walk away, Charlotte called out, "Be Jocelyn! Go for it!" My sister slapped Charlotte's arm playfully and made a gagging noise.

Wesley and I shared a confused look, but Henley patted me on the back. "That's a good thing, bro."

"If you say so," I replied as I stepped next to Daniella and reached for the passenger door.

I thought I heard her whisper something to herself, but I didn't understand what it was before she stepped between me and the truck and cupped my cheeks. "Kiss me again."

Did I hear her correctly? In the two seconds that I studied her, I saw her excitement shift to uncertainty as she began to pull back. Oh, hell, no.

I didn't waste any time as I dipped to bring our lips together and wrapped my arms around her waist. She went up on tiptoe, pressing her body against mine and deepening the kiss.

A horn honked, but I didn't care who it was. All I wanted was to lose myself in this woman. She had asked me to kiss her, and now that we weren't on the dance floor anymore, and there were shadows around us, I was happy to oblige.

I pressed her back against the side of the truck; she lifted her leg, curling her foot around my knee, and I groaned. I snagged ahold of her leg and pulled it up higher, my hand running underneath it to the curve of her ass, and I ground myself against her. She whimpered as her mouth left mine, and her head fell back against the truck.

A car rolled to a stop beside us, laughter floating through the air, and I clenched my eyes and dropped her leg. I glanced over my shoulder, and Wes had a brow lifted. "Maybe you should take that someplace else."

"Or not! Go, Jocelyn!" Charlotte yelled, and Daniella snickered.

Wes drove away, and I rested my forehead on hers for a moment. "Wes is right. We shouldn't be doing this here."

She stunned me with her next words. "How far away is your place?"

I shifted back, surprised by her question. "What?"

"How far is your place?"

"Um—" I was struck mute, and she immediately took it the wrong way.

Her hands pushed against my chest, and I moved away to give her space. "Sorry, I've had too much to drink. I should never have said that."

I took hold of her arm and cupped her cheek. "Hey, darling, I'm glad that you did, but you're right. You have had a lot to drink, and as much as I would love to have you in my bed, I don't want you to regret it in the morning." She pulled her bottom lip under her teeth again. "When I do take you to my bed, I want you to be there because you, Daniella, want to be there, not this Jocelyn person that you guys are joking about."

"She's a character."

"I think I might have figured that out." I chuckled softly between us. "Besides, I think Tigger might actually eat me if I didn't bring you home safely."

"Oh, no! I forgot about Tigger." She burst out of my grasp and yanked open the truck door. I made sure she got inside and then closed the door after she belted herself.

When I climbed in the other side, she was yawning, and I wondered if she would have even made it back to my place awake. When I passed my road, I glanced her way; she was breathing slowly, her lips parted, her head back against the headrest, and her body the most relaxed that I had seen it.

At the next stop sign, I turned to study her, and my heart squeezed tightly in my chest. Damn—I had a feeling that at that very moment, I fell head over heels for her, and I barely knew the woman.

CHAPTER NINETEEN

HUNTLEY

I pulled down the driveway at my parents and saw lights on downstairs. I was parking when Tigger dove off the back porch and made a beeline for my truck, barking a few times until he saw me.

I paused before I opened the door, still leery of the dog, but I couldn't sit out here all night. I pushed the door open cautiously, and he came around the door and popped his front paws on the ledge, his nose lifting as he scented for Daniella. His eyes hit mine briefly after he located her, and his tongue lolled out the side.

"She's okay, buddy. Just a little tired. Come on, get down so we can put her to bed."

Tigger dropped to the ground and backed up as I got out. He ran to the other side of the truck and waited, his tail wagging from side to side as I reached for the door. I barely had it open when he pushed his way in to check on her. I heard her mumble something, and then Tig turned and looked at me like he wanted me to translate her drunken gibberish.

"Your version would be as good as mine, Tig. Come on, get

down so I can get her out." He did, and I unbuckled Daniella and scooped her body into my arms.

Tigger walked beside us as we moved toward the house. "This is starting to become a habit of me carrying her around," I said to Tig as he eyed me carefully. "Not that I mind. She fits pretty good in my arms. Don't you think?"

Tig looked away, and I figured he didn't want to respond to that. The back door opened, and my mother stood there. "Oh, dear, did she get sick or just drink a little too much?"

"A little too much fun," I said to my mom as I passed by her. "I very much doubt that Daniella gets out very often, and I'm pretty sure she's not a big drinker. She's going to be hurting in the morning."

"Well, it's a good thing I have that vitamin water you all told me about. I bought some to keep on hand. You never know when Riley is going to need one."

I snickered. Riley was always out drinking and coming in late. "Let me get her to bed, Mom, and I'll be back down."

Tigger followed me up the stairs, and I set her on the bed. She hadn't moved a muscle since I'd picked her up, but her breathing was normal. After I set her down, I studied her. I didn't want to leave her in tight jeans and a blouse, but I wasn't sure she would like me undressing her either. I could ask my mother to do it, but then again, I didn't want to do that either.

"Tig, you want to help me get her changed? You can be my witness that there was no funny business, alright?" His jaw opened, and his tongue lolled out the side like he was agreeing.

I found the t-shirt from the previous night folded on the end of the bed, and I collected that before carefully unbuttoning her blouse. I had to set her upright to get the shirt off, but she didn't react to the jostling other than a slight mumble. I left her sports bra on and managed to get the shirt off her arms. After I pulled the t-shirt down, I laid her back, removed her shoes, and then unbuttoned her jeans.

I glanced at Tigger. "You know, I've never taken pants off a woman who wasn't awake and asking me to do so." Tig cocked his head, and I chuckled to myself. I couldn't believe I was talking to her dog as if he would understand me.

The jeans were skin-tight, and it was hard not to notice the sexy curve of her hips as I peeled them off. I sure hoped that someday soon, I could do this while she was awake. I had every intention of learning every inch of those elegant curves if I ever got the chance. I managed to get the jeans off with minimal fuss —or personal arousal—and then shuffled her under the covers.

Daniella had yet to move, and I was concerned about her sleeping so deeply while intoxicated. What if she got sick while she was passed out and choked on it? Damn—I wasn't sure she should be sleeping alone, but I wasn't sure she wouldn't freak out if she woke up and found me sleeping beside her. Wait, strike that. She would completely freak, but if she knew I was doing it for her safety, I'm sure she would understand—maybe.

"Tig, you stay and watch her," I told him, and he looked at Daniella and then me before he jumped on the bed and curled up against her leg. "Good boy." I closed the door most of the way and then went downstairs.

"Is she all tucked in?" my mother asked as she poured herself a cup of tea.

"Yeah, Tig's watching her. I'm a little worried about her sleeping alone with as drunk as she is. What if she vomits in her sleep?"

"Then maybe you should stay in there with her."

I laughed softly. "I had thought about that, but then I thought about how she might be upset if I did."

"I think if you explain to her that you were doing it for her safety and not your own pleasure, she will understand."

I laughed. "My own pleasure? Funny, Mom. I figured if I explained it, she'd understand."

"Besides, I'm not sure her dog would allow you to do

anything to her that she didn't want you to do," my mother added.

I snickered. "Of that, I have no doubt."

"Has she told you why she has him for protection?"

I shook my head, and my mother took a seat at the table, pointing to another one. I pulled it out and sank into it. "Did she tell you something?"

"No, she didn't tell me, but I think I know. I remember reading something about her a while ago, probably over a year ago. She had a stalker. That person broke into her house, but she managed to get to a phone and call the police, and he was taken into custody."

My heart dropped and then began to beat hard. The thought of someone hurting her or scaring her made me almost violent myself. "How do you know this?"

"I told you, I read about it. A friend of mine had seen the article in the paper. She knew I was a fan of hers. I remember thinking how awful it was for her. I think I remember hearing that the man was arrested, and he had read her books and believed her to be one of her characters or something like that."

"No wonder she doesn't want anyone to know she writes under another name."

"Yes, exactly. I get it now. I didn't remember at first, but I kept thinking about it, and then it came back to me."

"Mom, when was this?"

"Must have been about a year and a half ago, or it could be more like two years."

"Do you know where?"

She shook her head. "Not off the top of my head, but I could contact my friend and see if she remembers."

"Can you do that? It would be important to find out where that was and exactly when, if possible. Ethan and I both knew there was more to her story, especially after seeing how trained Tigger is."

"Sure, I'll reach out to her first thing tomorrow and see if I can find the article."

"Thanks, Mom."

She smiled and studied me for a few moments. "You like her, don't you, Huntley?"

I laughed a little uncomfortably. "Is that weird? I have only known the woman for a couple of weeks and barely spent any time with her." I shook my head as I leaned back in the chair, feeling as if someone had just knocked me upside the head. "I feel like I have known her for months, and yeah, I do like her, Mom. I don't know why or how it happened, but there is something about Daniella that just hits me straight in the gut."

She gave me a tender smile. "When the right person comes around, we just kind of know."

"Yeah, well, I was with Jessica for months before I felt anything even close to this."

"And she wasn't the right person, now was she?"

"No, she most certainly wasn't," I growled slightly.

"I suggest you go slow with Daniella. She doesn't seem like the type of woman to jump into a relationship with anyone or jump into bed with a man she just met."

I thought about the scene in the parking lot tonight. "Mom, do you know who Jocelyn is?"

"Jocelyn? I don't think so. Why?"

"Because when we were leaving tonight, Charlotte said something about being Jocelyn and going for it."

Her eyes widened, and she snapped. "Oh! Wait! I do know who Jocelyn is! She is a character in an earlier book. A strong woman who knew what she wanted and wasn't afraid to go for it. She also enjoyed sex with any man she found attractive, although she was picky." She laughed. "Jocelyn is probably the complete opposite of Daniella."

"Huh—" I pondered that for a moment. "Okay, that would

make sense, because after Charlotte said that, Daniella stepped in front of me and kissed me—like really kissed me."

"Maybe Daniella wants to be more like Jocelyn, and she used the liquid courage to do that."

"That's most likely what happened."

"Which means that tomorrow—if she remembers it—she is going to be very embarrassed by her behavior."

"Any suggestions that you can think of to help her not be embarrassed? I was not complaining."

She sipped her tea as she seemed to contemplate that. "Maybe just let her know that you enjoyed her forwardness, but I wouldn't make a big deal out of it."

"Okay, well, I think I am going to go up and try to get some shut-eye if her dog allows me on the bed. I don't think I want to leave her alone overnight."

"If Tig doesn't let you sleep on the bed, I can get you the air mattress, and you can sleep on the floor."

"Sounds like a plan," I told her and then kissed her cheek.

"Hunt," she called out to me as I began to walk away.

"Yeah, Mom?"

"Go easy on her. I'd hate to see her get scared and run away from you. I think the two of you could have a nice relationship, but don't push."

"I won't, Mom. Thanks."

"Night, Hunt, I love you."

"I love you, too, Mom. Night."

When I got back upstairs, I went down to my bedroom and changed out of the jeans and shirt that I had been wearing and put on sweatpants and a t-shirt. While I usually preferred to sleep in my boxers, I wasn't planning on climbing under the covers with her, so clothes were a better idea. I also grabbed a quilted throw to take with me.

Tigger eyed me carefully as I came back in and checked on

her. She was on her side, and I squatted down to check her breathing—still smooth and regular.

I went around to the other side of the bed. "Okay, bed hog, give me some room."

Tigger stretched his legs out as far as he could as if trying to make himself bigger. I shook my head and spread the blanket out before I climbed on the mattress. I had to push his front paws to the side slightly to make room for my body, and while he grumbled, he didn't try to bite me.

Once I was finally lying down, Tigger began to wiggle himself further up on the bed right between us. His spine rested against her back, and his paws pushed against my side.

I scratched the top of his head and then closed my eyes. A moment later, Tigger nosed my arm, and I went back to scratching him. He laid his head on my chest, and the two of us stared at one another.

"I won't hurt her, Tigger. You and I are on the same side."

He closed his eyes, and after a few minutes, both of us were asleep.

THE NEXT MORNING, I was downstairs when Riley arrived. "Is she alive?" she asked with a grin.

"She was when I left her at seven."

"What?" Her jaw dropped. "You slept with her?"

"I slept in the same bed as her," I told her. "She passed out on the way home and didn't wake up when I brought her in. I was worried she would asphyxiate if I left her alone."

"What did you do, lock the dog in the hallway?"

I frowned at her. "No."

"Tigger let you sleep in the same bed with her?"

Tigger was lying on the floor of the kitchen, watching us

with his chin resting on his paws. "We have come to a mutual understanding. We both want to keep her safe."

"Well, at least if she won't sleep with you, you have her dog to keep you company."

"Very funny," I muttered as my mother joined us in the kitchen and set a piece of paper on the table in front of me.

I glanced down and saw the headline, *Local Author Target of Stalking.* "Where did you get this?"

"I went back through my messages with my friend and found the article she had sent me."

Riley came to glance over my shoulder. "Oh, shit, was that Daniella? I remember when you told me about this, Mom."

I began to read how a local romance author had gained the attention of a stalker. The man, Lawrence Treadwell, had sent her letters and gifts by mail before he began to follow her personally and leave things like notes and candy on her car. It also stated that Treadwell had gone to her residence to speak with her. When she wouldn't talk to him, he smashed a sliding door and gained entry through that. Police arrested him when they found him trying to assault her in her office.

Riley gasped as she read from beside me. "He tried to rape her! That son of a bitch! No wonder she has Tigger now."

"It just says assault; it doesn't say sexual assault," my mother stated.

Tigger lifted his head, and we studied one another. It made sense now, and I was all for him protecting her. What I wondered was how far the man had gotten in assaulting her. I fisted my hands. "If I—"

My mom put her hand up. "I know what you are going to say, and you don't need to. I'm pretty sure we'd all like to do the same thing to that man."

"Yeah, well, I can think of a few things I'd like to do to him for sure," Riley muttered.

I stood, folding the paper and taking it with me. I needed to get my cellphone. I paused in the hallway. "Hey, Riley, don't say anything to anyone about this. When she wants to talk about, we'll let her. This is not something we need to bring up in conversation."

"I won't say a word, but you might want to let Ethan know."

"Yeah, that's what I plan to do right now." I headed up the stairs, Tigger right on my heel.

CHAPTER TWENTY

DANIELLA

The sound of someone panting broke through my groggy mind, and I groaned. A cold, wet nose brushed my cheek, followed by a big scratchy tongue. "Ugh! Tigger, oh god, please don't." My head throbbed, and my hand went right to my forehead.

Holy crap, how much did I drink last night? A footstep caught my attention, and I froze. Where was I?

The bed shifted as someone sat on the edge, and Huntley's low voice asked, "How are you feeling?"

Holy crap! Was I at his place? Was I dressed? Was I lying naked in his bed? Had we had sex? If we had sex, how could I have forgotten about that? The last thing I remembered was kissing him outside the bar—holy hell, what a kiss!—and asking how far away his home was. Wait—hadn't he said no?

I opened my eyes, winced, and closed them immediately before I slit my lids again slowly and glanced around. I was in Riley's room. My lids shut again, and I was thankful for where I was, but how had I gotten here? Had anything happened between Hunt and me last night? Ugh! What a fool he must think I am.

Tigger whined, and Huntley chuckled. "Don't worry, boy, she will be alright after she gets up and moving."

I shifted to my side, and my bladder screamed for attention. I opened my eyes again. Tigger stared at me, and I lifted my hand and let it drift down the side of his face and fall. That took entirely too much effort. Huntley chuckled again.

"I brought you a bottle of vitamin water."

"What time is it?" I asked.

"Almost ten."

"Ten?" I croaked and groaned. I never slept past seven—ever.

"Yep, ten." He moved off the bed.

I groaned again as I tossed back the covers and sat up. Huntley leaned against the doorframe. "Tigger's been fed, and he's been at the barn with Henley and Riley this morning playing with the horses."

"Riley is here?" I asked as I finally lifted my bleary eyes toward him. How could he look that damn good when I felt this damn bad? Oh yeah, he hadn't had a half dozen martinis.

"Yeah, she's been here for about two hours. I think she has more practice drinking than you do."

"No doubt. I don't think I have ever drunk that much." My stomach rolled.

"Well, drink that water now and then take a shower. After that, we can get some food into you and see how you're feeling."

I made a gagging noise. "You expect me to eat?"

"Yep, in fact, I'm going to make you a greasy hamburger and salty fries, and you are going to eat them."

I slapped a hand over my mouth and bolted for the door, almost tripping over Tigger as I did. Hunt jerked out of my way, and I managed to get into the bathroom and bent over the toilet before I expelled the alcohol still in my stomach.

On my rush to get in here, I hadn't had time to close the bathroom door, and if I had been feeling even the slightest bit better, I'd have been mortified that Huntley was witness to this.

At the moment, I didn't much care, though, as my stomach threatened to turn itself inside out.

The faucet turned on, and then Huntley squatted next to me, pulling my hair back from my face and wiping my cheeks with a cold cloth. He held my hair in a ponytail as I wretched a third time, and then he put the cold towel on the base of my neck.

"Ah—" I moaned. That felt so good.

He reached around me and collected some toilet paper from the roll and handed it to me. I could have done that, but I was using both of my hands to hold myself upright. I did manage to wipe my mouth, blow my nose, and drop it into the bowl all on my own, although he flushed for me.

"You need to do that more? Or are you done?"

"I think I'm done—for now," I murmured, and he pulled me against his chest as he sat back against the tub. I was between his legs, with my head resting on his shoulder, his arm around my waist.

"Feel better?"

"I think so." I sighed. "Sorry about that."

He brushed his lips against the side of my head. How could he kiss me after he'd just watched me barf? "Don't worry about it. We've all been there. Let's give it a minute, and then we can try to get off the floor." He was quiet for a moment, and then he chuckled. "Can't tell you how many times I lay here on the floor after drinking too much the night before when I was younger."

"Really?"

"Yep, Wes too. I don't remember Bradley ever doing it or Kayley."

"What about Riley?"

I chuckled again. "Oh, Riley had her share of floor naps. How are you feeling?"

"Okay." Tigger's nose touched my cheek. "I'm okay, boy."

I cracked my eyelids enough to see Tigger crouch down on his belly and lay his chin on Huntley's leg, worried eyes watching me. I pet him for a few minutes as we all remained exactly as we were. Every once in a while, Hunt's fingers shifted, and I found myself acutely aware of every flinch they made against my stomach.

"You ready to attempt moving yet? Or do you want to stay here a little longer?"

"I'd like to brush my teeth and pee, but I'm afraid if I stand, I'll pass out."

"Okay, hang here for a moment." He shifted so he could slide out from behind me, and I adjusted myself so that my back was against the tub while I rested my forehead on my knees.

He was back in less than a minute and put the lid down on the toilet to sit on it, holding out the bottle of water for me after he removed the cap. "Drink as much of this as you can."

I sipped it and wasn't sure I was crazy about the taste, but I almost began to guzzle it after swallowing a few times. I didn't, but only because I was afraid it would come right back up. I did manage to drink about half of the bottle before my stomach rolled slightly.

"That's enough for now."

"You feeling a little better?"

"Yeah, I think so."

"That's the problem with drinking; you get dehydrated."

"Would you believe I have never been drunk before?"

He cocked his head slightly and studied me. "You know if anyone else asked that, I might not believe them, but I can see that with you."

Lines creased my brows. "Why?"

"Because you are very reserved, Daniella. It's not a bad thing. You're careful as if you weigh your options before you do anything."

I dropped my gaze. "I guess I do, but to be honest, my stepfather was a drinker; I was never much interested in being like him."

"You didn't drink when you went to college?"

I shook my head. "No. I didn't have time for that. I was too busy working and studying."

He looked surprised at my admission, and I bet now he thought I was a loser because I'd spent all my time working hard and not being an average college person.

"Hey," He leaned forward and lifted my chin. "Why do you look so sad?"

"I'm not sad."

"Okay, then why do you look like you are?"

"It doesn't matter," I replied as I tried to get off the floor. Hunt took my arm and helped me get to my feet, not releasing it until I was upright and balanced.

"It does matter if it bothers you, Daniella."

"Can you give me a few minutes? I'd like to use the bathroom alone."

He nodded and set the bottle of water on the vanity. "Sure, why don't you take a shower, and Tigger and I will be downstairs."

I thanked him and then went back to Riley's room to find a change of clothes before I returned to the bathroom and closed the door. As I got undressed, I wondered how I had gotten undressed last night. I was in my t-shirt, sports bra, and panties, so either I drunkenly got myself undressed, or someone did it for me. That thought both made me uneasy and a little excited. I stood under the water spray a few minutes later, letting the hot water run down my body as I pondered that and more.

What else did Huntley think of me? He said I was cautious, and he was right, but did he think that was stupid? Did he think less of me because I hadn't partied in college? Or that my stepfather was a drunk? What would he think of me if he knew that I had grown up in a trailer park and not a beautiful house as he had? Would he think I was white trash like a lot of kids that I grew up with did?

Why did it matter what he thought of me? Hunt and his family were kindly helping me. That didn't mean there was anything else going on with us. Maybe his sister, Charlotte, and Roxy had only been nice to me last night because I was a guest here. I know they mentioned last night that they wanted me to join them again, but did they honestly mean that? Did I want that?

I sure didn't want the hangover, but I'd had fun last night—more fun than I'd had in years. Bits and pieces of the night floated back to me, the laughter, the jokes, the dancing, how easily the drinks had gone down, how Hunt had jumped in when the stranger had started dancing with me, and the kiss that Huntley had given me by his truck—or had I demanded that?

By the time I had gotten out of the shower, I was feeling a little more human—slightly aroused—and rather mortified at my behavior. I managed to drink the second half of the water bottle while I attempted to shove thoughts of Huntley and sex out of my mind.

I would need to thank him for not taking advantage of me last night. He easily could have, especially since, in my alcohol-pickled mind, I'd been Joceyln. A woman—okay, a character—who could do anything she wanted with her business. She could have any man she wanted in her bed, and she never once doubted herself. Well, not until she met Tripp. Then she had doubted herself, but that's what made her story compelling.

I rubbed my hair dry with a towel and pondered more as I tried to detangle it. It didn't make sense, but I had wanted to sleep with Huntley last night, which was completely irrational for me. I'd never had a one-night stand—ever—and both guys that I'd slept with, I had dated for a few months before we fell into bed. What was it about Hunt that made me want to act so wantonly?

Was it because he reminded me so much of Jake, and Jake

brought out those feelings in the women that he was with? Maybe—or maybe not.

I'm just glad that nothing had ended up happening—or had something happened after he brought me home? Crap! Maybe I should ask him, or perhaps I should just forget about it and pretend like nothing happened, including those incredible kisses on the dance floor and in the parking lot.

I snorted to myself. There was no way that I would ever be able to forget about those kisses. But just in case—I needed to sit down and write down everything I could remember about last night so that I could recall the feelings enough to describe them in my next book.

I dressed and hung my towel up and then went to find Tigger and Huntley. Tigger was barking outside, and I glanced out the window to see Patricia, Riley, and Hunt on the back porch. David was near the barn and was launching a tennis ball that Tigger took off after.

Wow, in my busy life, I had forgotten that dogs needed to have fun too. I was going to have to remember that in the future. I needed to make sure that he had playtime and got appropriately exercised. He wouldn't do me much good if he was weak and not in good shape.

With the way the fire had started, I was pretty sure that I needed to keep him in good shape. I knew that Ethan, Huntley, and the fire marshal had all suggested it was a random arsonist, but in my gut, I knew better. I had been targeted.

CHAPTER TWENTY-ONE

HUNTLEY

I collected my cellphone from my room where it was charging and took it down to my father's office, closing the door. He had a laptop that I could use on his desk, and I wanted to see if I could find anything on the internet about Daniella's incident.

I typed Lawrence Treadwell on the internet search bar and then pulled up Ethan's contact info on my phone, hitting dial. I clicked the first link that I found, and it was the same article that my mother had given me.

"Hey, what's up? How's Daniella feeling today?"

"She's still passed out," I laughed slightly. "What's your email? I want to send you an article that I found. Well, my mom found it and told me about it last night."

He gave me his email, and I jotted it down on a piece of scratch paper. "What's the article about?"

"It explains why Daniella has a guard dog."

"Oh, really? I knew there was a reason."

"Yeah, she had a stalker—a serious one—he got into her house and assaulted her. I don't know how badly, but the police arrived while he was there, and they arrested him."

"When was this?"

I put my phone on speaker and set it beside the laptop so I could bring up my email account. "About nineteen months ago."

"Okay, send me what you have on it."

"The news article gives the name of the police department."

"That's good. I'll give the department a call and find out the real story. I'll also try to get a copy of the police report and criminal complaint and find out if the guy was ever charged and if he's still locked up."

"Okay, good. Can you let Broadbent know?"

"Yeah, I'll fill him in as soon as I collect all the reports. I'm heading into the station in a few minutes, and I'll get working on it as soon as I get there."

"I thought you were off today."

"I am, but I needed to send some information to someone, so I might as well take care of this too. I'll call you later when I have it together."

"Alright, let me know." After I hung up with Ethan, I searched for Daniella's name and the town, but other than two articles about the incident that said the same thing, I didn't find much else.

I left the newspaper article in the office and went to check on Daniella. Tigger was lying on the floor outside her room and anxious to check on her too. She looked green when she woke up, and I wasn't surprised that she hightailed it to the commode. Did she think it was weird that I stayed there with her? That I held her hair back, let her rest in my arms? It wasn't odd to me; it felt right.

If she was uncomfortable with it or thought it strange, she didn't fight it, and I enjoyed being able to help her the little bit that I did.

While she got dressed, I went outside and spoke with my mom and Riley about what Ethan was doing. When I mentioned Ethan, my sister tensed at his name and looked away briefly. After I finished telling them what he was going to do, I turned to my sister.

"So, what's going on with you and Ethan?"

My sister's brows spiked high. "That's a weird question. Why would you ask me a question like that?"

"Because I saw how he was watching you last night. Are you sleeping with him?"

"Huntley," my mother stated as she shook her head. "Stay out of your sister's business."

"Why? She's always in mine," I retorted with a smirk.

"Why would you think I was sleeping with Ethan?"

"Because last night I was watching Henley and Wesley and saw the way they were looking at Roxy and Charlotte—as if they were their whole world. Then I looked at Ethan, and I'll be damned, but he was looking at you the same way."

"He was not," she blurted—a little too fast.

I laughed. "Oh, yeah, he was. Ethan looked like a man in love."

My mother snickered. "I have noticed that he does watch you when you are around."

"He does not," Riley growled and crossed her arms as she stared out over the yard.

I barked out a laugh. "Sorry, Ry, he does. So you going to tell us if you guys are an item?"

"No, we most certainly are not."

My mother and I shared a glance, and I wondered if she knew more than she was letting on. Maybe Riley had spoken to my mother about Ethan? Or maybe Ethan was really into my sister, but she didn't feel the same. Before I could ask Riley anything further, my mother spoke up.

"Looks like Daniella is up."

CHAPTER TWENTY-TWO

DANIELLA

*H*unt glanced at the window and smiled as I started to walk away. I paused by the coffeemaker and wondered if my stomach would revolt if I tried to drink a cup. The back door opened, and Patricia came in. "Are you feeling better, Daniella?"

"Well, I'm not one hundred percent, but at least I'm not heaving over the toilet, so I guess that's a good sign."

She patted my arm as she went around me. "So, do you want bacon and eggs or a hamburger and fries?"

My stomach rolled again. "Um, I don't think I could eat either of those."

"Believe it or not, they will make you feel better," she said as she paused in front of the fridge.

Another voice startled me. "Or I could just mix you another martini, you know, the hair of the dog and all."

I cringed at Riley. "No, thanks. Not sure I'll be able to drink another chocolate martini in my life."

She laughed. "It's the sugar in those drinks. Next time don't drink anything so sweet. Stick to wine or beer and a couple of shots."

"There is no way I am drinking any shots. I would make more of a fool out of myself than I did last night."

"You didn't make a fool out of yourself," Huntley stated from behind me. I turned so quickly that I got dizzy. He grabbed for my arm, and as soon as I appeared to be steady, he let go. "You were having fun, and you deserved to let off some steam after what you have gone through."

"Well." Riley laughed. "It was pretty funny watching you two make out in the parking lot."

"Riley," Patricia said as my cheeks turned bright red. "What? It was funny."

I closed my eyes, wishing that the floor would swallow me up. I felt Huntley's shoulder brush against mine as he leaned forward and whispered into my ear. "It was not funny; it was hot as hell."

I didn't know how to respond to him, and I could do nothing more than gawk at Huntley as he backed away. He winked and then passed by me. That man couldn't be more like Jake than if Jake came to life and stepped out of the pages of one of my books.

I took a seat at the table and began to pet Tigger who sat beside me. Riley set another bottle of water down in front of me with a wide grin.

"How are you so bright-eyed and bushy-tailed?" I muttered as I broke the seal on the water bottle.

"I do believe I have more practice than you do," Riley joked.

"I'm not sure I'd be proud of that fact, Riley," Patricia commented but was smiling as she did.

Riley shrugged and pulled out a chair.

"You'll be fine after you eat."

I turned to Hunt, who dropped a frozen hamburger patty into a frying pan on the stove. "You were serious about me eating a hamburger?"

"Absolutely," he said over his shoulder. "Grease, salt, and carbs will make you feel better. Fries are already in the oven."

My stomach rolled, and Riley laughed and got to her feet. "It will help. Okay, I have a few things to get done. I'll see you all later for dinner."

After Riley left, Patricia disappeared from the room, and the odor of the burger was making my stomach rumble. I wasn't sure if that was because it wanted to empty itself again or because it wanted food. I observed Huntley covertly from under lowered lashes as he moved around in the kitchen, every once in a while checking something on his phone when it gave him a notification. Then he'd reply before he went back to cooking. He looked so confident and so damn sexy as he worked. That was something that Jake didn't do. He didn't routinely cook for women.

A few minutes later, Hunt set a burger and fries in front of me and told me to eat slowly. I wasn't so sure about this, but I'd also never had a hangover before, so maybe he was right, and this would help.

He returned to the stove and broke open a few eggs into the same skillet he'd used for my food. I slipped a fry into my mouth and found the salty potato tasted better than expected. I slowly nibbled on a few of them as he cooked, and it wasn't until he sat down that I attempted a bite of the burger.

He watched me as I chewed and swallowed slowly. "You alright?"

I nodded and then wiped my mouth and chewed. "It's going down easier than I thought it would."

"Don't push it. Even if you only eat half of it, it will help. Just eat until you start to feel full." He dug into his eggs, and I laughed when I saw fries on his plate.

"Eggs and French fries?"

He shrugged with a laugh. "A different kind of hash brown."

"Ah, true," I replied.

"So, last night, I just want you to know that I didn't take advantage of you. You can ask Tigger; he was there the whole time I got you ready for bed."

The food stuck in my throat, and I coughed. "You got me ready for bed?"

He glanced up like the conversation was no big deal and we were talking about the weather and not taking my clothes off. "Yeah, you were passed out, and I figured you would be more comfortable in a t-shirt than a blouse and jeans."

Alright, maybe he was right, but that didn't mean it was okay that he did that.

"I also slept with you."

I froze, and he eyed me carefully, then grinned. "I meant to say that I slept in the same bed as you. Daniella, I promise I did not touch you inappropriately, and Tigger slept between us all night to make sure I behaved. I also slept on top of the covers."

"Why would you do that? I mean, sleep in the same bed as me."

He set his fork down and reached over the table to lay his hand on top of mine. "Because you were so out of it that I was worried you might be sick in your sleep. I didn't want you to choke on it."

"And Tigger slept between us?" I turned to Tigger, who was lying on his side on the floor watching me.

"Yes, he did, and he hogs the mattress."

I chuckled. "I'm so sorry about last night and this morning. You shouldn't have had to do that. I've been nothing but work for you and your family since the fire."

He squeezed my hand. "Daniella, don't think twice about it. You are dealing with a lot, and you needed to unwind. I'm sorry that you got sick, but I think maybe you needed that."

"Maybe," I replied and glanced at our hands. His touch calmed me more than it should have. "I'm sorry for what happened last night, too. In the parking lot, I wasn't myself."

He laughed louder and pulled his hand back. "No, you were being Joceyln, but I get it, and don't say you are sorry for that."

"Why not? That was not me. You probably thought I was some loose woman."

His gaze snapped up and locked with mine. "No, I didn't, and I never would. I'm not sure if you noticed this, Daniella, but I like you—a lot. I also really enjoyed kissing you last night, both on the dance floor and in the parking lot."

"You did?"

"Yes, I did, and I'm in no hurry to push anything between us. Yes, you turn me the hell on; you have since I lifted you into my arms the first time—hell, maybe even before that when you tried to barrel into your house while it was on fire—but I'm not pushing anything. If and when you are ready for more, you let me know. I would like to get to know you better, Daniella."

"You would?"

"Yes, I would. I've told you that before."

My heart sighed as the tension in my shoulders eased. "Thank you, Huntley. I think," I paused, "I think I would like to get to know you better too, and you are right, although I'm not sure I'm up to a relationship if that is what you are suggesting."

"How about we just take it one day at a time and see where it goes. No promises, no expectations."

Oh, my god! I swear I was sitting across from Jake and not Huntley.

"I'm on board, Daniella." He winked and resumed eating. I took a few more bites and realized that I was feeling better. Who knew eating these things would calm my stomach?

A few minutes later, he took our plates to the sink, and I followed him, intent on helping him clean up.

"How are things going at your house?"

"Okay, I guess. The crew is going to start tearing it down tomorrow."

"That's good. The sooner they do that, the faster your house will be built."

"Yes, true." I paused. "I still can't believe your father is coming out of retirement to help rebuild my house. Your family has been incredible through all this."

Huntley took me by the shoulders and moved me to stand in front of him as he leaned back against the counter. "Daniella, maybe where you used to live, people weren't like this, but around here, people like to help others. No, they don't know you, but they know of your situation, and they want to do something to help you. This is a small town, with small-town morals."

"I don't know how to repay these people," I said.

He cupped my cheek. "Darling, they don't want to be paid. They want to make life a little easier for you during a difficult time. Say thank you, that's enough."

"Thank you," I said softly to him, and his thumb stroked my cheek.

"I really want to kiss you again, Daniella." His voice was husky as he spoke the soft words between us. I nodded just the tiniest amount, and he leaned forward. I met him in the middle, and after two tentative brushes of our lips, he tilted his head, cupped the back of my neck, and pulled me tighter to him. I came willingly.

Kissing Huntley was like being part of the fire that had taken over my house. A small flame that quickly grew until it was roaring and attempting to take over everything that it could reach. I clung to him, lost in the way he made me feel. I didn't want it to stop, and as it continued, my mind began to memorize it.

When Huntley got tired of me, and this—whatever it was between us—was finished, then I would have these memories to fall back on, to use to build more intense romance scenes. He held me tightly for a few more moments and then slowly ended the kiss, resting his forehead against mine. Something that Jake always did after he kissed a woman so he could just breathe her in. Was that what Huntley was doing? No, I'd made that stuff up.

He took my cheek in his palm again and leaned back, dropping his gaze between us to where Tigger was pawing at his leg.

I laughed. "Tigger, what are you doing?"

"He's making sure I don't overstep my bounds." He looked at me carefully. "Was that okay? Too much?"

Too much? Oh, god! I wanted to say that kissing him would never be too much, but I couldn't admit that to him. "That was fine."

"Good." He kissed my forehead and stepped away. "How are you feeling now? You feel like getting out of the house for a little while?"

"And going where?"

I shrugged. "I don't know. What about a movie?"

CHAPTER TWENTY-THREE

HUNTLEY

I was at the firehouse on Monday, thinking back over Sunday afternoon with Daniella. I'd taken her to the movies, and she'd shared with me about her book coming out soon in theaters.

She told me that she'd even gotten a chance to visit the filming and how enthralled she was with the whole process. Everyone treated her like one of the stars, and it amazed her, but they kept reminding her that if she hadn't written the book, none of them would be there filming it.

I couldn't imagine what that would feel like to have something that you created come to life. Amazing.

I glanced up when I heard a vehicle park in front of the open garage door and saw it was Ethan. He stepped out of his police vehicle, his troubled gaze locking with mine for a moment. In his hand was a folder, and I slowly set down the piece of equipment that I was checking and went to join him outside in the driveway.

"You have information," I stated. It was evident that he did, and just how horrible that information was, was written all over Ethan's face.

He nodded and held the folder out to me. "Yeah, it's not good, but it could have been worse."

"What?" I glanced at the folder, afraid to take it from him. "Do I want to read that?"

He smirked. "No, probably not, but you will."

I crossed my arms over my chest and stepped back to keep from reaching. "Give me the important details."

He sighed and tossed the folder onto the hood of his vehicle, leaning back against it. I mimicked his stance beside him, the two of us lowering our heads and speaking softly.

"She was stalked for about four months. She filed a bunch of reports—I think there was six—but the cops out there didn't do anything."

"Why not?"

"Because they didn't have enough to go on. Dani was getting creepy phone calls, so they told her to change her number. That is exactly what I and anyone else in my department would have told her to do. Then she started getting notes on her car, but they weren't threatening; they were love notes. They talked about how beautiful she was and how they loved her stories. The cops told her she had an admirer and told her she should be flattered, not concerned."

"Are you kidding me?"

"Yeah, they sent me a copy of the notes; they really didn't have anything threatening in them, unless you take into account the fact that the guy said he wanted a future with her and that he could make her happy."

"That's not threatening?"

Ethan shook his head. "No, ninety-nine percent of the people who write something like that are dreaming, but not delusional to the point of violence."

"So, why did he escalate?"

Ethan shrugged. "No idea, but two days before the incident,

there was a report from one of her neighbors about a suspicious vehicle being in the neighborhood. They didn't connect it at first, but after Dani's attack, the neighbor brought it up to the officers again, and they realized it was him. They found the reported car parked a block away, and it was registered to him."

"Jesus," I muttered.

Ethan inhaled long and slow. "The attack was bad, Hunt."

"How bad?"

"He broke her wrist, used her as a punching bag." He paused. "He tried to rape her, Hunt."

I closed my eyes and forced myself not to react. "Tried or did?"

"He didn't accomplish intercourse, but he did penetrate her with a digit. The police got there in time to stop him."

I pressed my palms to the side of my head to keep it from exploding. "Tell me that son of a bitch is out so that I can hunt his ass down."

"He's out, but he's in a different kind of jail now."

I turned to him. "What, did he get out and break the law again?"

"No, he died in jail. His body is in a grave; hopefully, his soul is chained to hell."

I took a few steps away, feeling very agitated before I turned back and grabbed the folder off the hood of the SUV. Ethan didn't say anything as I began to page through the reports.

I skimmed the initial reports of harassment and then got to the one about the assault. I read the information in full, taking in every single detail. Daniella had opened the door, thinking it was a delivery, and the guy had tried to get in. She'd slammed the door on him, but then he had come around the back of her house and smashed in her sliding door. She'd gotten away from him long enough to grab the phone and dial 9-1, but she didn't get to finish the call before he was on her.

Luckily, I knew that if you dialed 9-1, it would automatically connect to 9-1-1 after a few seconds if there wasn't anything else pushed on the phone. The line had stayed open, and the call-taker on the other end had heard the assault and dispatched police.

I read the report, feeling ill, and then I turned to the next page and felt my knees start to buckle as I saw her written statement. I read it, wanting to vomit or commit murder when she talked about him twisting her wrist until she felt it snap and how he had torn her clothing, bit her breast, punched her in the face a few times, and then put his filthy hands on her. She said that he was over her, fighting to get control of her so he could rape her while he kept saying that someday she would love him. She heard her front door being smashed open, and then the cops were there, pulling him off of her.

I blinked back a few tears and was about to turn the page when Ethan put his hand over mine. "You might not want to go any further. The rest is photographs."

I felt ill as I closed my eyes, but I turned the page after he moved his hand—I had to see what he had done. The first picture was of Daniella's face. The side was red, swollen, and starting to darken with bruises. Blood had trickled from her mouth and nose, and her right eye was partially closed from the swelling. I shifted the paper and found a photograph of her chest. One side covered, the other uncovered to show a vicious bite mark on the side of her breast. "Fuck!" I said as a tear ran down my cheek.

Ethan grabbed the folder. "You don't need to see anything else."

I bent over at the waist, my hands on my knees as I tried to calm myself. The guy better be glad he was dead, because I wanted to kill him, and I had never been a violent man.

I stood up, needing to know. "How did that son of a bitch die?"

"Poetic justice, he was raped and beaten in prison."

I snorted. "Good."

"So the person who started the fire wasn't the guy who attacked her. That's good to know. Does she know this?"

"No, when I talked to the detective today, he said that he'd gotten a call from her a couple of weeks ago, but he'd been on vacation, then came back to a bunch of cases that needed his attention. He'd forgotten to return her call. He asked me to let her know."

"Okay, then let's go."

Ethan put his hand on my arm. "Hunt, I don't think you should be there when I talk to her."

"Why not?"

"Dani is a private person. How do you think she will react when she finds out you know the details of this? Do you think she would want you to know what happened to her?" He paused. "Maybe I shouldn't have shown these to you, but I wanted you to understand what she is going through—what she went through. I think it's going to be important if you want any future with her."

"Yeah, I guess you are right." I crossed my arms tightly. "You going to head over there now?"

"Yeah."

I nodded. "Okay, can you let me know how it goes?"

"Yeah, I'll give you a shout."

I shook his hand, told him thanks, and then watched him drive away. I hated that he would bring this up to Daniella, but if anyone was going to say something, I'm glad it was Ethan. I trusted him. I knew he would be respectful and kind.

To say that I was distracted was an understatement. I was inspecting the cabinets on the side of the truck. Usually, it took me about an hour to do them all. When Ethan reached out an hour later, I was still on the second one, not even halfway done.

I saw his text, and instead of reading it, I called him. "How did it go?" I asked the moment he answered the phone.

"She was stunned that I found out what happened to her. I had to tell her it was you that helped me figure it out."

"Was she upset?"

"She was. She said something about staying out of her business, but I think I might have gotten her to calm down. We talked for a long time, and I told her the guy was dead. She was relieved to hear that the same guy hadn't torched her house. We also talked about the possibility of her having another stalker, but she said that she hadn't had any emails, letters, or packages that would cause any concern."

"That's good, then her house being set on fire was random."

"Maybe."

"What do you mean, maybe?"

"Right when I was leaving, I got a phone call from the detective of her case. He said that on a hunch, he had looked into Treadwell a bit more after my call. He found out that the only person who visited him in prison was his brother. He sent a car over to the brother's apartment, and the landlady said that he's been out of town for a couple of weeks. She didn't know where he was, only that he paid next month's rent in advance and said he had family business to take care of."

"You think it might be his brother?"

"He has an arson charge on his record from his early twenties. Did two years."

"Shit! What did Daniella say about that?"

"I didn't tell her that part. Hunt, if it is him, I don't think that Daniella should be staying at your parents' house right now."

"You think my family could be in danger?"

"It is a possibility. I think we might need to figure out a better place for her to stay. I can offer my place—"

"Over my dead body," I growled. "I'll talk her into coming to stay with me."

"Do you think she will?"

"If I tell her that it's for her safety, she might."

"Well, if she doesn't, I don't mind letting her stay with me. I do have a guest room. I know how you feel about her, Hunt. I wouldn't come between that."

"How do you know how I feel? I don't even know how I feel."

He chuckled. "When you look at her, you are fascinated with what you see. If I'm right, you will do just about anything for her, and all you want to do right now is wrap her in your arms, keep her safe, and make her happy, right?"

"You know, it's funny, but that's kind of how you stare at my sister."

He was quiet for a moment. "No, it's not."

"Yeah, it is. I noticed it the other night at the bar. You stare at Riley just like Wes looks at Charlotte, and Henley looks at Roxy."

"You have no idea what you are talking about, Hunt."

"I think I do, and my mother has noticed the way you watch my sister too. Hey, I'm not upset if you do. I think you would be good for my sister, maybe too good."

"Nothing is going on with Ry," he stated, and his voice took on an edge.

"Alright, if you say so, but that doesn't mean I believe you."

"Look, why don't you focus on your own love life and leave mine out of it."

"Why are you so touchy, Winston? Did I hit a nerve?"

"Fuck you, Young! I gotta go. Talk to your woman, let me know if you need my help or if you see anything suspicious." He hung up before I could say anything else.

Hmm, wonder if he really did have feelings for Riley, but she had turned him down? Maybe that's why he sounded frustrated. Well, anything dealing with my sister was frustrating, but that was his problem, not mine.

I glanced at my watch. I had to get the inspection over, and then I could head over to my parents' house and talk to Daniella.

I knew she would be upset when she found out I knew, and she probably wasn't going to want to stay at my place, but what other choice did she have?

CHAPTER TWENTY-FOUR

DANIELLA

I couldn't remember that last time that I had gone out to the movies on a date. Not that Huntley said it was a date, but we both had said that we wanted to get to know the other better. Wasn't that what dating was?

During the movie, Hunt had held my hand. After the movie, he'd wrapped his arm around me, kissed my temple, and we'd gone back to his parents' house for a fun dinner with the family.

Everyone was there, and I was enthralled with the noise and activity. The kids giggled and ran around while Tigger chased them, and the adults laughed and shared funny stories from the week. There was food everywhere, and for the longest time, I tried to record every moment mentally, but I was so focused on trying to remember things that I wasn't enjoying myself.

Once I stopped and paid attention to what was being said and done and had tasted the food, I found myself happier than I had been in—well, forever.

I had written these types of scenes in my books, but I'd never been a part of them off the pages. I loved that this family had opened their arms and accepted me in. It was like in only a couple of weeks, I'd become one of them. I glanced at Huntley, who was across the room with Marisol, helping her with a puzzle. My heart was filled with something that I wanted to call love, but I was apprehensive about putting a name to it.

That night, after dinner, I walked Huntley out to his truck. He had leaned back against the side and pulled me into him. "You looked like you were enjoying yourself tonight."

"I was." I envisioned Jake and Arrabella doing this exact scene.

Above our heads, the stars were sprinkled everywhere, twinkling down on us like fireworks just waiting to explode when our lips touched. Jake pulled me closer, his lips so close, but not close enough.

"I'm glad. My family likes you." He paused. "I really like you, Daniella."

I leaned toward him, wrapping my arms around his neck. "And I really like you too, Jake." He blinked, and I started laughing. "Sorry, Huntley."

He frowned for a moment. "Do I really remind you that much of your character?"

"No, well, yes, but it was the scene. I was picturing Jake and Arrabella here doing this, and it just came out."

He looked slightly uncomfortable as he shifted and put some distance between us. "Well, you sleep well, and I'll talk to you tomorrow."

He started to step away, and I began to panic when I saw the disappointment in his eyes. I grabbed his hands. "Huntley, I'm sorry. I really am. I do like *you*, Huntley—a lot."

That seemed to appease him, and he cupped my cheek and kissed me slowly for a few seconds. "Get some sleep, and I'll talk to you tomorrow."

"Night, Huntley." I'd watched him drive away and was frustrated with myself for doing that. Man, I needed to remember to keep my character fantasies away from reality.

That night as I lay in bed with my laptop on my lap, I tried to remember every moment of tonight. I typed furiously as I tried to recall the sights, sounds, and emotions, and then I started typing up notes on Huntley.

Makes my heart beat faster by just looking at me. Watching him play with his nieces and nephew warms my heart. Strong but quiet, always willing to help. A sexy alpha male that will come to any woman's rescue. Any woman???? Okay, to his love's rescue and maybe her family. He's just like Jake, just as amazing, just as dedicated. Could he be someone that I love? Could I really love Jake?

I stared at what I wrote, and then I closed my laptop and rolled to my side. There was no doubt that I could love Jake. I did, even though he wasn't real. It was easier to love a fictional character than a live person. You didn't have to worry about disappointing a fictional character.

I curled my hand under my chin. In my books, I knew that even though they might have a misunderstanding—something that would come between them and seem almost relationship-ending—they would get over it. They would overcome the odds, and they would admit that they loved one another, and no matter what happened, they would survive and prosper.

That didn't happen in real life, did it? I thought about Patricia and David; they had been together for many years, and their love was powerful. The love of everyone here in the house was strong.

When Wes and Charlotte looked at one another, it was like no one else was in the room besides them. They radiated love. Henley and Roxy were similar, but they seemed stronger when they were touching. It was like as soon as they touched, powerful energy surrounded the two of them. I imagined rain-bows exploding around them when they touched.

Did Huntley and I have any of that going on? It was hard to see what was in front of you. Without being able to step back and look at it, I had no idea what we looked like together. If we expelled energy or if our feelings were visible to others. I closed my eyes, dwelling over that as I drifted off to sleep.

❄

THE NEXT DAY, I put aside my romantic notions and worked on a plotline for another book. Jake's book was off to Bea, and I was neck-deep in new characters and a new world to create.

There was a knock at the door. "Daniella, Ethan is here to see you."

"Ethan? Did he find something?" I asked almost excitedly as I set aside my computer and scrambled off the bed.

"I don't know, but he said he needed to speak to you for a few minutes." I followed her down the stairs. "I need to run to the store; David is over at your house working, so you will have privacy to speak with Ethan."

"Thank you, Patricia."

Ethan looked reserved but professional as I entered the kitchen. He was seated at the table, drinking a glass of tea, dressed in his uniform, and in front of him was a folder that looked to contain quite a bit of information. Wow, they must have figured something out.

We made small talk as we waited for Patricia to leave, and then after she did, he held his hand out for me to take a seat at the table with him. I watched him for a moment and realized that he appeared nervous.

"Ethan, what's wrong? What did you find out?"

He laced his fingers on top of the folder before he inhaled and exhaled deeply. "Daniella, I know about what happened where you used to live."

That was the last thing that I expected him to say, and I fought to hold back a shiver. "How? How could you possibly know about that?"

He stared at me. "Patricia remembered reading something about it, and she told Huntley. She shared with him a press clipping about the assault, and he passed that information over to me."

"What?" I was suddenly angry, and I burst from my seat. "How dare you go behind my back! All of you!"

Ethan leaned back in his seat. "Dani, we didn't do it to hurt you. We did it because all of us knew that you had Tigger for a reason. No one has a dog that is trained like he is if they don't have a reason. I work with trained K-9 units, Dani. I know what they take and why people have them. We asked you, but you didn't want to trust us to tell us. Why? Were you afraid that we would think differently of you?"

"Of course you do!" I walked away, arms crossed, and Tigger stood, looking between me and Ethan.

"No, we don't."

"We? Who knows about this?"

Ethan shrugged as I turned to look at him. "I don't know. Of course, Huntley and Patricia know, but I'm not sure who else in the house knows. Before you freak out more, know this. Tread-well is not the one responsible for your house fire."

My face snapped toward Ethan. "How do you know?"

"Because he's dead. He died in jail a few months ago."

I blinked and frowned as I considered what he said. "Good. I hope it was a painful death."

"He was raped and beaten, Dani."

I pursed my lips, wanting to sob. Raped! Just like he had tried to do to me! He was dead! That son of a bitch was dead! "Karma is a bitch," I finally muttered.

"Yes, it is."

I turned and looked at the folder. "Is that about my house fire, or—"

He shook his head and pushed it toward me. "No, the detective you worked with sent me over the entire file."

My jaw dropped. "The whole thing?"

He nodded.

"Please tell me that you are the only one that has seen that."

He glanced away, and I stepped forward. "Ethan, who else has seen that?"

"Hunt."

"You showed Hunt! You had no right!" I ran my hands over the top of my head. "I can't believe you showed that to him, Ethan! Why would you do that?"

"Because he needed to know what you had gone through, why you had Tigger."

"No! He didn't! That is none of his business, Ethan, just like it is not any of your business."

"That is where you are wrong, Daniella. It is my business. You moved here to get away from what happened. You refused to tell us what was going on. What if it had been Treadwell who started the fire? What if he came back and finished the job? What if he raped you and killed you this time? We wouldn't have any idea why or who. We can protect you, Dani, but only if we know about it."

I turned away from Ethan, staring out the window, and Tigger came to stand beside me, leaning against my leg and whining slightly.

"Dani, I'm sorry, but Hunt needed to know what happened to you."

I spun around, and as much as I didn't want to look, I went to the table and opened the folder, flipping pages until I got to the photographs. I winced, feeling the room spin as I stared down at the first one, then the second. I turned to the third one and put a hand over my mouth.

This picture was me fully naked and showed the bruises on my hip and thighs from his hands attempting to push my legs apart. "You showed him these?"

"He didn't see that one, Dani. Only the first two, and then he turned away. He couldn't look at them, and I didn't want him to see them."

I closed the folder and sank into the chair. "You had no right to show him this, Ethan."

"I'm sorry if you think that, Dani, but believe it or not, Huntley will not think any differently of you. You lived through something horrible, and to him, you are a fighter to have survived it and moved past it."

Tears filled my eyes. "Past it?" My laugh was shaky. "I haven't gotten past it, Ethan. I pretend it didn't happen by living in an alternate reality. I live in my books. I have no life; I hide from everything."

Ethan reached over and put his hand on my forearm. "I'm so sorry, Dani. Have you thought about going to therapy to talk about it? I think it might be time to deal with it."

"Why is now a better time to deal with it?"

"If you want a life again, if you want to live again and maybe find someone to spend your life with, then you need to deal with it."

"How could Huntley ever want to be with me after what he knows? After seeing this?" I pointed at the folder.

"Are you kidding? Right now, Hunt is trying to hold his shit together. After reading this, I know he wanted to race over here and wrap you in his arms and do everything he could to protect you. God knows that I wanted to do that, and I don't feel half of how he does toward you." He squeezed my arm.

Could he be right? Would Huntley want to be with me even after knowing this? Would Jake be with Arrabella if she had gone through this same thing?

CHAPTER TWENTY-FIVE

HUNTLEY

I was a little nervous as I pulled into my parents' driveway. Even more nervous when I saw Daniella sitting on the back porch watching me park. Tigger sat beside her as she ran a hand down his back over and over again. Was she comforting him, or was it the other way around?

I parked and climbed out, approaching her cautiously. We held gazes, neither of us saying anything until I was right in front of her.

"I don't think the words, I'm sorry, will do anything, but I am. I'm sorry that son of a bitch did that to you."

"Thank you."

"Are you upset that I know?"

For a few seconds, she stared at me, then she looked away. "I was, maybe I still am, but there isn't anything I can do about it now."

"Is there anything I can say to make you realize that this changes nothing?"

"What do you mean, it changes nothing?"

"It means I'm sorry about what he did to you, but that doesn't change the way I feel for you."

"Feel for me? How can you feel anything for me?" she asked. "You don't know me."

"I know more than you think I do."

"Whatever, Huntley."

I sank into the chair beside her. "Dani, I really do like you, and I do not want this information to change anything between us. Yes, maybe Ethan shouldn't have told me, but you should have."

She turned to me. "You think I should have come right out and said, hey, I was beaten and violated in my own house by someone who said they loved my books? I don't think so, Hunt."

"Daniella, when we asked you if there was a reason why you had Tigger, you should have said yes. You could have said you were a victim of a violent crime, and we would have understood."

She stared out over the yard, and her hand continued the movement on Tigger's back. "Maybe, but I guess that doesn't matter now since he didn't have anything to do with the fire." I sighed, and she shifted her gaze to mine. "What? Ethan said he was dead, so he can't have anything to do with this."

"You're right. Treadwell is dead, but his brother isn't."

She blinked. "His brother? What are you talking about?"

"His brother was the only one to visit him in jail, and—"

"And what?" she asked.

"And he was in jail for two years for arson." She continued to stare at me as if she knew there was more. "They sent officers over to his house to check on him earlier today, and he's been out of town for a couple of weeks. We don't know where."

Her hand stilled on Tigger's back, and after a moment, Tig nuzzled her arm before laying his paw on her leg. His eyes strayed to me as if to ask me what I was doing to bother her.

"Daniella, are you okay?"

"Do you and Ethan think that his brother is responsible for the fire at my house?"

"Maybe."

She was calm for a few seconds, and then she started to look around as if she were checking the shadows for someone hidden. I reached for her hand. "Daniella, we can keep you safe."

She started to get up, and I was on my feet immediately. "Daniella, where are you going?"

"I have to get out of here."

I took her hand. "And where do you think you're going to go?"

"I don't know, but I can't stay here! I can't put your family in jeopardy!"

"Look, Ethan and I already talked about this. I want you to come stay with me."

Her eyes bugged. "With you?"

"Yes, I can take some time off, and you and Tigger will be safe at my place."

"Huntley, I can't do that."

I hesitated. I didn't want to make the offer, but I would. "Ethan said you could stay with him if you didn't want to stay with me. He has a guest room."

"I can't believe you two are offering for me to stay at your homes! A lunatic destroyed my house, and he probably did it because I pressed charges against his brother. I can't stay with either of you! I will not put your lives at risk."

I took hold of her face. "Daniella, I put my life at risk every day for people that I don't know. So does Ethan. Why wouldn't we want to do it for someone that we know and care about?"

"Okay, I get that, but I can't ask you to do it for *me!*" She stressed the last word.

I brought her face a little closer. "Dani, you aren't asking us. We are offering. Please, stay with me. I'll keep you safe, or if you don't trust me, stay with Ethan. Please don't run from us. Let us help you."

Her hands rested on my sides. "Huntley, I would never be able to forgive myself if something happened to you."

I rested my forehead on hers. "Nothing is going to happen, Daniella. I'm going to keep you safe. Or Ethan will. Would you rather stay with him?"

She touched my cheek. "You. I'd rather stay with you unless you'd rather me not."

I cupped her face tighter, staring into her eyes. "Are you kidding me, Daniella? I want you with me. I want to know you are safe. If you had said you were staying at Ethan's, I would have camped out in his driveway."

A slight smile touched her lips. "Are you sure?"

"Yes, now, let's get your stuff and tell my parents what is going on."

"Do your parents know what happened to me?"

"My parents and Riley know that you were stalked and attacked, but none of them know the details of it, and I will never tell them."

She nodded, and we turned and went into the house. "You go pack, and I'll let my parents know what's going on."

She disappeared up the stairs, Tigger right by her side. There would be no distracting that dog from his job now. Nope. I wanted him one hundred percent focused on her safety.

My parents were in my father's office, and I knocked on the doorframe as I reached it. "Hey, you two have a minute?"

"We do if you are going to tell us what is wrong with Daniella?" my mother stated.

"She's okay. Ethan found the police reports of what happened."

"Oh? Why would she be upset about that news?"

"She was afraid we would think differently of her."

"Aw, that poor child," my mom murmured. "She was a victim. I'm sure it wasn't as bad as she thinks it was."

"No, Mom, it was worse. I read the reports. It wasn't good,

but I'm not going to tell you the details. That is for her to do if she ever feels up to it. She knows I am aware of it and that my opinion of her hasn't changed."

"It better not have. That is horrible, Hunt. Is she better now?"

"Well, not really, but that's because we learned that the guy who attacked her died in jail, but his brother is missing. His brother could be the one that is after her."

"How do you know that?" David asked, his voice filled with concern.

"Let's just say that the evidence kind of points that way, but don't worry. We are going to protect her. Daniella is going to come stay at my place with me."

"Do you think that is wise, Huntley?" Dad asked after peering at my mom.

"It's smarter than her staying here on the farm with you. If this guy comes after her again, I want to be there to protect her. Between Ethan and me, we will be able to do that."

"What does she say about that?"

"She wanted to run from here the minute she heard the information. She doesn't want to put you in jeopardy, but it took some convincing for her to agree to stay with me."

"Are you sure you want to take on that responsibility?" my father asked.

"Yes, I need to protect her. I want to. I'll do anything I can to keep her safe."

"Alright, son. If you need us to do anything, let me know."

"I will, Dad. Just keep an eye on her property. If you see anyone suspicious around there, call Ethan."

"You got it."

My mother came over to me and hugged me tightly. "You be careful, and keep her safe."

"I will, Mom. I'm going to go check on her and see if she needs help."

I went in search of Daniella and found her in her room on her phone. I paused in the threshold. "Yeah, I will. I'll keep you posted, Bea. I just wanted you to know what was going on."

Daniella glanced my way. "I need to go. Hunt is waiting for me. I'll call you tomorrow."

I glanced around the room and took in the small piles of clothes that she had accumulated since she'd been here stacked on the bed. She set her phone down. "I don't know how to pack this stuff. I don't have any suitcases."

"I have a duffle bag in my room. Just pack enough for a couple days. We can always come back for more later."

"Alright," she murmured as she shifted through her clothes and took out a few things. I went to get the bag, and as I returned, she went into the bathroom and retrieved her personal items there.

"Are you sure you don't mind me staying with you?"

"I do not mind," I stated. I didn't think it was wise to tell her that I was actually looking forward to it. While she finished packing, I shot Ethan a message to let him know she was coming to my place.

His response was two words: *lucky dog.* I wasn't sure if he was talking about Tigger or me. I assumed he meant me, but with Ethan, you never knew.

He also sent me a picture with a note. *This is Butch Treadwell.* I stared at the photograph. Holy shit! I had seen this guy. He was at the fire, standing behind me in the shadows, watching. I remembered his ruddy complexion.

I typed a message back to Ethan. *He is the one that started the fire. He was there that night. I saw him.*

Are you serious? You saw him?

Yes! He was there.

Alright, I'll put out an alert to locate him for questioning. Thanks!

I stared at the picture for a moment and then showed Daniella. "Does this guy look familiar?"

She frowned. "I feel like I have seen him before, but I can't place him."

"Well, that's Butch Treadwell."

She nodded and then looked up quickly. "He was at the trial. I remember him from there."

"You've never seen him around here, have you?"

She shook her head. "No, I don't think so."

"Okay. He was at your house that night, Daniella. I saw him." Her lips parted, and her eyes went wide. "Don't worry. Ethan is on it, and they are trying to locate him now. Let's get out of here."

It didn't take long for us to get her stuff into the truck, and my parents converged on her before we left the house.

"Dani, if there is anything that you need—ever, you call me. You got that?" my father said to her before hugging her tightly. My mother echoed the sentiment, brushed a hand down Daniella's long hair, and then sidled up to my father as we left.

Tigger jumped into the back seat, sniffing at his bag of food before poking his head between the seats. It was only fifteen minutes to my apartment, and I made sure to check for anyone behind us.

As we parked, Daniella looked around. "Are you sure it's okay for me to bring Tigger here?"

"Yeah, there are other dogs in the complex, although we will need to leash him to take him out."

"That's okay."

"Hopefully, it won't be for long, Daniella. Did you ever hear from the insurance company about a place to stay until your house is finished?"

"The only place they found was a few hours away. I was supposed to look, but I honestly forgot about it. I guess I need to start looking now."

We gathered her things. "Well, right now, you're staying with me until we figure this out."

"I can't stay here forever, Hunt," she said, and I wanted to reply with why not, but I kept my mouth shut.

I opened the door and let them in. Tigger put his nose to the ground and started sniffing his way around the apartment. It was large for a one-bedroom, but it suddenly seemed very small with her and the dog in it. I wondered what the price difference was for a two-bedroom.

She laughed softly. "I don't know why, but I expected sports posters on the walls, not framed artwork."

I grinned at her. "You mean like my bedroom at my parents' house?"

"Yep."

"Nah, I have grown up. I mean, I am thirty-one."

She turned and eyed me. "You're only thirty-one?"

"Yeah. How old did you think I was?"

She shrugged. "My age."

I laughed. "And how old are you, Daniella?"

"Thirty-four."

I blinked and looked her up and down. "Seriously? I thought you were younger than me."

"Nope. Guess not."

"Huh, I've never been in a relationship with an older woman before." Her eyes widened, and I stumbled over my next set of words. "Not that we are in a relationship. I meant, I'd never liked an older woman before."

She chuckled. "Yeah, never?"

I set her things down and came over to stand in front of her. "Never. Maybe you can teach me a thing or two."

Her eyes widened, and a little color slipped into her cheeks. "I'm not sure about that. I think you might have more experience than me in the relationship department."

"What makes you think that?"

"Because I've only ever been in two relationships before."

I shifted back, stunned at her words. "Are you serious? Are you talking about serious relationships or dates?"

She shook her head. "I have dated exactly two men; both lasted a few months."

"Wow," I said as I studied her face. How could this beautiful woman not have had men crawling after her for attention? The image of that photograph from the file filled my mind, and I clamped my jaw and turned away from her so she wouldn't see it.

Sadly, she saw something, though. "Sorry, I'm not who you think I am." She turned toward the door. "Maybe it would have been better for me to stay with Ethan."

I shifted around her quickly, taking her by the shoulders. "Oh, no, you don't. Stop saying you are not who I think you are. You are exactly who I think you are, and more. I look forward to being your third serious relationship, Daniella."

Her brows popped. "You do? What makes you think I am going to get into a relationship with you?"

I glanced around my apartment. "Well, you are aware that I really like you, right?" She nodded. "And we have already slept together."

"That didn't count."

I grinned. "In my book, it does, and now we are living together. So I call that a serious relationship."

CHAPTER TWENTY-SIX

DANIELLA

*J*laughed at Huntley. "Alright, call it what you want. I'm not putting any labels on it right now, and just because I am here doesn't mean I am sleeping with you. I'll take your couch."

"No, I'd prefer you in my bed—of course, without me."

"I can sleep on the couch," I told him as I stepped away from him. Like his parents' house, he had family pictures throughout the room, and I wandered toward several of them. There were many of his parents and siblings, but other people too.

"I'd honestly prefer you sleep in the bedroom. That way, if anyone comes in, they have to go through me first."

I turned and stared at him. "You realize that I have a dog that someone will need to go through before you, right?"

I glanced at Tigger, who had curled up in the middle of the room and sat watching us. "Alright, but I still don't want you sleeping on the couch."

I sighed. "It's no big deal, Huntley." I turned back to the pictures, and my eyes zeroed in on Huntley, who had his arm draped over a beautiful woman.

Huntley came to my side, his eyes following my line of focus. "That's Jessica. She was my fiancée for all of five minutes."

My face snapped toward him. "You were engaged."

"I was. Earlier this year. I thought Jessica was going to be my future, but she quickly turned into a thing of the past when I found her having sex with her boss on the couch here." I glanced at the couch. "Different couch. I tossed the old one and bought this one. It's rather comfortable."

"I'm sorry about Jessica."

He took the picture down and stared at it for a second. "I'm not."

"Why not?"

He set the picture on the shelf, with the back facing up, and turned to me, taking my face in his hands. "Because if I were still with her, I wouldn't be able to do this."

Huntley pulled me forward and kissed me with a passion that I'd never felt before. Not personally. I'd witnessed it with others, from actors to strangers, but I'd never experienced it before.

One of his hands curled around my neck to hold me close as his other arm slipped around my waist and pulled my body to his. In a matter of seconds, I was unable to think straight, unable to deny the feelings he was creating in me, and I curled my body around his.

Yes, Huntley had more experience than me, just as Jake did, but that didn't mean I couldn't use that experience to my own advantage. Hadn't I wondered how incredible it would be to make love to a man like Jake? Hadn't I fantasized about doing just that? I had my chance now. I had my own real-life Jake in my arms, and I wanted to know what it felt like.

Huntley's hands were both on my back now, one curled around me where his fingertips were resting against the side of my breast. It started to tingle, screaming for him to touch it more. The other hand shifted lower to the arch of my back, and

I pressed my hips against him, feeling his arousal. He moaned softly against my lips.

I held his face in my hands, loving the bristle of his jawline from his evening stubble. I let my hand drift down his chest to his waist and slipped my hands under the shirt he wore. He sucked in a sharp breath as I pressed my palms to his tight abdomen.

I already knew what his chest looked like, and I wanted to see it again. I wanted to trace the lines of muscle with my fingers. Would he think me odd if I did that also with my mouth? If he were like Jake, he wouldn't.

Huntley's mouth left my lips and trailed hot kisses down my throat. Goosebumps peppered my arms as my head dropped back on my shoulders to give him better access. "Daniella," he whispered against my neck. "Tell me to stop, or I'm going to take you to my bed."

I whimpered, unable to say in words that I wanted him to do just that. I held his face to my throat and heard the jingle of Tigger's collar. I turned my head toward him and gave a command. "Stay, Tigger."

Huntley lifted his face, staring down at me as I turned toward him. "Don't stop," I said.

In a quick movement, Huntley had me in his arms and was carrying me toward a door. Once inside, he stopped and toed the door closed. The entire time our gazes were locked, and I found myself lost in his beautiful green eyes.

"Daniella, are you sure?"

I glanced around the room. It was as I pictured Jake's room. Dark woods, burgundy comforter, heavy curtains to block out the light. Oh, I wanted this. If for only one night, I wanted my fantasy to come true.

"Yes, I want this. I want you." I gnawed on my bottom lip, and Huntley zeroed in on it, setting my feet to the ground.

He kissed me slowly, and my hands returned to under his

shirt. Although instead of touching his stomach, I began to lift his shirt. In my mind, I was Jocelyn. I was going for what I wanted. I wanted him, and I was going to have him.

He lifted his arms and separated our lips only long enough for the shirt to pass. He took my mouth with a hungry passion, holding my body tightly against his. He shifted, tugging at my shirt, and I stepped back and helped him get rid of it. His hands went to the back of my new bra and undid the clasp in only a second. I shrugged the garment away from me, putting our chests together as I curled my arms under his and splayed my hands over his muscular back.

His mouth returned to my neck, hot kisses, rushed breaths, and strong hands carried my passion to new heights, and I whimpered again. Huntley began to drop to his knees, his hands skimming the sides of my body until he got to my leggings. His thumbs hooked into the sides, and he stared up at me. He kissed my lower stomach, the heat of his breath filtering through the material. He moved lower, watching me as he kissed just above the apex of my thighs. My knees went weak, and he wrapped his strong arms around me to hold me up as he put his mouth over my mound.

The heat of his mouth caused my insides to clench. He kept his mouth there as he shifted one hand to my breast, staring up at it as he palmed it and pinched my nipple. My eyes closed as the exquisite pain radiated from my breast to my groin. My legs could barely hold me up as he began to pull my leggings down. His lips following them, kissing the sensitive skin as it was uncovered.

I was slightly frustrated that he had left my panties on, but I couldn't have voiced that if I had tried. Words were stolen from my tongue. My mind was in overload as he put his mouth back on the satin covering my sensitive flesh. The dampness of my core and his mouth mixed, and it was his turn to make noise. He murmured something against me right before he opened his mouth wide and covered me.

My hands went to the back of his head, where I held him to me. My hips pushed forward to get as close as they could. He released me for only a second, and that was to shift my panties to the side. His mouth covered my bare skin, and he moaned against me, causing my nerve endings to go into overdrive. I almost climaxed right there, but I held it in somehow.

His tongue slipped along the crevice, teasing the sensitive flesh until I thought I would faint. He shifted me back, causing me to shuffle and lose my balance, but I landed on the bed. He didn't give me time to even think about it as he pulled my leggings further down and put his mouth to my core again.

He managed to get one leg out of my pants and then shifted my legs further apart, getting closer. His mouth now had free rein as he shifted my panties further to the side. He paused, slipping his fingers through the moisture—his and mine mixed. He pressed one finger into me, and my hips rolled to meet him. My eyes clenched closed as my body held on to his finger. A second press inside of me, and then he added another finger.

"Jesus, Daniella, you are incredible." He moaned as he put his mouth back to my skin and tongued the bundle of nerves there. I felt myself climbing, felt myself getting ready to explode, and I curled my fingers into the comforter, biting my lower lip to keep from screaming as the world around me began to blur and then burst into blinding white behind my eyelids.

He kept it up, not letting me come down too soon. I started to struggle with the overwhelming sensations, and then he slowly began to stop, placing sweet, light kisses on the insides of my thighs and lower stomach. I was gasping for air, noting how fast my heart was pounding in my chest.

"That was incredible," he breathed over my skin, and I giggled, unable to control myself. I couldn't speak, not yet. I couldn't even lift my head, but I found his hand and laced my fingers with his.

I pulled on his hand, bringing him up to the bed where I lay. His chest reconnected with mine, and I stared at him. That was the most beautiful thing I had ever experienced with a man, and I was so glad that it was with him. I pulled his mouth to mine, tasting myself on his lips as I opened to him.

I wanted all of this man, needed to finish what we started. I needed to be able to say that I'd had my fantasy fulfilled. Our kisses became more urgent, and my hands went to his pants and began to unbutton them. He shifted away, getting back to his feet.

He leaned over me and removed my panties. "Move up on the bed," he whispered, and I pulled myself backward as I watched him remove his pants. My gaze locked on his pelvis as he stood upright again, and my jaw dropped at the beauty of him. I could not have ever written how perfect he looked or how much my mouth watered at the sight of his hard, thick cock. He gripped himself, and I fought to hold back the moan.

Before he came to me, he went to the bedside table and removed a condom, slowly opening it and sheathing himself as our eyes stayed locked. When he put his knee to the bed, my legs began to open for him. I wanted him deep within me. I needed to finish what I had started.

He shifted his body over mine, leaned down, and kissed me, nipping at my bottom lip as he moved his hips between mine. His hard cock pressed against me, and then he stared at me as he rocked his hips forward. He was perfect, and my eyes rolled to the back of my head as he filled me. I clung to him, holding him close as we kissed and moved our hips together.

I watched him, feeling everything I had ever felt for him coming to the surface. I would never forget this moment. Never forget how he made me feel. I loved this man, loved him with my whole heart.

He closed his eyes, straining to hold on as he moved faster. His neck corded, his eyes closed, and his mouth opened as he groaned his pleasure. He quickened his pace, and I felt myself building again. We were going to hit that top together. Never had I done that with anyone. I clung to him as we reached it. Our bodies compressed against one another so hard that I wouldn't be surprised if we had bruises later.

I gasped, and a single word slipped from my lips. "Jake."

He moaned, and then we were coming down, and his heavy body covered mine. My hands drifted over his back, committing every inch of him to memory.

I did love this man, and I would love him to the day I died. He was everything I had dreamed of, everything that I had written him to be. Jake was my everything.

CHAPTER TWENTY-SEVEN

HUNTLEY

I hadn't meant for that to happen, but it had. I was lying over Daniella, breathing in the fresh scent of her hair as my heart rate slowed when I suddenly remembered what she had said. She had called me Jake. In the very heat of the moment, as we'd both hit our climax, she had breathed his name. Or had I misheard her?

I leaned back and stared down at her blissed out expression, and I kissed her slowly before I shifted my body to the side. She curled against me, sighing in content.

I lay there wondering if I had misheard her. How could she have called me Jake? I kept trying to push the thought aside because I had to be wrong, but I couldn't. "Did you call me Jake?"

Her arm tensed over my stomach. "What?"

"Did you call me Jake while we were having sex?"

"No," she replied softly.

"You didn't? I could have sworn you did."

She started to pull away slightly but stopped. "No, I didn't. You must have misheard me. I said Hunt."

I lifted her chin with my thumb. "No, you most definitely

didn't say Hunt. You said Jake. Those two names are distinctly different."

She pulled her chin out of my hand and began to roll away. I stopped her, putting her body under mine. "Daniella, look at me." It took her a second, but she finally did. "You are aware that it was me, Huntley Young, that just made you orgasm twice, right? It wasn't a fictional character."

"Of course, I know that, Huntley," she said in a hoarse voice.

"Are you sure? Because I'm getting the feeling that you just used me to live out one of your fantasies."

Her jaw dropped, and her eyes widened and shot away. Holy shit! She had! I pulled back. "Are you serious? You just used me to get off on a pretend guy?"

I got off the bed and went into the bathroom to dispose of the condom and give myself a moment. I cleaned up, then rested my palms on the vanity, hanging my head. Did she really have sex with me and pretend I was a freaking fictional character? Holy fuck! What did I even do with that?

I could go in there and be pissed off, but I had a feeling that if I did, it would only push her away. Or I could go in there and let it go, make light of it, but was that better for her, or me? I hated thinking the only way I'd gotten her to sleep with me is because I reminded her of someone else. Someone that wasn't even fucking real! I raked my hands over my head. What. The. Fuck!

I inhaled slowly and released it three times. Then I looked at myself in the mirror. I didn't want to lose her. Maybe she was reverting to her fantasies because she was scared. Okay. I could give her some time to come around and make sure she knew it was me that was here in the flesh and bones and not an apparition of a character she created.

I returned to the bedroom after wrapping a towel around my waist. She was sitting up in the middle of the bed, my shirt over her body. If I thought that seeing her in one of my clean t-shirts was hot, seeing her in the shirt that I'd been wearing all afternoon practically gave me another hard-on.

"Huntley, I'm sorry," she said softly.

I sat on the side of the bed and cupped her cheek. "It's okay. I'm not sure why you said his name, and I hope you know it was me that was there with you, and not him, but I'm not upset. I was surprised; that's it."

She took my hand. "I do know that it was you. I really do know that, Huntley. He's just been such a big part of my life that it just slipped out."

I chuckled. How could I be mad at this woman? I couldn't. "You hungry?"

"Yeah, I could eat."

"Let's go find food, feed Tigger, and then we can take him for a walk."

"That sounds good."

I found track pants to put on and went to the bedroom door as she located her panties and slipped them on under my shirt. When I pulled open the door, I stopped in my tracks. Tigger sat two feet from the door, his eyes intent on mine, and he didn't look happy as he glared at me.

"Um, I think someone is a little upset that I closed the door on him."

Daniella glanced out the door and laughed. "Tigger, come here."

Tigger glared at me for one more moment before he got on all fours and trotted past me to her. She nuzzled him and spoke softly as I went into the main room.

While I cooked, Daniella walked around the kitchen and living room area, checking things out. She still wore my shirt, and I kept getting stuck on her bare legs as they moved around. Tigger sat off to the side and continued to glare at me.

I tossed him a piece of fat from the roast I was slicing up. His mouth snapped up and caught it before he returned to his glare.

My mother had given me a big chunk of the roast she'd made the other night. I loved cold roast beef sandwiches. I wondered how much of it I would have to sacrifice to get Tigger back on my side.

"What do you like on your sandwich?" I asked Daniella.

"Um, any way you want to fix it. I'm not particular."

"Okay, mayo, tomato, salt, and pepper good?"

"Sure," she said, and I frowned. I wondered if she was even listening to me. Part of me was still stuck back in the bedroom, wondering if she had really been there with me or if my fictional counterpart had been forefront in her mind the whole time.

DANIELLA HAD BEEN STAYING at my place for three days now. I had taken the week off from work so that I could stay close by her. Ethan and I had hopes that we'd locate the guy if he were in town. He had officers all over this section of the state keeping an eye out for Butch Treadwell and the older model truck registered to him. I wasn't sure what we were going to do if that went on for a long time.

Ethan and I had discussed it a few times, and I knew he was willing to take a shift or two to hang out with her while I was working. It was going to be rough since both of us worked shifts that changed on the whim of life. More fires meant more hours, and more crimes meant overtime for him.

During the day, I drove her from place to place to help her pick out flooring, fixtures, cabinets, and colors for her house. At night, I cooked while she worked on her outline and did research for her new series.

Despite me saying I'd sleep on the couch, I never had. Each night, Daniella and I had cozied up on the couch to watch television, and one thing had led to another. She hadn't called me

Jake again, and I had to accept that it had been a fluke the first time.

Over the past few days, she had opened up a tad and spoke about the incident. Mostly about the court hearing, but at least she was talking about it. She told me that she had gotten Tigger at the urging of her friend, Bea, and the process that she went through for selecting him and training him to be her companion.

Tigger and I had come to an understanding. He was allowed into the bedroom after we'd made love, but he wasn't sleeping on the bed. Instead, he took up watch at the end of the bed. His face always pointed at the door as if he were preparing to attack should someone enter.

It was Thursday night, and Daniella and I were going over to my parents' for dinner and to get the few other things she had left there. This morning, she'd gotten a call from her insurance agent, and they had found a place that was fully furnished that she could rent month to month and take Tigger. It was thirty minutes away, but at least she wouldn't be too far. The problem was, I didn't want her away from me—not until Treadwell was located. I wasn't sure she was all that thrilled to be on her own, either.

Anytime we were out, my eyes were always on the lookout for a black Ford truck. The problem was, around here, they were a dime a dozen. Most times, I was too far away to see the occupant or the tag of a vehicle we were passing, so I made a note of them and moved on.

When we arrived at my parents', it was getting dark, but that didn't stop Tigger from jumping out of my truck and taking off for the paddock. My father was inside with the horses, and Tigger got through the fence and started playing with Buttercup.

Daniella and I watched him for a moment, waved to my father, and then I took her hand, and we went into the house.

"Hey, Mom." I kissed her cheek as she stood at the counter, cutting potatoes.

"Hi, Hunt, Daniella. I'm so glad you could come tonight."

I glanced at the table, noting the extra plates. "Who else is coming?"

"Riley is going to try; she said something about bringing a guest."

"Oh, really? Is she finally going to come clean about her relationship with Ethan?"

My mother gave me an annoyed look. "Your sister said they are not in a relationship."

"That's a lie," I said as I took a beer out of the fridge and offered it to Daniella.

"Why do you think they are in one?" Daniella asked. "I'm pretty sure she said the night we went out that she wasn't involved with him."

"Were you all sober then?" I asked.

She chuckled. "Yes, we had just started dinner."

"Did you believe her?"

She shrugged. "I had no reason not to believe her."

"Yeah, well, I don't buy it. I saw the way he was looking at her and the way she looked at him. If they weren't involved with each other, why did he show up to make sure she got home alright that night?"

My mother shrugged. "Because they are friends. You know that Ethan is a gentleman."

I laughed. "Not when it comes to my sister." The back door opened, and Tigger rushed into the room and went to Daniella as Riley stepped through the door with a guy I didn't know. I frowned.

"Hey, everyone, this is Kent," Riley said, darting her gaze around. "This is my mother, Patricia Young, my little brother, Hunt, and his girlfriend, Dani."

I stepped forward, taking his hand and giving him a major once-over. Who the hell was this guy? "Hi."

"Nice to meet you," he said after shaking and turned to Daniella.

He eyed the dog for a moment. "Who is this handsome fellow?"

Tigger stood between Daniella and Kent. Did Tigger know something that we didn't? Or was Daniella's anxiety so high that he was picking up on that? I stepped around Tigger and put my arm around Daniella's waist. She was stiff as she stared at the guy.

"That's Tigger. He belongs to Daniella."

"He is very protective. What vet do you use? I just moved to town; I work at Delaney's Animal Hospital."

"What do you do there?" I asked as Daniella remained quiet beside me.

"Old man Delaney retired and hired me to replace him. I'm the new vet there. I just started there about three weeks ago."

Daniella started to relax beside me. "I remember Charles saying they were getting a new vet." She glanced at Tigger. "Friend, Tigger."

Tigger shifted back and sat on his haunches as she held her hand out to him to shake.

"He is a nice guy, isn't he?"

"Yes, he is." She laughed. "Actually, everyone in town is nice. I'm not sure I have met anyone who wasn't since I moved here."

"Oh, you're new to town too?"

"Yeah, I moved here almost seven months ago."

Riley stepped next to him and handed him a beer. "Remember, I told you that her house burned down?"

"Oh, yes, I read about that. I had only been in town a couple of days."

We all took a seat around the table, and Tigger, feeling satisfied that Daniella was safe with me and the other occupants of the room, barked to be let out so he could join my father with the horses again.

As I let him out, I glanced out the window, looking to see what kind of vehicle this vet drove and found a shiny black pickup in the driveway. My hackles began to rise as I stepped closer to the window and stared at the vehicle. In the growing darkness, I could barely make out the emblem on the front of the truck; it was a Dodge, not a Ford.

I laughed to myself as I returned to the table and the animated conversation between Daniella and Kent over being new to town. I was being overly suspicious of everyone.

CHAPTER TWENTY-EIGHT

DANIELLA

*T*he last few days had been lovely. I'd never lived with anyone, and while I wasn't officially living with Hunt, we were doing just that. It was strange being surrounded by all his things, and none of my own, but I was learning details about him on a daily basis.

While he preferred his rooms clean, his small walk-in closet was a mess. His shoes and sports gear were thrown into piles all over the floor. He also liked his ketchup in the same place in the fridge, and only in that place. He always brushed his teeth for two minutes, three times a day, and sang a song in his head while he did so he knew that he was brushing the correct amount of time.

I'd found these tidbits helpful, but none of them were as beneficial to me as our lovemaking sessions. Every night, I tried to memorize the physical and emotional touches that we shared. I knew that our relationship would probably eventually fizzle out, real-life ones did, so I wanted to remember as much as possible.

I forced myself to stay in the here and now and not think about Jake while we did. That little slip had almost cost me a lot, and I hadn't meant to do it. Just one time, I'd wanted to be with the man that I had created. Huntley was so much like Jake that it seemed natural to transpose one over the other.

Many times over the last few days, I'd had to shake myself out of that way of thinking. Huntley was Hunt, not Jake. Huntley was real, not Jake. Huntley was the one that took me to heights that I'd never been over and over again—not Jake. It was also Huntley that was escorting me everywhere and watched over me—not Jake.

When I got the call that they finally found a place that would allow me a month to month lease and have Tigger with me, I was torn. I didn't want to overstay my welcome, and I did like my independence, but with Butch Treadwell somewhere out there, I was nervous about being alone—even with Tigger.

Huntley and I pulled up to his parents', and I was looking forward to seeing them. Tigger was thrilled to be back, too, and took off like a child to play with his new friends.

When Riley came in with her companion, I was immediately uncomfortable, and I knew that Huntley was also cautiously curious about the man. Tigger stood in front of me, and I knew that he would have gone after the man immediately had he made one threatening move.

How terrible it would have been if Tigger had bitten his new doctor. Finding out who Kent was and that he was new to town put me immediately at ease, and the conversation quickly flowed. I was happy to know that I wasn't the only one learning about the ways of a small town.

Huntley had let Tigger out, and Kent and I mainly took over the conversation as Riley and Hunt helped Patricia with dinner.

A few minutes later, I heard Tigger barking. The sound of it was off, and I turned toward the window; it was dark outside now. I listened for a minute. His barking was continuous—deep, as if he were highly agitated. I got out of the chair, and Kent must have heard it too.

"Something wrong?" he asked as he came around. "He sounds like he's upset."

"Yes, he does." I paused at the window and felt a trickle of fear slip down my spine. "Huntley, the light isn't on over the barn door."

Hunt stepped up beside me, wiping his hands on a towel. "Why is Tigger barking?"

"I don't know, but something is wrong, Hunt. That's a warning bark. Tigger is upset about something."

Hunt began to turn for the back door, then spun around. "You stay here. I'll get Tigger."

"I'll go check on him," Riley said, but Hunt stopped her with a word.

"No!" He spun and went to Riley. "Stay here with her. Go get Dad's gun."

Her brow furrowed momentarily, and then she was rushing from the room. Patricia came over to the window.

"Do you see David?"

"No," I said softly.

"What's going on?" Kent asked as Huntley rushed out the back door.

Patricia put her hand on my arm. "Probably nothing, but—"

I knew she didn't want to voice what I was thinking. I covered her hand with mine, and suddenly the lights went out in the room, and Patricia and I jumped.

"It's just me," Riley said. "We can see outside better in the dark."

"Does someone want to tell me what's going on?" Kent asked from the other side of the room.

"Daniella had a stalker; he assaulted her and went to jail. That's why she has Tigger. A few weeks ago, someone burned her house to the ground; we think it was the guy's brother coming after her for revenge."

"Seriously?" he said, his voice rising an octave. I ignored

what else Riley was saying as I watched Huntley moving toward the barn. The light from the back porch didn't reach that far, and shadows quickly swallowed him. I squeezed Patricia's hand as Tigger's barking continued.

I heard Huntley calling for Tigger as he approached the barn, and Tigger's bark got faster. Huntley reached the door, and a moment later there was a flurry of movement as Tigger raced around Huntley and ran in a circle before darting off toward the back of the barn. Huntley took off after him just as I noted a strange glow coming from the back side of the barn.

"Oh, my god! The barn is on fire!" The words burst from my lips.

Before I could think of doing anything, Riley was running from the room.

"Riley!" Kent shouted. "Where are you going?"

She was already out the door, and we could see her streaking across the driveway to the barn. The top of the barn caught fire, and it quickly began to spread. I stood there, frozen, clinging to Patricia. Where was David? Where did Jake go?

Jake? No! Where did Huntley go? He had run into the darkness after Tigger. I tore away from Patricia and ran toward the back door.

"Dani! Don't go out there! You need to stay here!"

I didn't bother to answer her. I tore out the door, and I heard Patricia on my heels. When I reached the porch, I could barely hear Tigger barking, and then a gunshot rang out. In the distance, the flash of the gun went off in the field, and Tigger yelped and grew quiet.

"Tigger!" I screamed as I began to run down the stairs. Off to the side, I saw a police car, the red and blue lights flashing as the car pulled off the road, a spotlight shining into the darkness of the field, and there was Jake, facing off against another man. The two of them were too far to hear, but the man was pointing a gun at Jake!

I watched in slow motion as Tigger went from a crouch on the ground to flying toward the man with the gun. Another flash of the muzzle went off, and I watched in slow motion as Jake fell backward, his arms pinwheeling behind him as Patrica screamed behind me.

A louder gunshot rang out from the roadway, and the man with the gun dropped to his knees. In the back of my mind, I knew that whoever the cop was, he'd taken a shot with a high power rifle. It is exactly what would happen in one of my books. I raced through the darkness, praying that I didn't trip over anything as I ran to the area.

Flashlights were coming from the street; the glow of the barn fire was lighting up the area and making it easier to see, and I quickly arrived at the location to find Tigger lying over Jake as if to protect him.

I dropped to my knees, seeing so much blood on them both. I had no idea what to do. Tigger lifted his head toward me, whimpering, and I cried as my hand flitted over Jake.

"Jake, you're going to be okay! You're going to be okay." His eyes opened, and he frowned as his eyes closed again.

I lifted my gaze to the other man; his open eyes were staring at me, but he didn't say anything. Before I knew it, Ethan was there, and Riley, and Kent, and someone pulled me away as Kent went to work on Tigger, and Ethan and Riley helped Jake.

Only they kept saying Hunt, and I was so confused that I didn't understand why they were calling him that. I stared down at the blood on my hands, feeling dizzy as everything moved around me in hyperspeed.

Kent and someone else picked Tigger up and started carrying him away, and they told me to follow, but how could I leave Jake?

"Go! You need to go with Tigger." Someone was in my face.

"I can't leave Jake!" I mumbled back, and a hand cracked

across my cheek, snapping my face to the side. My eyes came back into focus as I gasped and put my hand to my face.

"This is Huntley! My brother! He is not a fucking fictional character! Now go make sure your dog is alive, Daniella!" She shoved me away as they lifted Hunt—Jake—oh my god! That was Hunt—to the stretcher. His face pale in the darkness, his shirt peeled back and blood everywhere. "Go, Daniella!"

I forced myself to turn, and then I ran to catch up with Kent and the officer carrying Tigger toward a pickup truck. I climbed into the back where the seats were up and sat with Tigger's head on my lap as I held a rag to the bullet wound on his shoulder.

Kent was talking, but I didn't hear anything. I stared out the window and watched as they put Huntley into the back of an ambulance. A moment later, I saw nothing but the back of my lids as I closed my eyes and let the tears streak down my cheeks.

How could I have thought Hunt was Jake? Did I do that because Jake was my hero? Because he had saved Arrabella?

I touched my cheek, where the smack back to reality still burned slightly. Riley had every right to smack some sense into me. There was no doubt that I deserved that and more.

Kent called my name loudly. "Daniella? You okay back there?"

"Yeah, I'm okay."

"How is Tigger?"

Tigger started to lift his head as if to answer. "He's hanging on. How bad is it?"

"Well, I won't know until I can get X-rays on him, but I don't think it hit anything major, or he'd be showing other signs. The biggest thing right now is to keep him from bleeding out. I already called the hospital, and they are bringing in people to help with the operation. I'll do everything I can for him, Daniella."

"Thank you, Kent. Thank god you were there tonight."

"Yeah, I know. Glad I was too, but I have a question for you."

"Yeah?"

He peered over his shoulder at me. "Are family dinners there always that exciting?"

A bubble of laughter burst out of my throat. "Let's just say they are never boring."

"We found David in the barn; he had been knocked out. But Riley and I got him to safety."

In all the madness, I had forgotten about David. I closed my eyes. I had brought so much trouble to this family. I had no doubt they wouldn't want to have anything to do with me ever again. "I'm glad to hear that. He's a good man."

He didn't say anything else as he slowed and pulled off the road into the animal hospital's parking lot. He drove around to the back and parked by the back door. The door to the building opened, and two people rushed out to help.

I leaned down and whispered to Tigger, "Don't you die. I need you, Tigger."

I let them take him from me, and I stared at the jeans I wore, covered in blood. I put my face into my hands and began to sob. What if I lost Tigger? What if I lost Huntley and his family? I wasn't sure which one hurt the most, and as I sat there and cried, I berated myself for falling into my fantasy world and thinking that Jake had been there when it had been Hunt. It had always been Huntley.

CHAPTER TWENTY-NINE

HUNTLEY

*T*he light should not be off above the barn door. The horses were snickering and throwing their heads up in the air, and the barn door was closed. Something was wrong. I felt it down to my soul. I told Riley to get my father's gun, and then I took off out the back door.

I paused as I stepped out the back door, scanning the darkness. I didn't need to walk into anything. Tigger's barking was incessant, and as I started to get closer, the odor of smoke filled my nose. The barn was on fire!

I rushed to the door where Tigger was scratching and barking like he'd lost his mind. The minute the door was open, Tigger rushed around my legs, turning in a circle with his nose in the air before he darted around the side of the barn. I ran after him; my other thought was to catch the son of a bitch terrorizing Daniella.

I wasn't far behind Tigger, and I saw the man running in front of him. Tigger jumped, and the guy yelled and then fired his gun. That stopped me in my tracks as Tigger yelped and fell to the ground. The guy held the gun on me.

"Back the fuck off, or I'll kill you too!"

"Why are you doing this?"

"Because she killed my brother!"

"She didn't kill your sick brother! He tried to rape her! He died in prison exactly where he should have died!"

"He wouldn't have done that to her if she had accepted him!"

"Accepted him? Your brother was a sick bastard! He was stalking her, following her everywhere she went because she wrote romance novels!"

"She is a perverted whore! If she didn't write that vile shit, he wouldn't have gone after her."

I saw red and wanted to go after him, but at that moment, Tigger leaped from the ground. I hadn't even noticed him moving around, but he went right for his hand, and Treadwell jerked, causing the trigger to go off. The bullet struck me in the chest, and I felt myself falling back.

As I landed, I wondered what had gotten into me to chase the guy in the first place. I was a firefighter, not a cop, and sure as hell not one of Daniella's fictional heroes. The pain was like nothing I'd ever felt before, and I couldn't seem to suck in a full breath. Another shot registered in my mind, and Treadwell landed on the ground with a thud ten feet away.

Tigger limped over to me and lay down over my chest. It made it harder to breathe, but I figured if I were about to die, at least I wasn't alone. Tigger lifted his face to mine and licked my cheek. Hard to believe the dog had finally accepted me, and it only took me being shot.

I closed my eyes, and a moment later, I heard someone shaking me and saying the name Jake. I managed to open my eyes and saw Daniella over me. She was calling me Jake again. I wasn't Jake. I would never be Jake, and because of that, I could never be with Daniella.

❅

I'D WOKEN up in the hospital after surgery and learned that everyone was alright. Dad had a minor concussion, but he would be fine. All my siblings were there, including Kayley, who had rushed from New York as soon as she got the call. Once Kayley saw I was okay, she excused herself and went home to be with our parents.

Henley told me that the barn had been damaged pretty badly, but the horses were fine. No one had said anything about Daniella, and I searched out Riley in the group. She glanced at me and looked away.

"Where is she?" I asked. "Is she okay?"

"I assume she is with her dog," Riley muttered as she crossed her arms. "Kent took her and the dog to the vet. I haven't heard from him. Who knows if I will after that mess."

"Why are you being so nasty?" I asked her. "What did Daniella do to you?"

"She called you Jake, Hunt! Like she was watching one of her books come to life. That is not normal. That woman is not normal."

I pursed my lips. Riley was right; that wasn't normal behavior, but I didn't want anyone saying anything negative toward her. "I'm sure it was stress."

"Stress!" she hissed at me. "No, that's being delusional."

"Enough!" I growled at her and winced.

Wesley stepped forward. "He's right, Ry, that is enough. He needs to rest. Why don't you all head out? I have to work in about an hour, so I'll stay with him for a while until he's back to sleep."

My siblings filed out after saying goodbye, and then Wesley pulled a chair up closer. "How are you doing?"

"I'm alright. Pain meds are wearing off. How long is my recovery going to be?"

"The bullet shattered your clavicle after it ricocheted off your chest plate. You're lucky it didn't go through that. It would have killed you instantly. It's going to take a while for that to heal, and then you're going to need some intense physical therapy. You can probably expect to be out of work for about six months before you'll be cleared to go back to full duty."

"Six months?"

"Yeah, the bullet tore a lot of your muscle tissue up. It's going to take a while for that to heal. It's also going to take time to get the strength back up to do your job correctly."

I shook my head in frustration. What the hell was I going to do for six months?

"You want to tell me about this Jake thing?"

"No," I said softly, but the thing was, I did. "Daniella has this character in her series that is named Jake. She said when we first met that I reminded her of him a lot. Once in a while, she would call me by that name, like she was in her head, or forgot who I was."

"When did she call you by that name?"

"You mean other than after I got shot? And yeah, I do remember her doing that tonight. It was like she didn't see me at all, but only him."

"Was tonight the only time?"

"No, she had used it a couple of times. Once when I kissed her, and the first time we had sex, she called me Jake."

"Did you ever ask her about it?"

"I did. She played it off as a slip of the tongue."

He shrugged. "Maybe it was."

"Wes, she was thinking of another man, one that wasn't even real, when she was having sex with me. Not to mention tonight, after I was shot, she was worried about him, not me. What the hell is that?"

"Wasn't Dani attacked?"

"Yeah, did Charlotte tell you about that?"

"Yeah, she did, said she had a stalker, and that's why she had Tigger."

"It was worse than a stalker, Wes. The guy who shot me tonight, well, his brother was the one to attack her in her house. He beat her up, tried to rape her. Police arrived in time. I saw the reports and pictures. It was bad."

"Maybe she does it as a defense mechanism."

"Does what?"

"Reverts to a safe place when she's upset or unsure. You said she called you Jake when you first kissed and had sex. Maybe that's her way of dealing with the trauma and moving forward."

"I doubt that, Wes, but it doesn't matter. If Daniella didn't even realize that it was me there tonight trying to protect her, I don't know what will get through to her. I can't do that to myself. Riley is right, she has some issues, and she needs help."

"You care about her?"

"I do, but I can't help her any more than I have, Wes. I wish her the best, but I can't help her with this." I winced.

"I hear you. Okay, you get some rest. I'll let your nurse know you need more meds. I'll check on you later. If you need anything, have them call me in the ER. Glad you're alright, Hunt."

"Thanks, man." I bumped knuckles with my brother and then let my eyes fall closed. The memory of being shot came back to me, and then Daniella's beautiful face over mine, calling me Jake. Yeah, I couldn't be who she wanted. It was time to let my fantasy go.

IT HAD BEEN seven months since that night, and I'd been back to work full time for six weeks. I hadn't seen or heard from Daniella since it happened. As far as I knew, no one in my family, except my father and Brad, had spoken with her.

I had heard a conversation between them the other day, stating that her house was finished, and they had gotten final payment, but she hadn't moved back in yet. What was she waiting for?

It didn't matter. I wished Daniella the best and hoped that she found what she was looking for.

Riley and I had come to Summersville to meet my parents, Wes, and Charlotte for dinner at a small Italian place. I wasn't sure why they asked us to join them, but Wes said he needed to talk to us about something.

It wasn't until after dinner that Wes approached Riley and me when we stepped out onto the street. "I need you two to follow me someplace."

"Where?" Riley asked.

"Just trust me on this, okay?"

Riley and I looked at one another. She rolled her eyes, and I shrugged. "Alright."

He nodded, and Charlotte grinned up at us as she took his hand and started down the sidewalk. We walked for two blocks before Wes and Charlotte paused outside a door. I glanced at the window and frowned.

"Why are we at a bookstore?"

Riley balked. "Are you kidding me, Wes?"

I noticed the sign by the door: Join us tonight for an author reading with New York Times Bestselling Author Veronica Raven. There was a glossy picture of Daniella, sitting on a stone wall, Tigger sitting beside her.

"Oh, her new book must be out," my mother stated with a smile.

"How do you know about this?" I asked my brother.

"Charlotte and I ran into Daniella a couple of weeks back. She told us about it."

"So, why did you drag us over here? I'm not going in," Riley stated indignantly.

I wasn't sure if I wanted to see Daniella or not. Wes held his hand up. "I think you should go in and hear what she has to say."

"No!" My sister took my arm and pulled on it. "Come on, Hunt, let's go."

"Riley!" my father snapped. "Behave yourself. We are here. We should hear what she has to say."

"Why? So she can call us all by other names? I'm not living in her fantasy world anymore."

"Grow up, Riley," Wes said. "Daniella went through a lot; I think you should go in there and listen to what she has to say. You might learn a thing or two about dealing with your own life."

Riley laughed. "I doubt that."

Wes turned to me. "Look, you don't have to speak with her; go in and have a seat and listen to what she has to say."

I turned to my mother. She nodded, and so did my father. "Fine, I don't want to talk to her, but I'll go in. Does she know we'll be here?"

"Well, she hoped that you would be. She asked us to get you here. We told her we'd do our best."

"Are you all serious? She brought a lot of trouble to our family, and she never even apologized!" Riley growled.

"How do you know she never apologized?" my mother asked her. "Maybe she didn't apologize to you, but she did to your father and me."

"She did?" I asked, surprised.

"Yes, she did. She came to see us, but that is neither here nor there. Let's go inside and see what she has to say. Besides, I want a copy of her newest book."

"I can't believe you are still reading her books!" Riley snapped.

"Riley Young, watch yourself. Now get in there and behave."

I took Riley's arm. "Come on, let's go see what she has to say."

The place was packed, and most of the seats were taken, but my parents, Wes, and Charlotte found some on the other side of the room. Riley and I decided to stick to the back wall in case we decided to leave.

We had barely gotten situated when a man stepped up to the podium in front and spoke. "Welcome, everyone. The author you are about to see is a local author to us, having moved to our area about a year ago. She now has fifty-three books published and three movies in the works. I'd like to introduce Veronica Raven to our shop."

Daniella stepped out from behind a bookshelf, her eyes scanning the rows of seats. She smiled brightly at a few people, and then her eyes jumped to the back of the room where they landed on me as if she knew exactly where I'd be standing.

One look into her eyes, and my feet were stuck to the ground. No matter what she had to say, I would listen.

CHAPTER THIRTY

DANIELLA

"So we are all set?" I asked as I shook Mr. Heller's hand.

"Yep, I'll contact your publisher and have an ample amount of books here for the signing."

"Perfect. I appreciate you allowing me to release this book here."

"I think your announcement will be huge news with your followers."

"I do too."

I left his office and meandered through the store, browsing over the titles until I got to the small coffee shop off to the side. I was checking my phone for an email when the couple before me turned.

"Daniella!" My eyes snapped up to find Charlotte and Wes Young. My stomach tightened with apprehension, but the look on her face didn't show anger, and as she stepped forward and hugged me, I welcomed it.

"Hi, Charlotte, Wes, how are you two?"

"We are good! What brings you to town?"

"I had a meeting with the bookstore owner."

Charlotte's eyes sparkled. "Please tell me you are going to be doing a signing."

I chuckled. "Actually, I am."

She squeezed my arm. "What series?"

"It's a new one. I'll be announcing it that night. I haven't said one word about it yet, so it's kind of exciting news to share." I paused, hesitant to remind them of what had happened, but needing to know as I looked up at Wes. "How is your brother?"

Wes smiled down. "His wounds are healed. He's back to work full time now."

"That's good." I didn't miss that he said his wounds and not that he was healed. Was Huntley still angry with me? An idea came to mind as I stood there. I wasn't sure if it would work, but this would be the perfect time to reach out. "Wes, can I ask you a favor?"

"Sure," he said after sipping from his coffee cup.

"Do you think there is any way you might be able to get your family to my book signing?"

"All of them?"

"Well, at least Huntley. I think what I have to say at that event might interest him—or not."

"I can try. What is it that you are going to say?"

I gnawed on my bottom lip for a moment. "I'd rather not say, but my new series, well, it was inspired by your brother."

Wes grinned. "I'll make sure he's here." His cellphone began to ring, and he stepped away to answer it.

Charlotte was studying me carefully. "You still care about him."

It wasn't a question. "Yes, and I can never say how sorry I am for what happened. I've actually been going to therapy to help me deal with all of it, and the therapy has made me see all my errors quite clearly. This might be a way to fix them—or at least apologize for them."

Wes returned and said that he had to get going, so Charlotte hugged me quickly, and I handed her one of the cards about the event before they rushed off. I wasn't sure if any of them would come, but I sure hoped so. I owed them all a personal apology—especially Hunt.

MY STOMACH WAS in turmoil as I stood behind the bookshelf, wondering if they would come. I kept peeking out, and the place was filling up, but there was no sign of them. Finally, with a minute to spare, Wes, Charlotte, Patricia, and David came into view and took a seat. Huntley didn't come? Damn!

I scanned the seats, not seeing him and feeling frustrated that he wouldn't be here for this. Right before I was introduced, my eyes landed on him at the back of the room. His arms were crossed over his chest, and he looked tense. Beside him was his sister, Riley, looking annoyed.

"Welcome, everyone. The author you are about to see is a local author to us, having moved to our area about a year ago. She now has fifty-three books published and three movies in the works. I'd like to introduce Veronica Raven to our shop."

I stepped around the bookcase, my heart in my throat as it pounded. I let my gaze slip around the seated patrons, and then as I took my place behind the podium, I lifted my eyes right to where I knew he was standing. I needed him to know that much of what I had to say tonight was for him.

"Hello, and thank you for coming tonight. I know that Mr. Heller introduced me as Veronica Raven, and for many years, I have been writing under that nom de plume. Much of that was for an air of mystery. Some of it was for safety reasons.

"Few of you might be aware of my real name, Daniella Knight." My eyes landed on Hunt as I said that, and his forehead lined. "A couple of years ago, I had a fan who was very aggressive and ended up finding me and attacking me in my home." There were a couple of gasps around the room, and I noticed that Huntley shifted, standing up taller.

I took a calming breath and continued. "I moved to this area to get a new start. Six months after I moved here, someone set my house on fire. When that fire happened, I found out just how incredible small-town life can be. See, I had this wonderful family that took me in and helped me.

"I grew up in a trailer park, and I'd never known the kindness of people like this family." I found David and Patricia and smiled at them. "For a little while, I tried to get back on my feet, but I was sort of in denial about a few things, but I didn't truly come to understand that until after another major incident occurred.

"Then I realized that the people I had come to care about had become part of a twisted reality in my mind. I hadn't recovered from the trauma of the first attack. The second one was so obscured that I wasn't sure what was real and what was part of my creative mind."

I sighed as I let my eyes drift over the crowd and settle on Riley. "It literally took a smack to my face to make me see what I had done to this family. Not only to the family but to a man that had come to mean a lot to me."

Riley pressed her lips together and gave me a slight nod. My gaze shifted to Hunt, and his lips parted. I tore my eyes off him as I continued.

"Because I hadn't recovered from my first attack, I had created a safety mechanism inside my head. At least that's what my therapist calls it. When something stressed me, I pulled myself into one of my stories. I saw the real people around me as characters in my books. In doing this, it protected me but hurt them, and they will never know how sorry I am for that.

"This brings me to the announcement of my new series,

Living in Fictional Reality, and for the first time ever, I will be using my proper name on this series." I shifted my gaze to Huntley as I raised the book in front of me to show the cover. "The first book in the series is *Falling for my Hero,* and I'd like to read the first chapter for you."

Huntley shifted and shook his head, but I wasn't sure if he was upset or confused.

I cracked open the cover, turning to the dedication page and swallowing the nerves that were threatening to choke me. "This book is dedicated to my hero. He might never realize how much he means to me, but I hope one day he does. I love you, Huntley."

Riley smacked her brother on the arm, and his jaw dropped. I brought my attention back to the book and turned it to the first page.

"Chapter one, Rebecca. *I flexed my hands to ease the tension on my fingers while I sat on my couch in the living room. I'd been typing like a woman possessed as I attempted to get this book finished. I was so damn close—so close—and I was determined to get it done tonight. I had every intention of stepping away from writing for a few weeks and enjoy the beginning of summer. I had one more chapter to blast out, and then I could type my two favorite words: The End.*

I rolled my shoulders, adjusted the pillow against my lower back, and prepared to get that final chapter underway. Unfortunately, my stomach grumbled madly, and I winced as I glanced at the digital clock on my computer. Holy crap! It was after eight!

When was the last time that I ate? One? Two? I couldn't remember, but that was normal when I was in my writing groove. I could go all day without moving from my spot unless my bladder revolted or some-thing else grabbed my attention.

Like my German shepherd, Revenge, who was now barking at the back door. "Rev, give me a minute."

I lifted my eyes from the page and found Huntley no longer

standing there. Riley was, and she was listening carefully, but Hunt was gone. I tore my eyes away and returned them to the story that was so closely tied to my reality.

AFTER THE READING WAS OVER, I answered questions for a few minutes, and I tried my hardest to keep myself together. Huntley hadn't come back, and the only thing I wanted to do was curl up in a ball and cry. I had hoped to apologize to him through my words. Did he not believe them? Did he not care? Maybe he was dating someone else. If he were, wouldn't Charlotte have said something? Maybe she had faked her excitement to see me that day, and this was payback for hurting her brother-in-law.

We took a ten-minute break after the reading before I started signing books, and I quickly disappeared behind the bookshelf. I closed my eyes, putting my hand out to hold me upright as the urge to crumble hit me.

When I had told my therapist my idea, he had thought it was fantastic. I had thought so too, but obviously, I had been wrong. So damn wrong.

"Is it true?"

I spun around at the voice and found Huntley standing two feet away. "All of it is true. Every word I said out there."

"You have been going to therapy?"

I nodded. "Yes, twice a week for almost six months."

"Who are you in love with Daniella? Me or Jake?"

I shuffled forward slightly. "Jake doesn't exist, Hunt. He was only a way to protect myself. I'm in love with you."

"How do you know that? How can you be sure it is me that you love? We haven't seen each other in over seven months, and we were only together for a short time."

"Before you, I had been in love a hundred times, but only

with characters. Never with a real person. I think I fell in love with you the night of my fire—the moment I looked up at you from the ground. But I knew that I loved you when you went after Butch. When I heard Tigger yelp, my heart broke with fear that he would die. But when I saw you get shot, all sense of reality vanished. I couldn't imagine a world without you, and my mind pulled me into my alternate reality. It was hard to breathe, hard to focus.

"Your sister literally knocked the sense back into me, and I saw you lying on the gurney, fighting for your life, and I knew it was you. I saw you, Hunt. Not Jake, not anyone else. I saw *you* and your sacrifice to protect me."

I smiled at him through tears. "Hunt, I should have found a way to tell you before, to find you and apologize, but I was learning how to deal with stress so that this wouldn't happen again. I know that you probably don't want—"

I didn't get to finish the sentence because Hunt took hold of my face and crushed his lips to mine. I clung to his arms as I heard a giggle behind him, but I didn't care who was watching. He wrapped his arms around me, deepening the kiss until I thought my knees would buckle.

He pulled back, staring down at me. "I want. Oh, man, do I want."

"Do you? Can you ever forgive me?"

"I can. Daniella, I have missed you so much."

"Have you?"

"Yes," he said before he kissed me again.

"Why did you leave after the dedication?"

He chuckled. "Because I went to buy my copy." I turned around, and Riley handed him his copy. "I figured that I would have a lot of time to listen to you read it to me later."

I laughed, and Riley stepped next to her brother.

"I'm sorry for hitting you."

I stared at her. "I'm glad that you did. I needed the wake-up call, and that did it. I think my jaw hurt for a week. I'm sorry for hurting you and your family. Will you forgive me, Riley?"

"Yeah, I guess. If Hunt can forgive you, I can."

I hugged Riley, and Patricia joined us. "Is that book really about meeting Huntley?"

"Yep," I told her as I put my arm around Huntley. "The entire story is about the whirlwind of meeting the Youngs and not only falling in love with their son but all of them."

There was a bark behind us, and I turned to see one of the employees bringing Tigger to me. The minute he was in reach, he pushed me aside and jumped up to put his paws on Hunt's chest.

"Hey, buddy!" Hunt ruffled his fur. "You remember me."

"I don't think he will ever forget you," I replied as Tigger licked at his face excitedly and then bounced down to see everyone else.

Hunt pulled me to his side, whispering in my ear, "You know, the doctors said that Tigger saved my life."

"He did?"

"Yeah, he climbed over my chest, compressing the wound closed so I wouldn't bleed out. If he hadn't done that, I might have."

Tigger came in between us, wiggling his head to put distance between us and sitting down as we all laughed.

After we left the bookshop, we said goodbye to his family, and I took his hands. "Come back to my place."

"Where do you live now?"

"About ten minutes from here."

"Oh, really?" He grinned and kissed my lips.

"Yes, really. I want to show you how much I love you."

"You do, huh?"

"Yeah, it'll be like the first time all over again."

He laughed. "You aren't going to call me Jake again, are you?"

I grinned. "Oh, no! But if you hear the name Oliver, don't mind it. He's my new hero."

Huntley tipped his head back and laughed loudly, and I felt my heart expand to a size it had never been before. I loved this reality.

The End

SNEAK PEEK: RILEY

**Enjoy the first chapter of Riley, Loving a Young Series,
Book 3**

Riley

"*I* thought we weren't going to do this again." A gravelly voice broke the silence in the semi-dark room, and I clenched my eyes tighter as the voice throbbed through my head. Man, how much did I drink last night?

A warm hand slipped under the covers and touched my leg. "You alive over there?"

I grunted. "Barely. Why are you here, Ethan?"

"Don't tell me you don't remember? You wanted me to stay. You practically begged me to tuck you in." He rolled to his side, spooning behind me, his hand curled around my hip, his morning hard-on pressing to my backside. "You don't remember that?"

I shook my head slightly and winced.

"Bad hangover?" I nodded, and he kissed my shoulder. "Want me to make you coffee?"

I nodded again, and he kissed my shoulder once more before he let his hand rub over my hip to my bare thigh and then slide away. I managed to split my eyes wide enough to watch his naked backside as he bent down to get his boxers off the floor. I'd have to be dead not to want to watch him naked. I closed them as he turned back to me and leaned over to kiss my brow.

"I'll be right back."

As soon as he was gone from the room, I forced myself to throw the covers back and literally rolled out of bed. On my hands and knees on the floor, I felt the room spin. My god, how much *did* I drink last night? I pulled myself off the floor and to my feet as my stomach rolled.

I managed to make it to the toilet and put my head in my hands as I used it, moaning softly. I'd gone out last night to celebrate Cinco de Mayo, and I remembered drinking a few beers, but that was normal for me. As I tried to remember what else I'd consumed, I suddenly had a memory of doing Jägermeister shots with Evan and my brother Huntley.

Damn them! I knew better than to do shots, especially on a weekday! It was hard enough recovering on the weekend. Dealing with a bunch of fourth graders was less than appealing with a pounding headache.

I stumbled to the shower, hoping the hot water would ease the pounding in my head, and tried to remember if I did beg him to stay. I couldn't recall it, but I'm sure I did—it wouldn't be the first time I had coerced Ethan into my bed. Coerced? Nah. That would imply I had forced him. Ethan always came willingly.

I sighed and pushed myself through the shower routine. Once I was done and my hair was pulled up in a messy bun, I returned to my bedroom with a towel wrapped around my body. On my dresser was a steaming cup of coffee. I scooped it up with two hands, inhaling deeply before taking a sip. Ah— perfect. I took another needed sip.

I glanced around and didn't see any of his clothing, but my bed was made. Maybe he left already. That was fine with me. It wasn't the first time we had slept with one another, although the last time was supposed to have been the *last time*.

I finished dressing, collected my phone and coffee, and went downstairs. I stopped when I entered the kitchen area. Ethan was sitting at the breakfast bar, his short hair flat on one side from sleeping, his dark-blue shirt wrinkled and untucked, and his attention on his phone.

"I thought you left."

He lifted his gaze to mine before his blue eyes skimmed my clothing. "No, I was waiting to give you a ride back to your car."

Whoops! I forgot about that. "Okay, give me a couple of minutes."

"How are you feeling?"

"I'll live." I dug around in the fridge for something to make for lunch and settled on ham and cheese. I made my sandwich, grabbed some precut veggies and bagged them, and then tossed it all into my lunchbox.

"Don't forget the dressing cup for your veggies. You want to grab breakfast on the way?"

"Oh, damn, thanks." I grabbed a single-serve dressing cup and tossed it into my bag before I glanced at the clock. "Um, I'm not sure I'll have time."

"Why don't I call in an order at Coral's, and we can grab it on the way to get your car? You can eat it at work while you read your email."

"Okay."

"You want your usual?"

"Yeah," I replied as I filled my to-go coffee mug. Ethan was just hanging up when I gathered all my stuff, and we headed out the door.

I climbed into his truck and rolled my eyes as he lifted my

bra off the seat. "I think you forgot something in your rush to get me in your bed last night."

Shit! I seriously didn't even remember that. "Give me that. I'd be pissed if I lost that. It's my favorite one." I grabbed it off his finger and shoved it into my tote bag, trying to hide my embarrassment.

He chuckled and started his truck as I put on my seat belt. "Do you even remember taking it off in my truck last night?"

"No."

He frowned, and I saw him glance my way after backing out of the space and putting his truck in drive. "Why am I not surprised?"

"Did I really beg you?"

"Yep, you did. You slipped out of your bra on the way home after you told me it was killing you, then when we got to your place, you climbed over the console to my lap and pleaded with me to come in."

I shook my head. "You could have said no."

He glanced at me, giving me a stern look. "I did tell you no, Ry. I reminded you that we had decided that we wouldn't sleep together anymore, but you kept saying just one more time. Come on, just one more time. You know you want to, and you know very well that I can't resist you, Riley, especially when you are rubbing that body all over mine."

I stared out the side window and pursed my lips. It sounded like something I would do. "You still could have said no."

"You are a hard woman to say no to, Riley. You know I can't resist you."

"I thought you were dating Karen," I stated.

"Kathy, and we went out a couple of times, but that didn't work out."

"Why not?"

His laugh was harsh for a second, and I glanced at him to find him shaking his head. "Same reason it never works. It just doesn't." His hand squeezed the steering wheel, and then he pulled into the small parking lot at Coral's Coffee Café and put the truck in park. "I'll be right back."

I watched him walk toward the building. His hair was still a chaotic mess, and his shirt looked like he had slept in it, but he didn't seem to care in the least. He waved at someone on the other side of the parking lot and held the door for a woman coming out with her hands full.

I sighed and rubbed my temples. We'd had a conversation a few weeks ago and had decided that we shouldn't be sleeping with one another anymore. It meant nothing to either of us—or I guess it didn't. I knew it was comfortable, easy, and well, pretty damn awesome, which sucked because I didn't want it to be awesome with him. I wanted it to be boring, so I wouldn't want to sleep with him anymore. He was practically my brother—only from different parents.

He returned a few minutes later and handed me a bag. "I got you a fruit bowl too. You always get hungry after a night of drinking around the mid-morning break."

"Thanks," I replied as he got on the road again. The silence between us was never uncomfortable, but today it felt a little tense. We pulled into the tavern's parking lot, and he parked behind my car and rested back against his seat, staring out the windshield. I knew the look. He wanted to say something, so I waited.

"Riley, we really can't do that again."

"I know," I quipped back.

He turned to look at me. "Do you? Because I seem to recall us saying this a couple of weeks ago, and I was pretty damn determined to keep my distance from you."

I shrugged and reached for the handle. "So, keep your distance, and I'll keep mine."

"I plan on it, Riley. I'm serious this time. I can't keep doing this with you. The only time you ever want to see me is when you're drunk and need a ride home and a good time. I can't remember the last time we had sex when you were sober."

I laughed. "Are you saying I have a drinking problem?"

His eyes looked serious for a moment. "Do you?"

"No!" I snapped indignantly.

"How often do you blackout when you drink, Ry? You don't even remember last night, and you didn't remember the last time either."

"Jesus, Ethan! Are you saying I'm a drunk?"

"No, I'm asking you to think about how much you drink and what happens when you do."

I snorted. "Just because I like to have fun and get a little tipsy, then have sex, doesn't mean I have a problem."

I shoved open the door as he spoke. "I didn't say you had a problem; you did, and it's never just tipsy, Riley."

I glared at him over my shoulder. "I do *not* have a problem. The only problem I have is you giving in to my every whim. It's not my fault you can't say no to me."

He frowned. "You're right. It's not your fault. It's mine, but I'm done, Riley. I can't keep doing this. I'm not going to enable you to drink more or be the guy who picks you up off the floor and takes you home for a good time because you're smashed. Not anymore."

"Then don't," I muttered as I scrambled out.

"I think you need to do some thinking, Riley."

"Who the hell do you think you are, Ethan? I'm a big girl, and I know what I'm doing."

"Do you? Because from where I am, it looks like you are kind of lost and hiding your frustration in a twelve-pack."

My jaw dropped. "Oh, my god! Just because I like to drink and have sex, you think I'm an alcoholic? You've lost your damn mind, Ethan Winston! Jesus, when did you become such a goody two-shoes?"

"No, Riley! I didn't say you were an alcoholic. I just said that you need to think about all of this, but I'm telling you that I can't keep doing this. I can't be the one that you call whenever you need a scratch itched or a ride because you have too much to drink—again. I can't do it anymore. I won't."

"Well, then, don't do it! I'm sorry I have infringed on our friendship so much. I thought that we enjoyed having sex together, and I didn't realize that getting a ride home from you was such a freaking hassle! I'll refrain from calling you in the future."

I slammed the truck door and began to dig in my tote bag. I heard the window go down on his truck. "Riley," he said sternly, and I refused to look at him. I didn't want him to see the tears in my eyes. "Riley!"

"Go away, Ethan. I think we have said all that we need to say."

He called my name roughly one more time, but I stepped away from him as I dug deeper into my tote. The jingle of keys rang through the air as they landed at my feet. I didn't even have time to pick them up before he was pulling away.

I was so furious that he would call me an alcoholic. Who was he to judge me for having a few drinks? And I got his ass to pick me up so he wouldn't yell at me later for driving under the influence. What a prick!

I snagged my keys off the ground and climbed into my SUV. I was done with him. *Done*! I didn't need him to drive me home or climb into my bed, and I sure as hell didn't need his bullshit! Ethan Winston could kiss my ass!

I frowned as I jabbed my keys into the ignition, thinking about a previous romantic interlude that I did remember, where Ethan had done just that. Whatever! I was over it. I should never have slept with him in the first place.

Riley, Book 4

Will Riley finally admit that she's in love with Ethan, or will she lose him forever?

Riley is always the life of the party, and Ethan is there to pick her up and keep her together. He knows her almost as well as she knows herself, and he knows she will never love him as he does her.

Now Ethan wants more out of life and love, but Riley continues to deny her feelings and insists they are only friends with benefits. When a training opportunity comes up that will get Ethan out of town for months, he jumps on it—finally, a way to get over Riley and move on.

With Ethan gone and a new guy in her life, Riley deals with several emotional issues without the help of her best friend. A family emergency has Ethan feeling lost without Riley to lean on, but he refuses to go to her and seeks solace with another.

Will Riley make the right choices and finally admit how she feels, or will she find herself alone and falling further down the rabbit hole?

LOVING A YOUNG SERIES

Wesley, Book 1

Traumatized by events of her past, Charlotte Bennett is not a
fan of strangers. When she sees a man touching her daughter at
the park, she reacts without listening. It's only later when her
daughter is rushed to the hospital that she realizes how wrong
she had been.

Doctor Wesley Young only wanted to help the tender-aged girl
he witnessed fall, but when her mother attacks him at the park,
he's left stunned. When the little girl arrives later in the
emergency department, he comes face to face with the mother
who makes more of an impression on him than the cut she left
on his face.

Things heat up quick when Marisol is no longer his patient, but
when things from the past are revealed, Wes isn't sure that
Charlotte is the woman for him. Can Charlotte find a way to
explain it all so that Wes will accept both her and her daughter
before it's too late?

Henley, Book 2

Being a wedding planner is hard, especially when someone is

always trying to steal your business, and your family doesn't support you. However, Roxanne Novak is determined to keep her business afloat.

When Roxy's in a car accident hurrying to meet a potential bride, she's injured and scared, but paramedic Henley Young takes good care of her.

Henley loves his job and thrives on the adrenaline of helping people in need. Maybe that's why when he meets Roxy, he's inclined to help her with more than just medical care. Hooking her up with his older brother Wesley and his bride-to-be could be just what she needs. It might also be the start of something between Lee and the spunky little wedding planner.

When a position at a country club is offered to Roxy, she finds herself rethinking her entire business plan. Excited to start someplace new, Roxy and Henley begin making plans for the future. Just after she starts her new job, Roxy learns of Lee's past relationship, and everything she knew about him is questioned.

Can Roxy and Henley put the past to bed and move forward to something that might be more than what both of them had ever hoped for?

Huntley, Book 3

Daniella Knight works hard to create suspenseful and romantic tales, but after a violent interaction with a fan, she wants to hide from the world. When her house catches on fire, her and her protection dog, Tigger, are forced to rely on the help of strangers.

Huntley Young loves being in the thick of the action. Well, as long as that action has something to do with his job as a firefighter. When Huntley stops the homeowner from going back into the house, he has no clue, that he just placed himself firmly in the hero department.

As they get to know each other, Daniella's creative mind is always building on what is around her, and before she knows it, reality and fiction are hard to tell apart.

When danger strikes again, will Daniella be able to see what is right in front of her, or will her past trauma keep her safely inside her romantic fictional world?

Riley, Book 4

Riley is always the life of the party, and it's Ethan that is there to pick her up and keep her together. He knows her almost as well as she knows herself, and he knows she will never love him as he does her.

Now Ethan wants more out of life and love, but Riley denies her feelings and insists they are just friends with benefits. When a training opportunity comes up that will get Ethan out of town for months, he jumps on it. It's the only way to get over Riley and move on.

With Ethan gone and a new guy in her life, Riley finds herself dealing with several emotional issues without the help of her best friend. A family emergency has Ethan feeling lost without Riley there to lean on, but he refuses to go to her and seeks solace with another.

Will Riley make the right choices, and finally, admit how she feels, or will she find herself alone and falling further down the rabbit hole.

Kayley, Book 5

Independent Kayley Young is a real estate agent in New York and loves her life as a single woman. She's not one to get tied down, and she has no desire to have children.

Officer Cameron Sexton is new on the job, a veteran of the military, and proud of his dedication to the job. Unfortunately, he finds himself annoyed at his lackadaisical sergeant who should hang up his gun belt before getting someone hurt. When Cameron is dispatched to a burglary, he meets Kayley Young and is instantly attracted to her. Cameron has a feeling she reciprocates those feelings, except she's a little leery of the fact that he is ten years younger than her.

When Kayley's life starts taking a turn for the worse, she finds herself depending more on the attractive young man she has let into her bed for fun than she intended. Her original thought of enjoying the moment starts to last longer, but Kayley's not sure that dating a man ten years her junior is smart for the long haul. Especially with the rest of the changes that have happened in her life.

Can Kayley come to terms with the age difference, or will her family sway her away from the younger man?

Bradley, Book 6

Bradley Young is the eldest sibling of the Young family, and the only one who had previously been married. After losing his wife to cancer several years ago, he's used to caring for his two kids alone. The thought of dating is not something he's interested in, now with a busy construction business, and a family that always needs help.

Nolan Nickels needed a change, and with the help of her good friend, Kayley, she left New York and came to Millerstown to take a teaching position at the middle school. She has always been a huge tom boy and loves to fix things with her hands and play sports.

With a new house in her name, Nolan seeks out the perfect plan to get the house ready so she can bring her two daughters' home, but is her fixer-upper more than she bargained for? When Kayley finally gets Brad to stop by the house to check something, Brad finds himself more than intrigued with the spitfire, Nolan. Will he finally find the woman to spend his life with, or will she be put a halt on any type of future?

LOVING A WINSTON SERIES

The *Loving a Winston Series* is a five-book steamy romance series that spins off of the *Loving a Young Series*. Characters from both series will appear from book to book. Each book is a standalone romance with suspense and spicy romance scenes.

Cara, Book 1

What happens when the man you fall for is all wrong for you?

Cara Winston has always been a bit of a rebel and an adrenaline junkie. As a helicopter pilot and paramedic, she relies on that to do her job.

When Cara and her team respond to a multi-vehicle accident involving motorcycles, she's expecting the worst. What she's not expecting is to find herself intrigued by the blue eyes of a man wearing motorcycle gang colors.

Ryan Vigilante rides the road, mostly on two wheels, not

four. When several of his club end up in an accident on the highway, Ryan never expects to see a future in the eyes of the intense female paramedic. The only problem is, she's way out of his league, and he knows that getting involved with her could only put her in jeopardy.

With Cara's family trying to keep them apart and Ryan's club breaking the law, Cara finds herself more of a rebel than usual. Will things work out for Cara and Ryan, or will Cara's law enforcement brother, Ethan, find a way to put a stop to it for good?

Evan, Book 2

What happens when she's not really who you think she is?

EVAN WINSTON IS DEDICATED to his job as a registered nurse in the ICU department of the local hospital. He's one hundred percent focused on the needs of his patients and his family, or at least he usually is. That all changes the day a woman visits one of his patients and turns his world upside down.

Laney Marshall wants nothing more than to help people who struggle. Especially those women and children who are fighting to survive domestic violence situations. After losing someone close to her to an abusive man, she is determined to do everything in her power to help.

Unfortunately, Laney has people that don't want her to do that. In fact, they don't even want her in this town or even the state of Pennsylvania. They prefer her on the other side of the country, where they think she belongs, living the life planned for her.

Can Laney and Evan find a way to build a relationship while keeping others from getting involved, or will the revealed secrets be enough to end any chance of a future before it begins?

Candy, Book 3

What happens when your lustful heart wins over your intellectual mind?

WHEN CANDY'S SISTER, Cara, was dating outlaw biker member Ryan Vigilante, Candy paid little attention to Ryan's club buddy, Bollard. Sure, Bollard, who works behind the bar at the local tavern, was pleasing on the eyes and made a mean chocolate martini, but he was an outlaw, and that's not the kind of person Candy associates with.

Michael Bollard is out of the club now, and he hopes to purchase the tavern. He had never wanted anything more than his bikes and the club, but now, Mike has hopes of building a future, a future that is colliding with sexy and intelligent Candy Winston in ways he could have never imagined.

Just when he thinks he might have his future figured out, a stranger enters the bar with a surprise he never saw coming. Will that surprise send Candy running for higher ground, or will it cement her future in the tavern with Mike?

Carmen, Book 4

What happens when your first love returns to town—twenty years later?

CHILD PSYCHOLOGIST, Carmen Winston, spends a lot of time at the schools, and when she come across a man and the name of a new student, she is thrown back to a time of young love and dreamy hopes of the perfect future.

Tim Kohl lived in Millerstown for six years before his parents moved him across the country. He never expected to return, and when he does, it's with three kids in tow. The last thing he expects to find in town is his high school sweetheart still beautiful as ever and single.

When sparks fly, can these two put the past behind them and plan a future, or will the years apart separate them before they can figure it out.

Coral, Book 5

What happens you overhear your family talking to the man you've fallen for?

CORAL WINSTON HAS FELT out of touch with her family since her mother passed away and throws everything she has into her coffee café. When her family forces her to take a vacation, they all decide to come along for the fun.

Landan Lancaster is the oldest of the eight Lancaster children, and he's still trying to deal with walking away from his cheating bride the night before their wedding many months prior. When a large family comes to stay in the Lancaster guest house on the lake, he finds himself intrigued by the woman standing at the water's edge.

On the slopes, Landan realizes he has met his match in more ways than one, and Coral begins to feel as if she has finally found where she belongs. When a conversation is overheard, Coral gets the wrong idea and flees, only to find a mountain of trouble waiting for her back home.

Can Coral overcome the issues facing her and find her way

back to the beautiful mountains and water of Lake Tahoe, or will Landan lose her before he can ever call her his own?

COMING IN 2025
Loving the Lancasters! Another 8 book Spin-off to keep the reading pleasure coming!

LOVING A LANCASTER SERIES

The Loving a Lancaster Series spins off of the Loving a Winston Series. In Coral's book, you are introduced to the Lancaster family while she is on vacation in Lake Tahoe. This series will consist of seven books, and stared with Leo.

Leo - Book 1

Leo Lancaster is coming home to Lake Tahoe. As a successful stockbroker and business owner, Leo has decided to open another office in Truckee and work out of that one instead of his Vegas office. Now, he must locate a house and get himself settled, and the last thing he expects to find on his return is love.

Heather McClain is a devoted mother of two teens, and a widow from Ohio. When her best friend encourages her to go on a girls trip to Lake Tahoe, she decides to take a break from the chaos at home and try to have fun. Only their antics are more than Heather bargained for.

Lucky for her, Leo is around to rescue her and the two of them quickly grow close, but is Heather ready to let go of her husband's memory and move forward into a relationship, or more importantly, are her children prepared to accept a new man into their mother's life when she surprises them with a trip to the lake?

Luna - Book 2

WHILE LUNA LANCASTER loves Lake Tahoe, she thrives in the outdoors near her home in Sedona, Arizona. When Luna's good friend, Sadie, plans a visit and decides to bring a guest, Luna is excited to show them the sights of the beautiful Red Rocks around her home.

Unfortunately, Luna's friend can't make it at the last minute, and Luna finds herself entertaining Trace Hampton alone. The chemistry between them sparks the moment they meet. The problem is that Luna thinks Trace and Sadie are a couple, and she does everything possible to hide her feelings and not act on them.

When Trace reveals that he is not involved with Sadie, Luna jumps at the chance to see what they could have, but when Sadie finds out, she's heartbroken that Luna stole the man she likes out from under her.

Will Luna save the friendship and lose the chance at a happily ever after with Trace?

Still to come: Lance, Lily, Laney, Lucas and Levi.

ABOUT THE AUTHOR

Stacy Eaton began her writing career in October of 2010 and, as each year goes by, she releases more and more novels. Stacy recently took an early retirement from law enforcement after over fifteen years of service, with her last three in investigations and crime scene investigation.

Stacy resides in southeastern Pennsylvania with her husband, who works in law enforcement, and her two dogs. She has a daughter in college and a son who is currently serving in the United States Navy.

Be sure to visit www.stacyeaton.com for updates and more information on her books.

Sign up for all the latest information on Stacy's Newsletter!

Join my Newsletter and get TWO Short Stories for FREE!

STACY BOOKS - PAPERBACK

Rise Again Warrior Series

The *Rise Again Warrior Series* is an intense and emotional journey through the lives of many service members, their families, and their friends. Focusing on the trials that they face after wartime is over, and they have returned home to a nation that sometimes seems to have forgotten what they were fighting for, and what all of these people sacrificed in the name of Honor & Duty. Books Include: Mission: Believe, Mission:Accept, Mission: Repair, and Mission: Courage

Loving a Young Series

The *Loving a Young Series* is a steamy romance series that consists of six books. While these books are all standalone romances, the characters will be seen across the series since this is a small-town romance series about siblings finding forever loves.

Books include: Wesley, Henley, Riley, Kayley & Bradley

The Loving a Winston Series

The *Loving a Winston Series* is a five-book steamy romance series that spins off of the *Loving a Young Series*. Characters from both series will appear from book to book. Each book is a standalone romance with suspense and spicy romance scenes.

Books Include: Cara, Evan, Candy, Coral and Carmen.

The Unexpected Series

The *Unexpected Series* is a steamy romance series where anything can happen and probably will. Each book in the series is a stand-alone happily ever after, or happy for now book. While they are stand-alone, the books are all centered around Safety Zone Security and the employees there. Characters from one book will continue throughout the rest of the series. Books Include: Unexpected Packages,

Unexpected Arrivals, Unexpected Trouble, Unexpected Storms, Unexpected Desires, Unexpected Ties.

Paranormal Romance:

My Blood Runs Blue Series

My Blood Runs Blue Series is an adult Paranormal Action/Romance Series with vampires and is intended for mature audiences.

Books Include: My Blood Runs Blue, The Pulse of Blue Blood, Blue Blood for Life, Mixing the Blue Blood, Blue Bloods Final Destiny,

The Return of Blue Blood Series:

This series is 40 years in the future after My Blood Runs Blue. It is a very steamy series intended for mature audiences.

Books Included: Kristin: Blue Blood Returns, Hugh: Blue Blood Compelled, Zander: Blue Blood Reborn, Lena: Blue Blood Desired, Reckoning, Blue Blood Finale

The Twisted Love Series

(Dark Crime Suspense)

with Amy Manemann Co-Author

The Twisted Love Series is a continuing Saga of intense police procedures and romantic suspense and contains nine books in total. It delves deep into the world of crime and how it is investigated. Due to that fact, the crimes continue from one book to the next and could leave you hanging till the next one. Not all crimes are solved in the pages of one book. These books also contain strong adult language, violence, and sexual situations. Books Included: Love Lorn, Love Torn, Love Inked, Love Drowned, Love Carved, Love Trapped, Love Crossed, Love Twisted, Love Lies.

Single Titles

Whether I'll Live or Die

You're Not Alone

Garda ~ Welcome to the Realm

Liveon ~ No Evil

Second Shield

Distorted Loyalty

Six Days of Memories

Second Shield II: The Return

Tempt Me Too

Finding the Strength

Finding Love in Special Places:

Stacy's Short Story Series

Sweet Romance about adult topics. Stories include: Finding Love on Christmas Vacation, Finding Love on the Summer Surf, Finding Love with Dear Santa, Finding Love with a Champagne Toast, Finding Love on the High Seas, Finding Love on a Dude Ranch, Finding Love at the Farmer's Market

Heart of the Family Series

The *Heart of the Family* Series is a small-town steamy romance series that is best read in order. Books Include:

Mistletoe & Cocoa Kisses, Roses & Champagne Kisses, Orchids & Hurricane Kisses, Carnations & Hot Toddy Kisses,

Heal Me Series

Love Spicy Medical Romance? Check out the rest of the Heal Me Series for sexy romances that will warm your heart as they deal with life-altering medical and psychological issues. These books do contain language and open door sexual relations. While each book in the Heal Me Series is a stand-alone book, the characters cross between books and are best enjoyed by reading them in order. Books Include: Cured, Revived, Mended and Rescued.

The Celebration Series

The Celebration Series: Celebration Township is made for family, friends, falling in love, and don't forget celebrating the holidays. The first twelve books bring two people onto center stage as they overcome odds and figure out what their futures may hold. There is laughter, love, romance and even suspense when you join these couples as they each find a happily ever after over a holiday. The thirteenth book brings all twelve couples, and even a few special guests, into final focus as the first couple in Tangled in Tinsel prepares for their wedding one year after they met. Books Include: Tangled in Tinsel, Tears to Cheers, Heathens to Hearts, Rainbows Bring Riches, Sweet as Sugar, Making Mom Mad, Sparklers or Spankings, Raffles to Rattles, Flirting with Fireworks, Working Under Wheels, Masquerading at Midnight, Blessing & Beans, Velvet & Vows.

The Sometimes Series:

The Sometimes Series consists of three romances where the passion is a touch spicy and there is a hint of suspense is in the air. Sometimes You Win is a stand-alone story that ends with a Happy-for-Now ending. Sometimes you Lose, Book 2 of the series does end in a cliffhanger and Sometimes You Play the Game will finally give the couple a Happily Ever After. In all three books, you will find adult language and situations. Books Include: Sometimes You Win, Sometimes you Lose, Sometimes You Play The Game.

Pleasure Your Fantasies Series

The Pleasure Your Fantasies series is an ADULT Series with coarse language and intense sexual situations along with suspense. Books Include: Mistletoe Fantasies, Whispered Fantasies, Secret Fantasies, and more coming in 2024.

List Updated 9/6/23